Charles.G.Fournel grew up in a small seaside town in Suffolk, England. He is a divorced, devoted father of two. He started writing short stories at the age of ten and since has expanded his genre to World War Two. He has family connections in both the Allies and Axis during the war. This is the reason for his extended interest in this era. He has grown to have great respect for resistance groups who, without any military experience, took up arms for their country. Other books by Charles.G.Fournel: *Rise of the Maquis* and *A Quest to Get Homebound.*

In the memory of my father Christopher Robin Fournel, he will be sorely missed.

Charles.G.Fournel

A Soldier's Conscience

Austin Macauley Publishers™
London * Cambridge * New York * Sharjah

A CIP catalogue record for this title is available from the British Library.

ISBN 9781398453159 (Paperback)
ISBN 9781398453166 (ePub e-book)

www.austinmacauley.com

First Published 2022
Austin Macauley Publishers Ltd®
1 Canada Square
Canary Wharf
London
E14 5AA

Prologue

Genuine photo of Mont Valérien, made by Clemens Rüter.

The year is 1941, it was eight years since the tyrannical Nazi party took power and the German invaders occupied France for just over a year. The previous French government was exiled to the South to control the 'Free-zone' under the collaborating Vichy regime, who worked alongside the Nazi powers.

At a secret isolated fort, just over twelve kilometres west of Paris, was where the Nazis had a top-secret base and executed more than one thousand resistance fighters and other hostages during the Second World War which was the largest number of executions in one single place in France. The Nazis arrested Resistance members and many Communists and Jews that were arrested in reprisal for the death of German soldiers; they were then sentenced to death, by firing squad, in military tribunals.

The men and women were sent to Germany after the execution and decapitated so as not to enrage the local population. They had previously been attached to five wooden poles in a clearing, blindfolded and shot by a group of sixty fusiliers. The firing squad was large so that no German knew who he had shot. One random gun always carried blanks. No photographs were allowed of these executions, due to Nazi fears they would be used for anti-Nazi propaganda purposes.

Chapter 1

The young man was excited as he packed his sack with the few personal items that he was entitled to take. He had only been out of his hometown, of Dresden, once and that was to attend 'basic training' at Leipzig, one hundred and ninety kilometres from the country's capital, Berlin. Now, he would be leaving his country as a soldier to defend a 'top-secret' base in France. It would be hard leaving his Italian mother but was comforted by the thought that his two childhood friends, Carl and Stefan, had also been assigned to the same post.

His name was Siegfried, known as 'Siggie' to his friends. He had short dark blonde hair and piercing marble blue eyes that he had adopted from his father, who was an officer in the Schutzstaffel (SS), but his true Arian features stuck out even more by the eighteen-year-old's faint olive skin, the one thing he had gotten from his Italian mother. This complexion had always made him very popular with the fairer sex, yet the young man had never taken advantage of this and had retained his virginity, despite many advances.

The military post he and his friends has been assigned to was only twelve and a half kilometres from the French city of light, Paris. Siegfried had always wanted to visit the great capital city, he had often heard of the magnificent architecture, the fine wine and cheese, the fair French maidens were renowned for their beauty and after hearing soldiers talking, who had returned back home on leave, at a local café, about the notorious Paris red-light district, the young German was ecstatic to be able to visit the grand settlement. Yet when listening to their stories, there was one thing that put fear into every German soldier who had ever been deployed to France, the savage peasants who would kill you for looking in their direction, they were the French resistance or better known as the Maquis.

"Siegfried! You best hurry, the taxi will be here in a couple of minutes." Came an Italian woman's voice from downstairs, Siegfried's mother only ever spoke to him in her native Italian tongue, making him fluent in both Italian and

German. The young man stuffed a black and white photo of his dear mother into his sack and sealed it shut.

"Coming, Mama!" he called back chucking the bag over his shoulder, he was already wearing his very smart, ash grey Wehrmacht uniform.

After a tearful farewell, Siegfried tried to act as upset as his mother but was unconvincing. He was in the back of a taxi on the way to Leipzig where he and the other new recruits would be put onto buses to be deployed across the Nazi occupied world.

Five hours later, the recruits were standing at attention in three ranks, ready to swear the oath to the führer, in unison:

"I swear to god this sacred oath that to the leader of the Herman Reich and people, Adolf Hitler, supreme commander of the armed forces, I shall render unconditional obedience and that, as a brave soldier, I shall at all times be prepared to give my life for this oath."

The training camp's officer looked at the men he had cussed out and trained for the last two years proudly, like a father watching his child's first steps. They had spent the last two years being trained in a wide assortment of weapons, grenades, hand to hand combat and various explosives and now they were ready to defend the Reich that they all served.

"I am proud to look upon you all, the best recruits that I have ever trained, you should be honoured to go off to serve our glorious führer and our triumphant fatherland!"

He then directed to one of his subordinates to hoist the Nazi emblem up the flagpole. The black swastika in the white circle on the blood red background waved in the breeze, over the new recruits proudly. The training officer raised his right arm in a fascist salute and said loudly "Heil Hitler, Sieg heil!" and showing the results of the continuous doctrine of Nazi ideology, the young conscripts retorted, raising their right arms in salute

"Heil, Heil, Heil." It gave Siegfried a tremendous warm glow in his chest beneath the eagle adorning the swastika emblem on the right breast of his uniform, he had met the führer once before and it was the most illustrious moment of his life, it was the most memorable experience that he ever had and a day that he would remember until the day he died.

He was twelve years of age when scouting was abolished and he was transferred into the Hitler youth instead. Being part of the first Hitler youth paramilitary organisation in Dresden, they were honoured by an official visit from the führer, who shook each of the young members by the hand, asking their names. After Siegfried informed their glorious leader of his name:

"Ah, Siegfried, the famous dragon slayer. Your name is one of a true brave soldier." The great leader put a hand on the boy's shoulder and gave a small chuckle before moving on down the line. Every time he heard the great man on the wireless radio, it filled his heart with electrifying patriotism but this was the moment that he had decided that he would be willing to take on the noble deed to fight and die for the prominent leader.

"Dismissed!" the order snapped Siegfried from his memories. The troops turned to their left in unison and ran to collect their haversacks, then queued at three previously set up wooden tables where they would give their name and be assigned to one of the waiting buses that would transport them to their designated destination.

The dark navy buses with the emblem of the imperial eagle, its wings outstretched above a wreath encasing the swastika on its sides, they were not designed with leisure in mind, the windows were grated, the seats were made of hard, solid, splintering wood with no cushioning and the rough floor was covered in mud and by the smell, worse. This did not discourage the young conscripts, whose only experience of war was the bombing around their great cities and the German propaganda messages at the cinema and on the wireless radio sets that every family had in their front room.

They were going onwards to their own greatest adventure, like the great Germanic heroes of legend. If they had been sensible, they would have taken the next eighteen hours journey resting but the new Wehrmacht troops were too excited to relax and as the bus lurched forwards, the teen occupants gave a delighted cheer and began singing raucously, the Reich national anthem, Horst-Wessel-Lied, as they watched the German terrain past them by at speed.

As the vehicles drove down the streets passing the residents of the German cities, they received cheers and waves as the German citizens held the greatest respect for their troops, in high regard. This reception quietened down as they travelled between the worked fields but the young blonde female farmhands would run up to the road waving and blowing kisses to the 'brave soldiers of the fatherland'.

After a couple of hours their excitement waned and the men began playing card games with the hope to expand the small amount of money that they had taken with them to spend in the glamorous French capital. One of the new recruits, a rebellious chap who had found himself in the brink more than a couple of times for his unruly behaviour, named Clemens Rüter, had smuggled in a couple bottles of schnapps, both pear and cherry flavoured. He passed the bottles around to his travelling comrades, each taking a generous sip.

The atmosphere on board soon became turbulent once again, as the journey became fuelled with the distilled spirit. The betting became ridiculous, songs (some not really befitting the Nazi regime) were sung and slurred jokes were made with the occasional ending in a small tussle when someone took offence. This continued late into the night, when the excitement waned, a mixture of fatigue and alcohol took over, the green soldiers fell into an alcohol fuelled slumber on the hard wooden benches. No one was conscious enough to notice when they had left Germany and entered the Reich state of France.

The military transport violently jolted to a turbulent stop, forcing some of the young troops to fall from their perch where they had passed out the previous night and littered the mud baked floor with their bodies. The sliding door at the front of the bus snapped open and in stepped a short, brick-built man with a grim face and square jaw. He looked at the shamble of 'fresh meat' before him. Without a word he picked up an empty schnapps bottle that had rolled to the front of the bus, his eyes then turned back to the hungover recruits, his face then cracked a grim, sly, wicked smile before bellowing at full strength.

"Okay, ladies, this is not a summer camp!" the officers voice echoed in the ears of the men who were all feeling worse for wear. "Out of the bus! This year gentlemen!" The teenage soldiers wearily rose and disembarked the bus.

"Come on, three ranks your disorderly lot, I have seen Jews with better order!" This was an offensive statement, for a German, as Jews were considered the lowest form of life on the planet. As the camps officer made his commands, it was evident that he was speaking louder than that was usual as some sort of torturing punishment.

Once the men had finally organised themselves into three ranks, the driver of their transport was chucking the men's bags from the belly of the bus into a disorganised pile, whilst some tired, bored looking troops boarded the vehicle, the new recruits were obviously being moved in as relief core.

"Welcome to Mont Valérien. This is a top-secret base and it is exactly that *top-secret*! Any photos or information of the operations of this facility is highly forbidden. Anybody found disregarding these facts will be shot." The troops were too hungover to react to this direct threat.

"I am Fledwebel Wachtmeister,"—equivalent to a staff sergeant— "Schultz, you are now mine!" he smirked as he looked as the shocked faces, they had not been used to such a harsh treatment. "These two charming men beside me", he indicated to a pair of corporals who stood either side of their superior with crooked emotionless faces, "are unteroffizier Müller and unteroffizier Böhm. You report to them and they report to me. This base has one objective, to eliminate that constant threat of the terrorists to the third Reich, the local ones call themselves the Maquis, but we also have the communist and Jewish infection."

The staff sergeant paused and observed his men for any reaction, yet received none, this did not please the officer, he waited for the bus to pull away, the diesel exhaust blew into the soldiers faces making them cough and splutter, before he continued:

"Now, fortunately, for you men, it is Friday afternoon and every weekend we send you to Paris for some R&R, as directed by our commander and chief, Reichsführer Himmler." Siegfried looked along the ranks to see if anyone else had noticed what he had, Heinrich Himmler was the head of the Schutzstaffel and the man who had orchestrated the concentration camps for the 'untermensch' (undesirable, labelled this for their race or religion), this camp was becoming all the more mysterious.

"Today you will find out where you will be living, your sleeping quarters, duties and rotas. Five men must stay guard every weekend; this will be done by drawing lots. The lucky five who will be staying on guard with me, whilst your comrades will be drinking and whoring are, soldat Krämer, Dietrich, Kühn, Pfeiffer and Beckermann."

Siegfried gave a sigh of relief, his name had not been mentioned but, disappointingly, Pfeiffer was the surname of his good friend, Carl. The three young men had discussed visiting the city of light together. But that group excursion would have to wait until another time.

"The rest of you will be going to Paris. Now, collect your bags and my two associates here", he directed to his two subordinates "will show you to your new home. Dismissed!"

The young soldiers, their heads sore through no fault but their own, collected their haversacks from the pile and were led by the pair of sour faced corporals, over a grassy ridge, that overlooked what could only be called a pit and in the centre was a line of five thick wooden posts, the rest of the area was sparse. This confused Siegfried and a few of the others, of course a top-secret base would need to be hidden and disguised in case a French hunter should stumble upon it or an allied reconnaissance plane was to spot it from the air but this was not what they had expected at all.

They were led to a wooden built barracks, on the other side of the ditch, secluded by the natural trees of the French woodland, surrounded by a barbed wire fence, which they were told was 'for security' but it looked more like a mini prison camp. The inside was nothing particularly special, it was a single room with twenty, three storey bunk beds along the walls neighboured by three lockers, one for each bunk, two stoves at each end of the room and four tables with six chairs for each.

"The trees are your toilets," laughed the corporals, "you do not want to be smelling your shit during the summer, so you will want to go deeper into the woods."

The men began claiming their bunks and lockers, personalising them almost instantly, by putting up pin-ups or pictures of family and loved ones. Siegfried stuck up the picture of his mother on the wall behind his lower bunk bed. The privates then lined up to check their duties and rotas from a clipboard. Siegfried and Carl were on perimeter guard duty, where Stefan had been assigned catering duty. The two friends were taking the mic out of Stefan, telling him to watch out when peeling the potatoes, when Clemens Rüter appeared among them.

"What did you get?" question Stefan trying to deflect the attention from him.

"I've been assigned as a motorcycle, prisoner escort." replied Clemens proudly.

Siegfried was puzzled 'prisoner escort?' He thought, *what kind of base was this?*

Chapter 2

The following morning there was a sense of excitement around the camp, as the recruits dressed in their uniforms, they had to be smart. They were going into the great 'City of Light'; they must make a good impression to the French peasants of Paris.

They took a roll call before boarding military transportation lorries and the atmosphere was full of anticipation. Siegfried and Stefan had agreed together that on their first trip to this foreign land that they would try the two specialities of Paris, the French wine and cheese delicacies that this country was famous for. The travel was only a short trip and only took them half an hour to arrive into the capital city.

The young soldiers were agog as they dismounted the truck, the architecture was astonishing and the men lingered at the rear of the truck to absorb the area, in the distance they could see the iconic Eiffel Tower standing tall and proud over the beautiful city. The two friends began to walk into the large city, neither had ever seen such a picturesque settlement, they had both grown up in the German city of Dresden, which did not compare to this historic place.

The duo found a quaint little traditional French café where there were already many Nazi soldiers frequenting, enjoying the city's wares. Germans tried not to mingle with the French peasants to avoid familiarity. A tall waiter came out of the building to take the newcomers order, Stefan who had been studying the French language placed the order and minutes later the couple were enjoying a bottle of Château Musar, red wine and a platter consisting of five various cheeses which were full of flavour and had a pungent odour, so unlike the bland cheeses that were available in Germany.

They had been enjoying the French delicacies for a near two hours when their comrade Clemens Rüter joined them, proud of his most recent purchase, a Canon IIB camera.

“We should take some photos” he suggested, picking a small wedge of cheese from the platter and ate it without asking. “Souvenirs of our first visit to Paris.” the two friends looked at each other, gave a shrug, why not?

The three men continued to travel deeper into the great city, with Clemens snapping away with his newly acquired camera at every turn. The group paused outside a tobacconist store, in thick white paint on the business window was the Star of David and the word ‘Juden’, Jew, pasted on the door was a sheet of paper with writing in French and then German, stating that the proprietors of the business were Jews and enemies of the Reich. Anyone who was to enter or purchase anything from the establishment would be arrested; if the perpetrator was a soldier, then they would be arrested by the Gestapo, secret police and tried for treason.

Siegfried was horrified seeing the actions taken by the German forces. He had been brought up to believe the Jews were the enemy of the German people and were ‘unter menschen’, the lowest form of life and had no rights to own any personal possessions, yet he had never expected to see such persecution. However, his comrades seemed unfazed or even proud of this vulgar display, so Siegfried hid his disgust and the group continued on. It did not take them too long, soon they saw and past many other shut down Jewish businesses.

Passing a tailor’s shop named ‘Weinstein clothing’, they saw a small throng of people shouting abuse and obscenities at the proprietor who was being beaten by some khaki shirted men wearing the national socialist, blood red, swastika armband, kicking and throwing violent punches against the helpless, downed man, who already had a swollen black eye; blood was streaming from his fractured nose, matting his black beard a shade of crimson, yet the assailants never faulted there beating.

The three recruits watched the spectacle, Clemens and Stefan seemed to get caught up in the scenario and began yelling encouragement to the aggressors with such words as “Lynch the Jewish scum” and “All Jews should be slaughtered”. As one of the Nazi goons began to beat the demobilised body brutally with a wooden baton, Siegfried was horrified by what he saw and was shocked by his friends’ interactions, yet he could not show his sheer disgust, he felt dumbfounded. He did his best to seem uninterested and bored of the savage display, so continued on followed by his friends.

Soon they were looking up with admiration at the pulling iron structure, towering above them with the large white letter ‘V’, for victory, as symbol used commonly by the French resistance and the Allied forces. This was later adopted by the Germans as a claim to their conquered territory.

There were a few beautiful French maidens who approached the trio, flirting with them, they took the three men by surprise as many of the Paris residence tried to avoid the occupying forces and kept their eyes to the ground so as not to make eye contact with the foreign invaders. These three soldiers were not going to reject the amorous advances by the gorgeous brunette maidens who had attached themselves to the Wehrmacht soldiers.

Clemens began snapping photos of his associates with these three lush females in front of the giant structure. Two of the girls, seemed very attracted to Siegfried's olive-skinned complexion, leaving Clemens feeling a bit jealous. Yet the females, without a word, immediately dispersed, when four Frenchmen passed by the group, giving the girls stern looks.

"I would bet that those men are with the resistance," whispered Stefan.

"Shouldn't we place them under arrest or something?" Siegfried questioned, feeling a bit concerned that they were being observed by these apparent ruthless murders.

"What for? Anyway that's not our job" dismissed Clemens.

The men looked around the surrounding city; they felt a bit lost in this foreign land. But they made a point of exploring the notorious red-light district. They were even propositioned by a few 'ladies of the night' who were standing in the street. All three were greatly tempted as they observed the scantily dressed, beautiful working girls, in the many red lit front windows of the brothels. Though Siegfried was very tempted to sample the wares, especially when he saw a long-haired blonde prostitute with pale white skin but was unsure that if he wanted to pay for his first time.

As they exited the district, Clemens came up with an idea, "Shall we get some proper Scottish whiskey and American cigarettes?" he suggested, Siegfried did not smoke but was favourable to the occasional whiskey. He knew only too well that the flavour of the German whiskey did not even compare to the true Scottish whiskey in the slightest.

"Where the hell can we get that?" asked Siegfried, "We can't get British and American stuff anywhere."

"Not a problem. I was talking to a Panzer commander earlier and he told me of a German speaking black-market dealer nearby."

"But they are all connected to the resistance, aren't they?" Stefan asked concerned.

"Apparently so, but I think they care more about money. I was told they are happy to deal with us," urged Clemens.

Siegfried had to agree that it would be worth the risk if they could get their hands on some good quality whiskey, even if it meant the risk of dealing with the Maquis. The trio roamed down the cobbled streets of the grand city, led by Clemens and then to a small secluded side street, stepping aside to allow a smartly dress Frenchman, who had almost bumped into them, as he passed, leaving the alleyway with a small canvas bag most likely containing some illegal or rationed wares.

They descended down the dark damp passage where they found a gruff looking man wearing a white collarless shirt with the cuffs folded up, a black striped waistcoat and a black armband on his upper left arm. The alley had come to a dead end and was littered with wooden crates, it was filthy and bleak. The man noticed the three young soldiers dressed in their uniforms and spoke in fluent German with a strong Bavarian accent, which took them all by surprise.

"Good morning, gentlemen, how can I help you today?"

"You're German?" asked Siegfried.

"Non, I am a Frenchman, of course," the man replied handing the young man his 'ausweis', identity card, which Siegfried flipped opened, the photograph matched the man before him.

"Didler?" asked Siegfried, observing the unusual name, handing back his papers.

"Oui, how can I be of service?" He offered, acting quite relaxed but that was how these illegal marketeers were.

"We understand that you can get us some Scottish whiskey and American cigarettes," said Stefan quietly, they weren't sure but it was possible that they could get in trouble if they were caught trading with these underground dealers.

The man scanned the three men in front of him, before replying, "Oui, but it will not be cheap," advised the black-market dealer.

The three men rifled into their pockets and passed Clemens half of their Reichsmarks, this was his idea so he could do the deal. He showed the French trader the money who inspected it and went over to one of the crates and began rummaging through the straw contents. Siegfried continually checked behind them nervously, he was getting all the more nervous, if they were discovered down here then they could very likely get into trouble.

Even though it was widely known through the ranks that the German occupiers often used these back-alley dealers but it was known that they had close connections with the French resistance, the Gestapo, was always trying to shut them down. The marketeer pulled from the crate a single seventy centilitre bottle of Scottish Highland whiskey and two hundred Lucky Strike cigarettes in two cartons; he passed them to the young soldiers in return for the money.

"Merci," said the gruff man as he watched the trio leave.

They retired to the boarding house they were staying at, casually saluting officers as they passed. In their room they remained, playing cards, drinking the whiskey as Stefan and Clemens made their way, chain smoking the newly acquired tobacco products. The lads had, at first, intended to have an early night but the motorcycle escort driver decided that he wanted to go and visit one of the many brothels that they had seen in the famous red-light district and persuaded his two friends to accompany him. The excessive amounts of alcohol had diminished their morals and they agreed.

They spent the remainder of their money to spend the following couple of hours in the arms of the desirable beauties the brothel offered, drinking a lot of the un-rationed champagne that was offered, before returning satisfied and slightly intoxicated back to the boarding house and the next morning they refused to rise from their beds. Only rising to be sure that they were able to catch the only transport truck back to base.

Chapter 3

Upon their return to the covert military base, they were surprised to hear that Fledwebel Wachtmeister Schultz was not as acrimonious as he had appeared at first and had paid for a group of high-quality working girls, who had arrived shortly after the other men had left on a small bus with blacked out windows, to entertain the men left at the camp. If that wasn't enough to boost the remaining soldiers' moral, they had also enjoyed roast venison with honey glazed vegetables, a selection of fine cheese and some top-quality French port for dinner.

They were also informed that the lieutenants were not as generous as their superior and would go so far as to make the weekends miserable, they were also the men that would be in charge of the next two weekends of guard duty. Siegfried and Stefan both secretly crossed their fingers hoping their names would not be called for guard duty on the following two weekends. Still slightly hungover from their two days of free living, many of the soldiers of the secret base retired to their bunks with the intention of sleeping off their pounding heads. And like most of the troops, Siegfried promised not to drink again, a promise he intended to keep, until the next time.

As the next day dawned, the men's heads had cleared and as every morning at the hidden stronghold, the alarm for roll call sounded, waking the man from their deep, rejuvenating sleep, which would have seemed to have its desired effect. The young troops, quite literary, sprung from their firm mattress, slipped into their matt ash grey uniforms, grabbed their Mauser Karabiner Kar 98k rifles and formed three ranks outside in the bases yard.

The gruff Fledwebel Wachtmeister watched as one of his subordinates called each man by name "Köhn".

"Jawohl," Siegfried replied, standing to attention. Instead of dismissing the men directly after the roll call the Fledwebel Wachtmeister stepped forwards.

“I hope you all had an enjoyable time in this country’s capital city.” There was no sound of sincerity or thoughtfulness in his tone, it sounded more like an order:

“But now your duty begins. We are fortunate not to get much trouble here in the middle of the French woodland, except for the occasional hunter or logger who should stumble in our direction. I know that I do not need to remind you that this is a top-secret installation. So if you were to see anyone, no matter how innocent they may seem, you either arrest them or shoot to kill, this place cannot be reported to the resistance or Allied forces! Shoot to kill, no exceptions!”

He stopped and scanned his men’s faces for some sort of reaction, yet these new recruits had been trained well and just looked dead ahead with stone like expressionless faces as they absorbed the words. This reception seemed to please the garrison’s commander to some extent.

“Now go to your duty and keep this base protected from unfriendly eyes! Dismissed!” The parade fell out and took up their assigned duties.

Much to Siegfried’s jealous dismay, Carl had been placed to man a Fallschirmjagergewehr 42, light machine-gun bunker. There were twelve of these surrounding machine gun positions around the ridge encasement, each having a wide field of fire, when the other guards had to carry the standard bolt actioned Mausers. Each guard patrolled between the machine-gun posts to assure the whole terrain was observed and no one could absent-mindedly wander into the encampment.

Siegfried had listened carefully to every word his superior had said and three words had stuck in his mind, ‘shoot to kill’, the young Wehrmacht soldier could not fathom what could be so secretive that the order would be such. But who was he to question it? He had been given a direct order by a superior officer and as a soldier he had to abide by the command, anyhow the Fledwebel Wachtmeister did say that it hardly ever happened. Siegfried prayed that this was true.

Up upon the ridge the scenic view was astounding, on three sides was the deep green forest in full bloom, while on the fourth side were beautiful grassy knolls as far as the eye could see. There was a mild chill in the air, despite the morning sun, yet there was no breeze to speak of. They could hear the faint low roar of approaching lorries accompanied by the roaring sound of a motorcycle revving from the other side of the complex which intruded like a profanity. The noise ceased together in a moment.

They had been on guard duty for half an hour when there was a single ear-splitting blare of the alarm. A platoon of sixty SS fusiliers, all wearing the jet-black uniforms and the 'Toten Kopf' emblem signifying that they were prisoner of war or concentration camp guards, they marched smartly into the arena below them.

"Hey Siggie," Clemens greeted him cheerily, as if appearing out of nowhere, wearing the Reich's motorcycle leathers.

"Hi," Siegfried replied, his attention fixed on what was happening below them. "Aren't you meant to be doing some kind of escort?" With a hint of boasting in his voice Clemens replied

"Done it. We had to get up before the rest of you guys, I guess it is so you do not have to wait around for too long."

"Wait? Wait for what?" Wondered Siegfried out loud and as if answering his question three men all appearing to have been beaten, wearing dirty tattered clothing and one thing the young man had noticed, none of the three men were wearing any footwear, they were being savagely dragged over the rough gravel flooring barefooted. The men were being taken from the 'Restricted Zone' by a few brutal looking SS soldiers, this was an off-limits area buried into the side of the rock face. No one except for base commanders and now it would seem the Schutzstaffel were permitted to enter.

The three men were tied to separate posts, blindfolded and got a white square of paper, harshly pinned to their left breast. Siegfried could not believe what he was seeing, he had often heard his father speak of this exact procedure, the white square were the targets for the marksmen to aim for, this was an execution. Siegfried looked at the bound men, these were not soldiers, they were civilians. Shooting unarmed non-combatants was not an act of war, it was cold blooded murder.

As horrifying as this act was, the young Wehrmacht trooper could not tear his eye from the scene unravelling before him and he was not the only one witnessing it. This disgusting display had seemed to have caught the attention of all the new recruits, but none, except for Siegfried, seemed to be affected by what was unfolding in front of their very eyes. No one seemed to notice that the victims were not military.

"Who are they?" he asked Clemens, hoping that he was mistaken.

"Resistance, communists, Jews, who knows?" Clemens said coldly, not taking his eyes from the condemned men for a split second "Who cares?"

The Schutzstaffel commander barked to his men to take aim, the SS platoon took aim with their rifles simultaneously, like a smooth operating machine, at the three men. One of the three condemned men bellowed at the top of his voice, "Vive la France!" Ignoring this outburst the Nazi officer commanded his men to fire

"Feuer!" The firing squad fired simultaneously, the shots echoed against the rock face walls, as the three men slumped to the bottom of the logs. The SS officer withdrew his Luger revolver and went from one to the next of the victims, firing a single shot into the skull of each of the corpses for good measure. Siegfried looked towards his new friend and comrade, Clemens, who had a wide almost smug smile on his face, he had obviously found this display rather entertaining, when Siegfried felt sick to his stomach to such an extent that he was worried that he may vomit. He was finding it hard to register what he had just witnessed, had this been real or just some awful nightmare? But not even the worst of nightmares could make him feel this ill.

He had to respect the deceased man's courage, when facing death in the face he still displayed his infidelity for all to see. Clemens had disappeared after saying something about the dead bodies needing to be dispatched back to Berlin, yet the young soldier was too terrified to be listening, he dared not move, he stood stock still as he watched the deceased men being dragged back into the restricted area. Only once the corpses had vanished from view did Siegfried continue on his guard duty, trying to determine what he had just observed, it was unbelievable, beyond excusable. He continuously saw the scene in his mind's eye as if in a loop, he could hear the words of the patriotic civilians and the deafening explosion of the gun shots.

He marched from machine gun post to machine gun post as if in a daze. The rest of the morning was uneventful, except for seeing a beautiful red fox dart out of the forest brush with a limp rabbit in its mouth then seeing the Nazi encampment, he disappeared as quickly as he had arrived, otherwise they just watched the lifeless surroundings. Stefan came out with mugs of 'Ersatz Kaffee', acorn coffee, which the men welcomed; this static job did not use much energy to warm themselves up.

That same afternoon, things had changed; dark clouds had formed above them. They had just finished their boil in a bag army rations which they had cooked over small fire stoves without leaving their guard posts, which Siegfried, unlike many of his comrades, rather enjoyed his military issue rations, yet the feelings that had engulfed him from what he had seen that morning, made the food taste like ash in his mouth and he heard nothing of what his friends said, as the scenario of what had happened played through his mind in slow motion when there was another ear-splitting blare of the alarm. All eyes once again turned towards the lower court, as before the sixty strong SS firing squad had formed and like before the condemned men were roughly brought out, all in the same demoralising stake.

This time the victims consisted of two men, a woman and a boy who could not be any older than Siegfried, the inhumane executions had just taken a turn for the worse. Siegfried could not visualise that this kid being an enemy of the Reich. As before the detainees were blindfolded and had the small tear of paper pinned to their left breast. The two men raised themselves, as if standing to attention, which was not easy in their bound state and as loud as they could, they began to sing La Marseillaise, the illegal French national anthem, outlawed under Nazi law, at the top of their lungs. The female and youth then joined in with the raucous display.

The guards were watching this patriotic display with utter disgust, yet Siegfried felt a feeling of deep respect for these people, even when staring death in the face, they stood firm for their country. Something caught Siegfried's eye, to his left he saw hunkered down concealing himself behind a prickly shrub, was Clemens with his new camera. Seeing Siegfried looking in his direction, he put his finger to his lips motioning him to stay silent, as both men knew only too well what would happen to Clemens if he was found and Siegfried would not be dealt with any the less harshly, for having knowledge and not reporting this act of disobedience. Clemens gave a small smile as he snapped three photos of the detestable punishments being handed out to the French freedom fighters.

The Schutzstaffel commander had to bellow his commands at the top of his voice to be heard over the monotone voices of the prisoners. Siegfried watched the young detainee, it was obvious this young Frenchman was scared, taking his lead from his fellow older prisoners. The shots rang out in unison and the four French civilians crumbled to the ground before the officer made his final shots to the head of each corpse, for good measure. As if he had telescopic vision, Siegfried could see the petrified look on the young man's face which etched itself into his mind, he was at least two years Siegfried's junior.

That night many of the camps Wehrmacht guards ate heartily, all that was excepted for the young trooper, from Dresden, who could not get the image of the poor child victim and wondered how many more children had been and would be slaughtered here, the child's face was embedded in his mind.

The following week there were two group executions a day, victims of all ages, of both males and females, no matter how many lives he saw extinguished, by the firing squad it affected him all the more.

Chapter 4

The following days it was the same story, groups of between two to five men, women, the young and the old, with no one spared, every morning and afternoon people were being unmercifully slain. After the third day of executions, the guards no longer paid much attention to the massacre happening beneath them. Every night Siegfried would wake in a cold sweat with the image of the young, now deceased, boy that had been murdered under the tyrannical regime of the Nazi powers, that he was now ashamed to be an instrument of. The scenes he witnessed on a daily basis and the persecution he had seen in the city tormented his mind every night. After a week of disturbed sleep, was enough to send the clearest mind mad, Siegfried had to do something extreme and now.

Friday soon arrived and the lots for the weekend duty, under unteroffizier Böhm, were drawn. Everyone was holding their breath with the hope that their name would not be called and that they would be able to visit the grand city of light. Siegfried listened as each name was called and there was a huge sigh of relief after the five men had been chosen. Siegfried knew what he had to do, even though it was risky and he could not do it whilst being stuck on the base. If he was discovered, then he would be as good as dead or even worse in the hands of the ruthless Gestapo whose notorious methods and inventive torture methods were infamous, they could put the fear into the hearts of the bravest of men.

Siegfried sat in compete silence on the military transportation journey, even when Carl and Stefan spoke to him, he only gave short curt replies, he had more pressing matters on his mind. They had soon arrived at beautiful city of Paris and disembarked the vehicle. As Siegfried roamed down the cobbled streets, he no longer noticed the extraordinary superb architecture or the beautiful French maidens that would have normally caught his eye. He purposely led his friends into the popular red-light district, he knew that they both had a decant sum of money as he had made sure that they had won it from him before leaving camp.

As soon as they had entered, they were swiftly surrounded by a small flock of working girls like bees around honey. This is exactly what Siegfried had anticipated, his close friends were soon preoccupied by the lush ladies of the night which gave him the chance to slip away un-noticed. He tried to recall the route that he had taken with Clemens and Stefan the previous week, he was on the way to see the black-market dealer, Didler, he needed the man's assistance, he would be the only person who could get him in touch with the only organisation who could help him, the Maquis.

He saluted a Generallentnant who walked from the necessary alleyway, carrying a suitcase, possible filled with illegal wares that had just been procured from the illicit trader. The German officer ignored the private and continued on his way, this suited Siegfried just fine. The young soldier checked the street, making sure he was not seen or being followed, this was not going to be a simple purchase, before he descended down the back passage.

"Ah, hello again," said the gruff man recognising the junior soldier, the man lit a cigarillo before continuing "more whiskey? Or is it cigarettes?" the young man was unsure how to proceed, He stammered as he forced out his words.

"I need you to…to arrange a meeting for me with…with the resistance."

The gruff man was naturally taken back by this curious and bizarre request from a German soldier. He looked around, to be sure that this was a genuine appeal and not a Nazi ploy and that they were not being observed or being eavesdropped upon.

He took another deep drag on his tobacco product before replying, "And why do you think I would be able to do that?"

"I was told that a man with a black armband could get me anything" replied Siegfried, hoping to play on the man's vanity, "plus it is not a secret that you illicit traders have connections with the resistance".

The marketeer smirked at this reply, "Now why would a German want to make contact with the Maquis?" The man studied the young soldier suspiciously. Siegfried knew only too well that he had to be convincing, otherwise this whole attempt would be a bust and he had no plan B.

"I need—," the marketeer cut the young man off with a raise of his hand as a Frenchman turned the corner.

The pair of Frenchmen spoke briefly in their native tongue, Siegfried could tell his presence was making the newcomer nervous, yet the salesman reassured him and handed him a brown paper bag, in exchange for a small wad of Franc notes. The Parisian left making sure he did not make eye contact with the Axis soldier observing him. They waited for the capital city's resident to vanish before the German was invited to continue:

"I need help to get out of the army, I cannot be a part of what the Nazis are doing, I am a soldier, not a murderer," he said sincerely. Didler studied the man for any sign of deception but he could see the conflict in the soldier's face. Didler gave a small nod in thought.

"Alright, I will talk to my boss," he stated. "Meet me back here, tomorrow morning and I will have an answer for you."

"Danke," thanked the young soldier and left the alleyway. He wandered around the city streets aimlessly; this may be his last chance to admire the buildings of this historic settlement; he visited the iconic Arc de Triomphe and the breath-taking cathedral of Notre-Dame.

That afternoon he had met backup with his two childhood friends who had not noticed his absence as they had spent most of their money in the loving arms of the Paris whores. The three mates had agreed to meet up at a local French café, popular with the Nazi occupiers. Siegfried decided to retire to bed early. Even though the extreme stress of the whole situation had made him fatigued, he found it hard to drop off to sleep with the fear of what tomorrow may bring and what message the Maquis had in response to his request.

The following morning Siegfried woke early in the room of the boarding house, his partners were still deep asleep signified by Carl's deep snoring. The young soldier quietly dressed himself, slipped covertly from the room and began walking along the bleak city streets, it seemed that the residents of the capital rose late, a couple of newspaper vendors, market stall traders who were setting up their wares and the occasional German soldier who seemed to have had a bit of a heavy night enjoying what this city had to offer, looking a bit worse for wear after a night of drinking and whoring, otherwise there were very few people on the cobbled streets.

Siegfried hardly noticed the few civilians as he had only one thing on his mind and it was all going through his head at a tremendous rate, it was giving the young Wehrmacht soldier a fierce headache. He eventually found his way to the desired alleyway, he hesitated briefly at the entrance, if the illicit trader had not trusted him or the resistance were overly suspicious that this turncoat was anything but sincere, he could be walking to his fate. But he had come too far to turn back now, no matter how he felt his stomach was jumping in knots. He looked one final time along the streets, there were a mere few people, except for a group of three Frenchmen smoking, all stood around a barrel fire, this was nothing out of the norm.

Siegfried took a deep breath, straightened out his uniform and descended down the dim red bricked passageway. He turned left into the clearing and was met by seven men, all armed, dressed in everyday civilian clothing. Siegfried looked behind him, two of the three men, who had been outside now stood behind him with sawn down shotguns, which they had been concealing under their coats, whilst the third stood guard blocking the entrance of the alleyway.

"Welcome," said the man in the centre, in German with a strong French accent. He rose from the wooden crate he was seated at; he was a clean-shaven middle-aged man who had long black hair going down to the bottom of his neck, tied back in a ponytail and deep brown eyes, he was wearing a sky-blue polo neck jumper, a brown, wool lined, leather jacket.

"I believe you said you wanted to meet with us?" Siegfried looked around at the men who had congregated in this back passageway and seemed amused by the young man's confusion and concern.

"We are the Maquis," confirmed the man, turning the collar on his coat to reveal a brass pin of the Cross of Lorraine, the symbol of the French resistance

"I am Pierre, leader of the Paris resistance. And you are?" he asked in a friendly tone, producing a hand. Siegfried was nervous, he was in front of a group of men who had openly killed German soldiers.

"My name is Siegfried, Siegfried Köhn," he forced out taking the resistance leader's hand.

"Welcome, Siegfried, now I am afraid that my German is not the best and I have almost exhausted my supply. But first tell me what would your parents think if they knew that you were consorting with the French resistance?"

"My father would disown me, he is an officer is the Schutzstaffel," he confessed sadly ashamed.

"And your mother?"

"She is Italian. She would respect my decision, even if she didn't agree with it," he replied, Pierre nodded in understanding, the relationship between mother and son needed no explanation.

"Well, my friend here will be able to translate for us, from now on," Pierre said presenting a man. "This is Yosef," he introduced.

The man was in his mid-forties, with dark slicked back hair and distinct Jewish features, stepped forward. Pierre spoke to his associate, who then translated it in German in a distinct Kölsch accent, an accent which was near impossible to imitate.

"Our leader, Pierre, would like to know, what we can do for you?"

"You're German?" question Siegfried, taken back by this man speaking fluently in his native tongue.

"Yes, I am a German Jew. I fled Germany when the reality of the Nazi party came to light." The man had a comforting, soothing tone, like he was talking to a young child "Where are you from?"

Siegfried was not naive he knew this question was to put him at ease.

"Dresden," he replied, the Jew just nodded.

"And why did you wish to speak with us?" he persisted.

"I need to leave. I am working as a guard at a top-secret base at a fort called Mont Valérien," he saw the Frenchmen stand up straight and take notice at the name of the fort. "It is an execution base where they are shooting people who they consider as enemies of the Reich, like Communists, Jews and resistance." The young soldier paused, allowing Yosef to translate what was being said to his boss. "I am a soldier, not a murderer. I am *not* a Nazi!" he said, his voice was almost pleading.

Pierre spoke to some of his associates in a low tone and was replied to in hushed voices, before their leader once again turned and spoke to Yosef who in turn translated to the young soldier.

"We know that not all Germans are Nazis and we have heard of Mont Valérien. Do you know of a resistance leader named Jean Moulin?"

Siegfried shook his head, the name meant nothing to him.

Yosef continued, "He was captured recently and sent to this fort of yours for execution, we have considered a rescue but the base is too heavily guarded." The Jew hesitated, looking a bit distressed about the next thing he had to translate. "We will help you but only if you help us. You must smuggle him out of the camp and take him to a hidden logger cabin in the woods just outside the base. It is a safe-house and from there we can get you out."

Siegfried had not expected this, he had not even been to the area where the prisoners were confined, there had to be another way and he voiced his concerns to the Jewish, Maquis soldier, Yosef passed it back to Pierre, who gave the young soldier the once over and his reply to Yosef to translate.

"There is no other way, my young friend. If you want us to trust you then you must do something for us. You do this, we will help you escape."

Escape sounded a bit over-dramatic but he guessed that that was exactly what he was doing, escaping the Third Reich.

"If I do this, I will never be able to, be able to return home, you understand?" he said.

Pierre then spoke up, "No, you cannot, you will be a wanted man, just like us, you will be marked as a criminal and a traitor, then we would be the only people able to help you." He was blunt but to the point "do you agree to our terms?"

It was evident that he had had enough of the idle chit-chat. With the knowledge that rejection could result in his life being extinguished by the resistance, he replied, "I have no choice," said the young man dully, his mind full of doubt.

"Bon, we will see you in two days at the woodman's cabin. Jean will know the way, he built it," said Pierre turning back to German and the men began to slip from the secluded alley, leaving intervals between each man so as not to arouse suspicion, until the young German was alone. Still struggling to absorb what he had just agreed to.

Chapter 5

Siegfried's head was in a daze as he left the alleyway, he had set the wheels in motion, things that couldn't be changed now. But first, he had to risk his life for some high-profile resistance fighter that he didn't even know. Why the hell hadn't he just done his R&R and then absconded, become a deserter and not returning to the secret base? He could just let his hair grow long, not shave and become a logger or hunter in the French wilderness, after all he came the top of his class in target practise, instead he was breaking his oath and doing the bidding of the Maquis, traitors of the Reich, he didn't even know if he could trust these people, after all he was a soldier of the Wehrmacht.

These thoughts ran through the young Germans head like a freight train. Siegfried did his best to put the depressing thoughts out of his mind; he couldn't let anyone see his anxiety. For a while he wandered around aimlessly, he felt a strange sense of freedom in the grand city, there was a visible throb of history in the grand Parisian architecture. He saw his friends Carl and Stefan at a quaint, traditional French café, with a bright green blind to protect the patrons from the sweltering Paris sun which had finally made its appearance.

"Where the hell have you been?" Carl cheered as Siegfried joined them and took a seat at the outside table.

"You need to ask?" Stefan answered, "he has been to one of them brothels, making one of those French whores squeal."

Siegfried turned red in the face at the thought of it, which his friends took as confirmation, making then to laugh out loud.

"Café?" asked a young brunette appearing from inside the establishment.

"Ja…oui," said the new soldier. For the remainder of the day he sat with his friends relaxing and laughing, almost forgetting the strenuous and potentially dangerous quest ahead of him.

On their return to the base, the reality hit Siegfried like a ton of bricks, he had to find out what jail cell this Jean Moulin was in, smuggle him out of the base without raising the alarm and deliver him to the resistance who would be waiting for them at a hunter's log cabin deep in the forest. *It sounds easy if you say it fast,* thought Siegfried, trying to make himself feel better and more comfortable with the situation, without success.

He hadn't even thought of how he would smuggle a condemned prisoner out of the heavily fortified base without arousing suspicion. That night the young private hardly slept, his plan was racing through his mind, he had to get the timing exactly right down to the second or the whole operation could be an utter bust. After a long night of tossing and turning, the sound Siegfried had been both longing and dreading, the morning roll call was sounded, his rescue attempt was to be today.

The Wehrmacht troops enthusiastically jumped from their bunks, hastily dressed into their uniforms and grabbed their assigned weapons before they rushed outside for the headcount. Before leaving the camps barracks, Siegfried grabbed the black and white picture of his mother, folded it in half and slipped it into his pocket. Siegfried was almost shaking, he was so scared he could not deny it, so many things could go wrong, so much was going through his mind he nearly missed his name being called.

Once the order to be dismissed was made, everyone ran to their posts, everyone except for Siegfried, who slunk straight into the restricted area of the base, the prisoners' confinement area. An area built into the side of a hill, with reinforced concrete, it was dimly lit by single lights on the walls, every twenty feet between each other, the floor was uneven with the occasional puddle which you could not see until it was too late.

Siegfried got out his Daimon air right angle flash light and began to scan the walls for some sort of clipboard or some indication of who occupied the dark, cold cells. The smell down here was one of sweat, blood and human waste, the damp air seeped into the young soldier's skin, chilling him down to his bones. He could see movement in the darkness of the prison cells as he passed. He saw a light streaming from an open doorway ahead. He froze for a brief second, switching off his torch, before continuing, if the room was occupied, the operation would be over before it had begun.

He listened for any notification of any occupancy, he heard nothing and continued cautiously, flinching when he made the slightest noise, stopping every few steps to inspect for any sign of life. It took him twice as long to reach the open doorway, he nervously peered in. It was vacant, the room was an office, illuminated by a single desk lamp, there were three old wooden filing cabinets, overflowing with what seemed to be execution orders, sat on the desk was the one item that Siegfried had been looking for, the clipboard. On the sheet it had the cell numbers, from one to thirty, neighboured by the name of the occupant and then the date of the execution.

The young German scanned through the names and found J. Moulin written in bold red ink signifying that he was a prominent and significant member who had orchestrated attacks against the occupying forces in France. His adrenaline rose, with the unmistakeable knowledge that being found here would result with himself being shot. He checked the resistance leader's execution date; it was today, that very afternoon.

He then checked his cell number, cell twenty-two, *very apt*, he thought, the letter used abundantly by the resistance was 'V' for victory and that was the twenty-second letter of the alphabet. He grabbed a long, thick, fur lined, Russian trench coat, that was hung on the back of the antique style, swivel chair with red leather padded cushions, he had seen the rags that the prisoners wore and this long coat may help disguise the fact that this man had just escaped a Nazi execution camp.

There was a map of the subterranean cell on the wall, yet something else caught his eye, up on top of one of the filing cabinets sat a Luger P08 revolver, carried by most German officers, this was perfect, it was much easier to carry and conceal than his rifle. He slung his rifle on his back, they may need the fire power to escape, retrieved the pistol and replaced it with his coal scuttle helmet, there was no going back now. Only then did he check the map, the cell was only two doors back from the way he had just come.

He was just about to leave the room, when he froze in the door way, the keys; he needed the prison cells keys! He could have kicked himself; it had totally skipped his mind. He turned back into the office, the jail guards had a set each, but they had to keep a spare set somewhere in here. He checked the walls for a hook, nothing, he looked on the desk to no avail. He opened the centre draw to the desk, there was a carton of pistol rounds for the luger, which Siegfried slipped into his pocket, they may come in handy, but still no keys. He opened the left-hand draw, if they were not in here, he would have to resort to checking in the filing cabinets.

Upon opening the draw a half bottle of Scottish highland whiskey caught his eye, probably brought from one of the black-market dealers in the capital city of

Paris. Without hesitation Siegfried picked up the bottle, took out the stopper and took a large swig for 'Dutch courage' before slipping the bottle into his pocket, the French leader may need some enticement. He turned back to the draw, rolled his eyes and gave a small sigh, as he saw a huge set of brass keys, each one had a number painted on it, indicating the cell in opened. The young Wehrmacht soldier flicked through the keys until he found the one, he needed and detached it from the rest, it would make less noise that way, whilst he carried it.

He ducked behind a wooden filing cabinet as a couple of SS guards marched a small group of men to the arena, to be the victims of that morning's execution. Once he was sure they had passed he checked the hallway for any other sign of life, there was none. Then in total silence, he ran to the cell door, slipped the key into the lock and carefully opened the door. The pungent smell was much stronger in here and nearly made the young man vomit as the overpowering stench singed his nasal hairs.

Inside the small concrete room, it was bleak and dark, there was near no light, except for a small stream of sunlight which came through a two-inch open slit at the top of the wall. There was a rusting bucket in one corner for the detainee to take a call of nature, there was no straw bedding or any type of furniture, the entire room was surrounded in concrete which was scrawled with names, dates and the slogan 'Vive la France'. Curled in the darkness of one corner of the room in a state of nakedness sat a man, aged in his late forties or early fifties, he had long, unkempt, matt greying hair with a matching beard and was unnaturally thin from malnutrition.

"Monsieur Moulin?" Siegfried asked nervously. The man wearily rose to his feet, the prisoners physic was worse than the German had seen at first, his ribcage was sticking from his body and the stomach was a pit in the man's torso, making the pelvis look larger than normal.

"Monsieur Moulin, I am here to get you out." The young man informed him, hoping he sounded convincing. The frail man replied in fluent German, "I will not be falling for any more of your tricks, German." Siegfried checked the hallway before replying.

"Pierre sent me," urged the young Wehrmacht soldier, he handed the coat, rifle and bottle of whiskey to the man. In the worn detainee's eyes there was a small glint appear at the name of the leader of the Paris resistance.

"Pierre?"

"Oui, but we must hurry," the young soldier was getting more nervous by the second. Jean, full of suspicion slipped on the coat that Siegfried had stolen from the office, covering his bare body the Frenchman then slung the rifle over his shoulder and took a swig from the whiskey bottle before slipping it into the coats oversized pocket.

"Come please, we must go!" The German pressured the Frenchman, once again checking the tunnels for any patrol. The French freedom fighter approached the German, wondering if this was some kind on Nazi trick to get him shot. Siegfried, with the pistol drawn, began to lead the resistance soldier down the dark corridor, not entirely sure where they were headed, the Frenchman noticed the German was disoriented.

"Where are we going?" he asked his liberator.

"There must be a back exit, where you were brought in after you were caught and where they take the dead bodies out," explained Siegfried franticly, looking around in a panic.

"This way!" the Frenchman directed, rushing down a side passage. Siegfried turned and followed the escaped man, as he turned the corner, to his horror he saw the escapee pinned against the wall by his throat, the aggressor was Siegfried's childhood friend Carl, he had his arm across the escaped Frenchman's neck, starring at him grimly. He glanced towards Siegfried and made a double take.

"Siggie? What the hell do you think you are doing?" Carl interrogated in surprise without easing his grasp on the escaped prisoner

"Let him go, I need to get him out of here, just let us go." Siegfried pleaded with his friend.

"Have you lost your god damn mind?" Carl spat, not taking his eyes off the Frenchman "He is a traitor!"

"He is a soldier, like you and me, he is fighting for what he believes in, for freedom." Explained Siegfried to his childhood pal, the prisoner was choking under the unwavering pressure of the man's arm across his oesophagus. Without thinking Siegfried raised his newly acquired Luger pistol and aimed it towards Carl and then, his voice stern and composed, with just a hint of begging he said "release him". His mate took a swift glance towards Siegfried and then back to the Frenchman.

"Are you fucking mad? I can't let you do this!" the assaulting soldier said removing his bayonet, preparing to gut the enemy of the Third Reich. Without a thought Siggie squeezed on the trigger, the bullet met its target and hit his friend, penetrating the young man's skull, killing him instantly. The sound echoed down the underground tunnels, ricocheting from one reinforced concrete wall to the next.

Jean gave Siegfried a thankful nod, yet the German hardly noticed, he was stuck where he was, looking at the deceased, crumbled body of the childhood friend that he had just murdered, he had never killed anyone before and never thought that his first confirmed kill would be someone he had known all of his life. A set of heavy footsteps could be heard running down a neighbouring passageway, this sound of impending doom approaching snapped the young German back to reality, he looked around him franticly to find somewhere to hide.

He saw a door with the word 'Lager' (the German word for storage) written in the common Fraktur text, he strode straight over to the door, it was unlocked, the two men, without looking first dived into the room and closed the door behind them. It was pitch black in here and as the young German pressed his ear against the door, as the Frenchman tried to figure out what was in this room as the smell was somehow familiar.

"Give me your torch" he whispered to his German associate, who was still listening to the activity happening just on the other side of the door and was hardly daring to breath, without moving from his position he removed the torch from his pocket and blindly passed it behind him to the French resistance leader. He could hear as least five Germans on the other side of the door in the hallway, then there was a shout and the boots began running towards the cells.

"Mon Dieu!" Exclaimed the Frenchman, drawing the young man's attention back to the room, what he saw shocked him to the core. Hanging from meat hooks in three rows were the bodies of the innocent victims of the Nazi firing squads. The two men were dismayed by this gross display of annihilation and total disrespect. The Frenchman walked along inspecting the corpses, mentioning names as he recognised some of his rebel brothers in arms. He stopped by the boy Siegfried had witnessed being executed a week ago.

"You see this boy?" He asked sternly, "he was only sixteen years of age. He is not a soldier. He posted flyers, that was it. This is what those philistines, your people do, murder children!" The man was clearly angry with this horrendous display, "do you know what your Gestapo did to him, to me?"

Siegfried was not sure he wanted to know, the unconventional methods of the Nazi secret police, the Gestapo, was notorious to say the least and it was not only the enemies of Hitler's Third Reich who had reason to fear them but everyone, civilians and even officers of the Nazi war machine could fall victim to these brutish tactics, no matter your rank or position in the Reich, nothing could protect you from the Gestapo.

"They stuck matches under our fingernails and lit them, they tore off our toenails with pliers, we swear an oath to hold out for two days but these patriots, men, women and children, they held out to the very end, without saying a word, they could have ended the pain and torture then and there, but they resisted, they are patriots, heroes. And this is how they are honoured?"

Siegfried looked to the ground, ashamed of his people's methods.

"I understand, they take them to Berlin as trophies," he stammered, hoping that would help the situation in some way.

"Or dumped into a mass unmarked grave." The French resistance member was quite obviously fuming but seeing the distress in his young associate, he calmed. "That soldier, he was a friend."

Siegfried nodded sadly, the Frenchman nodded in understanding, he put a comforting hand on the young man's shoulder and said "You help me get out of here and we can both put this place and what has happened here behind us. Forever!"

Jean then without an explanation started undressing one of the deceased men and pulled the clothes from his fallen comrade onto himself.

"You should change Mon ami, the German uniform is not favoured where we will be going," he advised.

So Siegfried, understanding the Frenchman's logic, stripped off the uniform he had once proudly worn as part of the oppressive cult and dressed himself in the brown woollen three-piece suit of one of the resistance fighters, with a khaki shirt and matching dark corduroy trousers, they were still loose enough to cover his strangely comfortable jackboots and the revolver which he slipped into the trousers belt, Siegfried mentally pulled himself together and they left for the exit.

Chapter 6

The duo darted down the dimly lit passageways, jumping for cover, in doorways at the first sound of approaching footsteps. Eventually exiting through the back door, they were confronted by three giant, grey transport trucks, each with the black and white Balkenkreuz on the side doors. They had to time their next step carefully after finding the corpse of the young Wehrmacht soldier, Carl, the entire base would be on high alert and by now they would have found out that they had a prisoner missing, along with Siegfried's absence, they could only come to one conclusion. Which could only mean one thing, if they were caught, then they would be shot, without any kind of trial.

Whilst the truck drivers and guards were distracted trading cigarettes, the two men hastily ducked beneath the last of the three lorries and waited for the engine to rumble to life. They did not need to wait long, they heard the lorry cab doors slam shut and after a cough and a splutter, the engine roared to life. The two men hoisted themselves off the ground and tucked themselves beneath the undercarriage. The lorry stopped briefly as the three-vehicle convoy travelled through the bases back entrance.

Siegfried glanced over to the escaped convict, who seemed to be having the time of his life, the dirt ground beneath them was passing at an alarming rate, only once they were sure that they had travelled far enough from the hidden base, so as not to be seen, by the large guard concrete towers at the bases exit, did they simultaneously let go and allow the truck to pass over them, before disappearing into the thick woodland on foot.

For a man who had almost been starved to death and tortured on a near daily basis, Jean travelled through the dense forest at tremendous speed and agility, as the sense of freedom filled him. So much so that the eighteen-year-old German was struggling to keep up with the escapee. Branches scratched against their faces and roots made them trip forwards as they raced through the bush, trying to get as much space between them and the Nazi stronghold, as possible. Jean seemed to know exactly where they were going, as he led the way, moving without hesitation, happily humming La Marseillaise, the French national anthem as they got closer to their destination.

They had been going through the French wilderness for a good couple of hours when Siegfried was just about to go and give in, insisting that they take a brief break when, the Frenchman raised his hand, allowing the younger of the two, to catch up to him. Jean was looking straight ahead.

"Follow me, slowly, watch where you put your feet. Just because they are expecting us does not mean they will not shoot first," advised the Frenchman.

Siegfried peered through the trees, ahead of them, he could see a small wooden log cabin, this must be the hunting lodge that was previously mentioned, the so-called safe house. Jean led the way cautiously, watching his every step, one snap of a twig or pine cone and they could be killed by the hand of the resistance. They worked their way forward towards the hut and ducked behind a couple of giant oak trees. They could see the cabin clearly from here, it was a rather well-built property.

Sat on a pair of garden chairs, out the front of the building, beneath a moss-covered porch, were a couple of armed men, one had a sawn down shotgun nestled on his lap when the second man had a Nazi MP40 machine gun slung on the back of his chair. The door to the cabin opened, Siegfried instantly recognised the man who had just emerged, it was Pierre, the head of the Paris resistance. He had come out with three metallic cups, steam was rising from the hot contents, he handed one to each of his comrades before sipping on his own. All of a sudden Jean yelled out in German, loudly enough to be heard at the wooden property.

"You sit around drinking coffee, whilst your friends are risking their lives to escape the clutches from the National Socialist scum," he gave Siegfried a friendly wink, letting him know that he was not to be offended by the last bit.

The three men all drew their guns and were scanning the forest area around their camp, for the source of the German voice. Then with his arms raised to his sides, Jean emerged from the tree revealing himself to the resistance soldiers, Siegfried followed, copying the Frenchman. It took Pierre a few seconds to recognise the two men. It would be the normal protocol to welcome the two guests and share a meal or at least a beverage but this was war torn France and this was too close to a Nazi base to be candid or over-relaxed. The two newcomers slowly approached the trio, who had not yet lowered their weapons, their leader examined the duos faces, it softened slightly as he recognised the former Wehrmacht soldier and after studying the second man's face, squinting slightly, before his expression quite literately lit up.

"Jean?" he asked almost jumping with joy.

"Oui," Jean said casually.

"Jean, Mon ami," the leader of the Paris freedom fighters holstered his weapon and passionately kissed his old friend and fellow resistance leader on both cheeks. This was making Siegfried feel uncomfortable with this display of male affection and he nervously shuffled from one foot to the next, after this daring rescue, he was still unsure what the French Maquis had in store for him.

"I misjudged you, my apologise." He produced a hand to the young German. "Thank you for getting our friend out, this will help raise support for our cause." Siegfried hesitated for a moment before shaking the man's hand.

"Siegfried, my young friend, I would like to introduce you to a couple of young female freedom fighter friends of mine, this is Simone Segouin," he said as a young lady with a brown bob haircut and a blue and white spotted blouse emerged from the property, kissing Jean on the cheek. "She had been involved in armed actions against enemy convoys and the destruction of trains, attacks against enemy troops and she is a master of sabotage. She is one of the purest fighters of the heroic French Resistance. Also I must introduce you to my dear friend and fellow resistance leader, Yvette."

The large man looked around and then turned to Pierre. "Where is mademoiselle Lundy? You said she would be here," he asked still speaking in German for his new friend's benefit. Pierre looked sheepish as if he did not want to answer his resistance comrade, the other men looked just as uneasy finally he replied.

"The Gestapo arrested her last week, she is in Saarbrücken concentration camp."

"What?" Jean bellowed loudly, outraged. Siegfried had heard rumours of the concentration camps, they were meant to be the final solution for the Jewish question, the stories were of mass executions and gas chambers, nothing that the young German had believed, until he had witnessed the mass of executions, first hand and saw how Jewish business owners in Paris were being treated, he had learnt that he had been mistaken by a great many things."Come let us go inside, you must tell me everything," he continued in German, once again for Siegfried's benefit.

The man called Pierre gave a coded knock of two slow knocks followed with three in quick succession before opening the door. The three men entered the warm cabin, leaving the lady with the other two men back on guard duty outside. The log cabin consisted of four rooms, two bedrooms, a bathroom and the lounge area with two settees, four armchairs, which formed a square around a pine coffee table, there was a strong smell of cooked onions and grilled cheese that filled the air. Huddled in the kitchen area there were another four men inside the property, they all carried a form of side arm revolver from an American Colt .45, French Modèle 1892 or like Siegfried the German P08 Luger, against the wall beside the door was a small collection of rifles, such as the German MP40 and British Lee Enfield rifles.

Jean took off the Mauser Karabiner Kar 98k that Siegfried had given him previously, that he still had slung over his shoulder, and he put it alongside the others. The men greeted the two new comers with pats on the shoulder to Siegfried and much kissing and embracing to Jean. The German recognised each one of the men from the alleyway. As the group congregated in the kitchen area, Siegfried settled into one of the armchairs, this type of modest luxury was non-existent in a military barracks.

He was admiring a painting above the fire place of a truffle hunter with a pair of dogs and a pig on a rope lead, it looked like a quiet modest life, in the distance you could see the architectural Paris skyline, with the iconic Eiffel tower looming in the centre. The German Jew Yosef handed the young man a soup bowl which had some sort of mixture with a cheese over-bake.

"It is a traditional French onion soup, a treat for Monsieur Moulin's return," he said producing a steel spoon. "Is there something troubling you?" he asked concerned, seeing the German youth's solemn look.

"What is going to become of me? I can't go home and my face will be pasted on wanted posters all over the Reich." He nearly cried thinking of the shame and humiliation that he had inflicted on his family. Seeing the young man's distress, Yosef took a seat in the armchair beside the youngster.

"You said your mother is from Naples?"

"Ja," the younger of the two Germans looked at his counterpart with curiosity.

"Do you speak Italian?"

"Ja, fluently."

"We have some friends over the border, the brave Italian partisans, they need a translator who can speak both Italian and German. You will not only be fighting the Nazis but Mussolini and his Blackshirts also. You will be totally safe there; you will have a different name and no one will know who you really are." Assured Yosef.

Siegfried had heard of Benito Mussolini, often considered as Hitler's 'lap dog'. He was the fascist dictator of Italy and his private militia, the notorious Milizia Volontaria per la Sicurezza Nazionale, better known as the Blackshirts, before the war they would produce a national service but at the commencement of the conflict, it became made up of criminals and thugs released from prison to serve the Italian paramilitary unit which consisted of over five hundred members and much like Hitler's Brown shirts, who helped, mostly by the use of violence, their leader take power. The two axis forces joined and signed a pact of steel and then Japan joined the two armies and the three forces signed the Tripartite pact and became known as the Axis alliance.

Just then the two men and one woman who had been left on guard outside the log-built property, ran into the property.

"Allemands des centaines d'entre!" They said alarmed by something.

"Sheisse!" Yosef blurted in his own tongue "Germans, hundreds," he translated to Siegfried, who was lost by the trio's alarm, he rose from his seat, now also rather alarmed.

"Merde ! Comment ont-ils nous trouver si rapidement ?" Pierre asked questioning the speed at which they had been discovered. One of the men from outside, turned to the new German guest and stepped towards Siegfried with a menacing glint in his eye and said in broken German.

"Maybe our new friend here is a bit of a blabber mouth or more likely is that he is not as innocent as he seems." The man was glaring daggers at Siegfried who was lost for words, he had expected some distrust but had never suspected that he would be accused of treason against the people who were meant to help him get out of the perverse sect of the Nazi army. Yosef rose and stood beside his fellow countryman.

"Don't be so bloody ridiculous," he said in the young man's support.

"Well it is not such a stretch," the man continued, scowling at the two Germans, "he claims that he wants to quit the army, but I state that this is a rouse, so they can ambush us and get rid of two resistance leaders, along with the rest of us. I don't know what you guys think but to me it seems a little susp—."

"Don't be so stupid!" Interrupted Jean, stepping in between the two men and standing face to face with Siegfried's aggressor. "This lad rescued me from a Nazi firing squad, risked his own life and got me out of that place, even killing one of his own friends to save my life. He is in as much crap as the rest of us and anyone who disagrees will have to go through me first!"

This was an unexpected side of Jean that, even slightly scared Siegfried, obviously the man had found his superiority again.

"And me," added Yosef.

The young man appreciated the faith these two men had in him. Before any more could be said, they heard the sounds of approaching dogs barking. Jean cursed under his breath.

"They are getting close," Yosef said quietly.

"Vite, nous allons sortir par le tunnel," Pierre said and without a moment's hesitation, two of the resistance soldiers removed three wooden panels from the wall to reveal a small hidden alcove and a wooden ladder going down into a hole in the ground. Jean turned to Siegfried.

"Come, Mon ami, we have an escape tunnel," he said comfortingly.

Pierre had gone into an under counter cupboard and handed out handheld lanterns, the group then passed around a lit spill to light their lanterns and grabbed their weapons before descending the ladder. Pierre went down first followed by Jean, then Siegfried, Yosef and then the other resistance members followed after refitting the planks back in place to hide their escape route.

The tunnel was tight and damp, shored up with strips of wood, it was so cramped that they had to crawl through it on all fours, apart from some small holes in the roof every twenty feet for air, the only light they had was from their handheld lanterns. Siegfried had never been good in small or refined spaces, ever since he had been a child.

Himself, Carl and Stefan had been exploring an abandoned mine, when there was a cave in that half buried them and they were not discovered until the next day, so ever since then any prolonged stretch in a contained space, stressed the young German to the point of panic.

The only thing which kept Siegfried calm were the small air holes, where he could feel a small breeze as he passed and the knowledge that he would soon be away, fighting with the Italian partisans in the East. There he could reinvent himself as a new person and put this traumatic time in the past. He tried to keep these thoughts in his mind and concentrated on keeping his breathing steady.

After an hour of crawling through this dirty cavern, Pierre opened a hatch above them streaming sunlight into the dark space, the troop clambered out into the centre of a Parisian Forest. Siegfried breathed in the fresh, sweet forest air and the claustrophobic trauma waned, he felt an overwhelming sense of freedom. Yet, the other members of the group were preoccupied defending their position, as they were still in enemy territory.

Pierre and Jean were deliberating quietly together in French, giving quick glances in Siegfried's direction before the two men came to a decision. Yosef gave the young man a comforting smile as the two resistance leaders approached them.

"We will be staying at a safe house until everything has quietened down," said Jean.

"Yosef, you take them," added Pierre, "we must return back into the city." Pierre then took Siegfried to one side and spoke to him quietly, "What is your mother's maiden name?"

"Giordano."

"You will have to leave your name of Kühn behind you. Where does your mother come from?"

"Naples."

"Bon, we will get a fake identification card made for you and deliver it to the safe house. Give me your military papers," he directed, the young German did as he was bid and passed over his military identity booklet and the French man examined it, slipping it into his waistcoat pocket.

"Bon chance," he smiled.

The Maquis fighters shook each of the three men's hand, with a 'Bon Chance', except for the man who had accused Siegfried previously, he said his farewells to Jean and Yosef yet totally ignored the former soldier entirely, Siegfried had expected this, he did not take offence, after all they were the French resistance and according to most of them all Germans were the enemy.

He had never been disillusioned and had not expected a warm welcome but had hoped that his defection may be enough evidence that his change of allegiance was genuine. The six-man strong resistance group went over a hill and dissipated from sight; the three remaining men watched as their comrades left and vanished from view.

“We had best go, it will be dark soon,” recommended Yosef, looking up to the sky, so following the German Jew they made their way to the temporary dwellings.

They had only walked for fifteen minutes when they crossed over a hillside and to their delight there in the middle of freshly ploughed farmland, beside an old rusting tractor, sat a small red brick two floor built farmhouse. They leisurely made their way down the slope to the quaint cottage, always observing the surrounding area in case of an ambush. It was a rare occurrence for the occupying forces to venture this far from the big city but this was a rare situation.

Once they arrived at the peeling blue painted door. Yosef gave the peculiar coded knock, three fast knocks followed by two slow. The front door cautiously opened, by an elderly lady in her mid to late eighties. Wearing a blue and white stripped apron and a red bandanna covering her white hair, she looked at the three strangers inquisitively and then recognised the Jewish resistance fighter, her face lit up and she allowed her guests to enter, gesturing them in, looking around before closing the door behind her.

“Madame Bubois, Puis je vois présente Monsieur Moulin et Monsieur K”

“Giordano,” whispered Siegfried harshly, understanding that this was an introduction.

“Monsieur Giordano,” Yosef corrected himself, “de la résistance.” He introduced his two accomplices; the elderly lady gave the two men a polite nod of the head.

“Avez vous les quelque chose ?” Yosef questioned her and without a word, she lifted up a couple of loose floorboards and picked out a large canvas sack, she put it down with a loud thud onto the dining table before going back to washing her clothes in the kitchen sink.

For Siegfried’s benefit Yosef changed back to his native language as he addressed Jean.

“These are your things; we had put them into storage awaiting your return.”

The French resistance leader seemed overjoyed by the consideration and delved into the bag, pulling out an old clay ‘oily’ pipe with studded amber beads.

“Oh Gott! I almost forgot, I also got you this,” the German said presenting the man with a small box from his pocket. The man opened it and gave a small smile it was brand new rose-wood pipe.

“Merci, Yosef,” he said thankfully patting the man on the shoulder, turning to their young comrade he asked, “Do you smoke?”

Instinctively Siegfried was about to say no but he *was* going to reinvent himself, so instead said, "I do now."

The resistance leader casually chucked him the old pipe, Siegfried examined it, he had never smoked a day in his life. The resistance leader gave a small smile and removed an oval pair of spectacles and put them on.

"Ah, perfect!" he said seeing the world in all its splendour once again, the glasses had totally changed the man's appearance, but that was the French resistance, the master of disguise, hiding under the enemies very nose.

The three men sat in the living area of the small remote farmhouse with Jean teaching his young German friend how to pack and smoke his new pipe which made Siegfried cough violently, the two resistance soldiers could not help but hide a smirk. Yosef revealed a one-gallon glass flagon of very strong home brewed cider which contained a high alcohol volume and as they drank and smoked, they regaled each other with the tales of their lives.

Yosef told his horrendous tale of fleeing his home city of Düsseldorf, when the Nazi party took power, leaving his friends, family and loved ones behind. Siegfried had always suspected such stories but having someone telling you the story face to face and seeing the man's emotion, brought it home. All because of one man, a man that he had once compared to a demi-god, a man he had met, which had been the proudest moment of his life, how deluded had he been? How had he ever worshipped a man this barbarous?

Madam Dubois brought over a small bowl filled with small charred balls.

"Châtaigne." She smiled, placing them onto the table, the three men thanked her and she waddled off. Siegfried gave Yosef a confused look.

"Roasted chestnuts," he translated, taking one and peeling off the shell, to get to the sweet flesh inside.

After another couple of hours the men continued reciting memories before the world had been plunged into the turmoil of war. Siegfried and Jean ended up going to bed early, neither had slept much since the previous night and the strong cider was beginning to take its toll. Yosef on the other hand had opted to stay guard, it was unusual for Nazi troops to venture this far into the wilderness but they were looking for two fugitives, so anything was possible.

The young German found himself crying himself to sleep, he had kept hidden his emotions for such a long time, whilst he was a Nazi soldier, he sobbed uncontrollably, yet as tears fell from his eyes, he felt a great feeling of release.

Chapter 7

The following morning after a relaxing, deep sleep, in a soft mattress, Siegfried was awoken by a rough knocking on the front door. He was still dressed in case he had to make a quick getaway, instantly grabbed his luger that he had previously placed on his bedside table and crept to the door to his room, straining to hear what was being said, it could be a Nazi squad checking the properties in the vicinity, all he could hear were French voices, one he recognised as Yosef who sounded quite laid back and relaxed, with not a note of fear or anxiety in his voice, as would be expected when talking to the occupying troops.

The young German exited his room, made his way to the end of the landing and to the top of the stairs, still holding the revolver, he stood with his back against the wall, listening intently and heard the visitor leave. He slipped his Luger in the front of his trousers and descended the stairs into the living room where Yosef was standing looking at a couple of brown paper booklets.

"Ah Siggie, I have your new identification papers. Your new name is Vito Giordano from Naples." He smiled broadly, Siegfried wiped the sleep from eyes and took the identity card from his German associate, slipping it open directly to the information page, he read his new name multiple times to allow it to sink in. Siegfried Köhn was no longer and Vito Giordano was born.

Chapter 8

Later that morning, Yosef sat the young man down and went through recreating his story with him, apparently if his new Italian comrades were to learn the truth of his past life, then it would be brought to a swift end.

Vito Giordano was born in Naples to a widow and went to study engineering at Dresden university, which would explain his slight German accent, even though he was fluent in Italian, he could not hide the German 'twang'. He then fled Germany with the refugees when war broke out and has been hiding in France since the occupation, with the will to join the cause to save his country from its malicious dictator, Mussolini and the Nazi goons stationed there. Any other information he would have to make up as he went. The resistance members fired rapid questions to him, which he had to give a quick response, making sure that the story stuck in his mind and eventually, the young German began to believe in the fabricated story.

It was midday when Yosef decided that they should leave, so as a fond farewell, Jean presented Vito with a small pouch of pipe tobacco and thanked him once again for rescuing him and saving his life. The two Germans then set off towards the French/Italian border. All Vito carried was the Luger pistol that he had tucked in the front of his trousers, while Yosef carried a wicker basket that contained a bottle of French wine, five wedges of French cheese, three large truffles and a couple of sandwiches, which were for the travellers, the other French delicacies were for the Italian partisans, as a 'sign of respect'.

It would take them a long three days and nights before they got to the border; they trekked over ploughed fields and uneven wasteland where the mud stuck to their boots making them feel like lead. They avoided roads and populated areas as much as possible. Only having a couple hours sleep in run down desolate buildings or in caves and deep crevasses in the rocky terrain. Whilst one slept the other would take guard and then they would then swap, before they continued their journey, throughout the night. They hardly spoke, except when Yosef decided to give the young man a spot quiz on his new history, but the ex-Wehrmacht soldier had it all the much sussed and it was now what he considered as his true past.

It was early on the second morning when they arrived at a small secluded farmhouse, after a quick examination of the property showed that the occupants of the small home must have left in a hurry, probably escaping from the Italian fascist army that had approached from the East some years before. The cupboards were still full of canned goods, with five set places on the dining table with plates and cutlery, there were clothes still in wardrobes, with the beds still made, apart from the eerie silence, it was quite inviting.

Yosef lit the cast iron stove to warm the home, cooked a pot of stale coffee and took guard looking out of the front window, whilst Vito grabbed a tartan patterned blanket, curled up on the settee, to catch as much needed sleep as he could after the struggling journey that they had had that day. This was the most comfortable place they had stayed in since they left Madam Dubois' home and the sleep absorbed him swiftly.

"Siegfried, wake up my friend," Yosef called harshly from the window.

"It's Vito," the drowsy reply came. "Is it my time to take guard already?"

"No! It is German troops! They are heading here!"

This instantly roused Vito from his lethargic state, those were the two words he least wanted to hear. He sprung from his makeshift bed and ran beside Yosef, looking out of the cottage window. Travelling at an alarming pace in their direction, kicking up a cloud of dust, down a dirt road were six sets of headlights and in the morning light you could make out the ash grey coloured vehicles, of three troop transport lorries, two A7V Sturmwagen and an armoured jeep.

"We must get out the back door!" Yosef said in urgency.

This was good enough for Vito and the two Germans rushed for the door. The older of the two chucked his coffee onto the fire in the stove, putting it out, and grabbed the wicker basket before following his comrade out of the back door. They ran across the stone-slabbed back courtyard and darted behind a red brick wall. They listened intently as the vehicles came to an abrupt stop before the property and heard the front door crack as it was burst open.

Vito looked around for an escape route. They were in an apple orchard, encased with the brick wall, he scanned the brick divider; at the end he spotted an open archway leading into the deep, thick woodland, this could be their escape route. The two men were both hoping that the empty property did not warrant a more extensive search of the rear outbuildings. But they could not take the risk, the duo only had a single pistol each, not enough to fight off a squad of Nazis, no matter the size.

"Over there!" Vito pointed the opening to his friend.

Yosef replied with a single nod and the two men ran between the apple trees, through the arch and into the dark woodland. Neither man slowed for at least a mile until they had no option but to stop from complete exhaustion.

"How the hell did they know we were there?" Vito questioned, gasping for air.

"I am not sure they did," Yosef replied, also catching his breath, leaning against a giant pine tree. "I am guessing that they were just trying to find a place to get their heads down."

It took them a few minutes to recover their breath before they continued the cross-country trek. They were soon travelling over a thick black charred, rocky terrain, as they walked over the hard boulder covered ground, Vito would notice unnatural, man-made, metallic domes, slits in the rock face and even pillboxes. Seeing Vito's curiosity, Yosef explained:

"Welcome to Ouvrage, the Italian part of the Maginot Line, we are just four miles from Italy. It is a miraculous piece of engineering. After the Germans invaded France, they left just a few of the more inexperienced French forces here, whilst the more experienced went to fight, leaving it wide open for the Italian forces, they put up a good fight, they held off the Italians for forty-six days. There is a small self-contained fort, in the tunnels beneath our feet. When the fortifications were abandoned, they were left empty and are now just a relic of France's history," he explained, "This is where you will be meeting Sal, Salvatore, the head of the Italian partisans and your new leader," he smiled.

They worked their way down the rickety ladders, which had been fitted to the sheer rock face, down to shingle flooring. The duo looked around the surrounding area, there was no sign of anyone around. Yosef did not seem worried by this.

"They will be hiding somewhere, watching us. They do not trust anyone," he said quietly, "Come, we will sit and wait, by the entrance to the tunnels. They will make themselves known to us when they are ready and not before."

Vito sat on a large rock, got out his newly acquired pipe, packed it with the tobacco that Jean had given to him, striking a Vesta match against the rough side of his seat and began puffing on his accessory. In the meantime Yosef checked that they had not lost anything during their escape from the unexpected Nazi visitors.

They had been seated on the cold rocky terrain for three hours, Yosef had built up a small camp-fire, from dry twigs, to warm them up in the rough rocky surroundings. When there was a sound of boot steps on concrete, coming from behind them, that made the duo spin and aim their side arms towards the doorway, into the pitch-black abyss of the French made fortifications.

Chapter 9

Out of the shadows, a lean, perhaps skinnier that would be normal for a man of his size, he was no shorter than six foot four inches. He wore a white shirt and grey sleeveless jumper, a dark navy-blue suit trousers, a thick pair of brown military boots and a coal grey fedora tilted hat on his head, he had an unlit cigarette hanging from his lips.

The stranger struck a match on the wall and lit his cigarette, illuminating his face, he had thick, jet-black hair sticking out from beneath his broad brimmed hat, his eyes were deep chestnut, a crooked nose that had clearly been broken and reset multiple times, but similar to Vito he had light olive skin. With a red, white, green armband, with a yellow, five-pointed star and the letter CLN in the centre, which stood for 'Comitato di Liberation of National Liberation' on each of his arms.

"Good evening, gentlemen," said the new man in Italian. "Are you lost? This is Free Italian territory."

The man approached them unfazed by the weapons pointing in his direction, carrying an Italian OPV sub-machine gun, Yosef gave a small smile and slipped his pistol back into his belt.

"Yosef," replied the German and then said something in French, that Vito did not understand, from Yosef's tone of voice Vito guessed it something such as 'do not be such an idiot, you almost got yourself shot!' Which made the man laugh out loud, his rasping jolliment echoed around the cavernous, reinforced concrete corridors of the famous fortifications.

Yosef handed the thin man the gift wicker basket, the partisan inspected the goods with grunts of agreement and once he had made sure that the gift was acceptable, did he hand the older German a brown paper bag, it did not seem like a fair trade to the younger German. Yet Vito could sense that the Italian had a coldness towards the German. Yosef seemed happy by his gift, opening it and gave a wide smile, he then removed a green olive and popped it into his mouth, spitting out the pit, his expression told you everything, true Italian olives were a rare treat and you could not get anything so flavourful in occupied France. Vito was not surprised when Yosef slipped the bag into his pocket, without offering his young friend one.

"Incroyable, merci," thanked the German and then speaking in broken Italian said, "I am introducing you to Sie, Vito Giordano, he be speaking Italian and Germany."

"You are Italian? Where are you from?" the man interrogated.

"Naples," Vito said confidently, recalling the details of his forged identification card.

"How is it that you speak German?"

"I studied at university in Dresden, I left when the Nazis took power and have been trying to get back home and fight against the fascist dictator who ruins and terrorises our great country."

The Italian man judged the young man carefully for any sign of deception.

"My name is Salvatore, you may call me Sal, I am the head of the Italian partisans. If you truly wish to fight against Mussolini and his Blackshirts, then you will join us. And if you can speak German then you will be of use and welcome," he spoke coldly and bluntly.

"I would be proud to join your ranks to free our historic land." Vito had totally brought his new identity to heart but hoped that he was not coming over too strong.

Salvatore gave Yosef a sharp distinct nod and said, "Come, Vito, I will take you to your new home." Vito went and shook his new German friend by the hand, Yosef whispered to him in German,

"You are a new man now. Forget your old life, be safe, my young friend."

Siegfried in turn, whispered his reply, "Thank you for everything."

This was one man who had had faith in him from the first time he had betrayed his previous brothers in arms and got in contact with the French Maquis. Now, he was leaving his past behind him. He was part of the Italian partisans, to face a new enemy.

As Vito followed the Italian rebel leader, men dressed in similar attire to the partisan leader, carrying a large array of weaponry began appearing from behind large rocks or vegetation, giving their superior a nod of the head or a flimsy, casual two fingered salute. After three hours of travel at a steady pace, where Vito had to continually remind himself that he was no longer German. The group had became seven men strong when they entered thick woodland.

“Welcome to Utopia,” said Sal gleefully looking around. “This is our hidden forest headquarters”.

Vito looked around the camp, there were clothes lines hanging between the trees, small fires with metallic kettles or pots were boiling. Above them the dense foliage of the forest canopy gave them perfect cover from any type of air reconnaissance. There were wooden poles erected leading to a door built into a giant mound, that lead into an underground bunker. Around the camp there were between forty to sixty dirty looking men, like the other five men who had accompanied them on their return trip to the headquarters, they all had the similar matching armband to Salvatore’s but only one on their upper left arm.

It had been previously a communist symbol but was later adopted by the Italian partisans to become the logo for the Italian resistance against the fascist plight destroying the country. All the forest dwellers were smoking cigarettes, chewing on gum or eating some kind of food source. The area seemed almost surreal; he had never seen anything like this, not even in his dreams.

“Now, we see if you are worth belonging to our movement.” Salvatore said with a small grim smile.

Great, thought Vito, *now I have to take an audition.*

“Okay,” he said reluctantly, with an unenthusiastic shrug.

“You speak German?”

“Sì.”

“Good, come with me.” the leader commanded, Vito followed Salvatore into a ravine where two more resistance members were guarding a man, down on his knees, dressed in a near navy blue uniform, with stitched Nazi insignia.

“We captured this man when we attacked a Blackshirt controlled fuelling depot. We want to know what he was doing there. Start by asking him for his name.”

Vito looked at the man, he was shaking with fear and looked in a poor state, his clothes were in tatters and from the bruising and cuts around the face, it was clear that he had been savagely beaten. Vito squatted down to look the German directly in the eyes.

“Wie heißt du?” Vito questioned the man in his native tongue, who seemed surprised to be spoken to in German, giving the impression that all his interrogators in this small civilian band, only spoke, a single language, Italian.

“Herman,” stuttered the man. “Herman Brandt. Please, I am only a transportation driver, I am only here to drive goods to the führer," the man pleaded.

It was a pitiful display, making the observers sneer in disgust. Vito translated to the partisan leader.

"A transportation driver? What is he delivering to his fanatical leader in Germany?"

But before Vito could ask the German driver, the man blurted out.

"Nein, not Germany, I am to go to the Berghof!" The driver corrected in German, yet indicating that he understood at least a few words of Italian.

The rebels glanced at each other in surprise, the Berghof was Adolf Hitler's private residence, it was a lavish property surrounded by the private properties of his inner circle, built just four kilometres from Berchtesgaden in Austria, a town where only true members of the Nazi party were allowed to own property.

"The Berghof!" Exclaimed Salvatore. "What is he supposed to be delivering?"

Vito continued his translations, if it was to be delivered to the Berghof, it would mean that whatever was delivered was for the German führer personally and not the Nazi treasury.

"A tribute, from Mussolini to my führer, Adolf Hitler. Gold and art work. A gift," explained the captive, not hesitating for a moment, for fear of any reprisal. "Please, mein Herr, please, I have a wife and two young daughters, I am just a driver, not a soldier."

The man grovelled, it was a pathetic spectacle, yet Vito did not ignore the man's pleas for mercy but did his job by once again translating it for Italian leader. Sal, totally disregarded the man's overture for benevolence, strode over to a makeshift table, which consisted of just a plank of wood perched on a couple of tree stumps, grabbed a sheet of paper from the top and put it on the floor in front of their prisoner, putting a rock on each corner to hold it down. It was a map of northern Italy.

"Tell him to show us the route he will take!" Salvatore ordered; Vito demanded the German to point out the road he would take. The detainee examined the map carefully for a brief moment before pointing out a road. It was as they had all expected, the shortest route through the Alps, directly into Austria.

"Good. When?" Vito asked the captive

"He says three days' time."

"Grande! Take him away!" Sal ordered the pair of guards. They followed their commander's order.

"Where are they taking him?" queried Vito.

"Germans are hung, but the Blackshirts are our kin, so we shoot them." Salvatore said quite calmly, as if he had just ordered a meal at a restaurant. The Italian resistance leader removed one of his partisan armbands and handed it to Vito.

"Welcome to the Italian partisans," he smiled.

Vito slipped in onto his upper left arm. Even though he was worried, that he had he just traded one execution camp for another? Well at least these were not civilians they were executing, but soldiers and this was war.

The two men strolled back to the centre of the camp and sat by an open fire, with a pair of skinned rabbits roasting on a spit. Vito looked around the partisan residents, most were male and dirty, there was even one man who would sit on a tree stump knitting constantly.

"That is Eliseo. He makes clothes for the orphans of the war," explained Salvatore, before he delved into his new wicker basket and removed a small wedge of pungent blue cheese, offering a crumble to Vito who graciously accepted it. It had a deep strong flavour which sparked his taste buds, this was one thing he would miss from France, the huge array of cheeses, not to mention the wine.

After being introduced to many of his new comrades, they dined on the roast rabbit and shared a woodland made potato skin brewed beverage which singed the young former Germans throat, he had never experienced something so strong, not even the home-made cider that he had shared with Yosef and Jean at Madam Dubois' house, was this strong. The alcohol session continued until well past one o'clock the next morning, when the throng slowly broke apart and the men began disappearing below ground to their home-made bunks.

Vito stumbled through the reinforced door, into the subterranean sleeping quarters. The whole area had been encased with planks of wood, protecting them from any collapse from the surrounding earth. For an underground base it was very clean and vast. It had around twenty underground rooms, with three bunk beds in each. He had previously been informed that there were no designated sleeping arrangements, so the young man collapsed into the bottom bunk of the first bed he came to and fell into an inebriated fuelled deep sleep.

Vito awoke six hours later and with his head splitting he carefully walked back outside, the camp was bare apart from a couple of men carrying an assortment of weaponry.

"You look rough, my young comrade," said one of the men, passing the bewildered man, Vito had met him the day before a man that was called Flavio. "Come with me, a cool bath will see you right," he recommended.

Vito did not quite follow what the man was suggesting but followed him through the woodland at any rate, until they ended at a tranquil looking, meandering river, the deep blue, molten snow, water that trickled along the pebble stream bed. Without another word Flavio stripped down naked and entered the small tributary. Vito hesitated before also stripping down and entering the cool water, the shock totally revived the young rebel fighter. More members of the partisan band joined the two other men, with a large amount of splashing and laughing.

Then after couple of hours of relaxation, six further men, carrying sharpened poles entered the river, downstream from the bathing men, standing in a straight line, one beside the other and began spear fishing, chucking any impaled pike and trout onto the bank. Vito had never seen such a beautiful, yet still violent display, it almost had an operatic feel to it. Looking around it seemed like a sort of luxury, back to nature, summer holiday camp, it was as if there was no war, no Nazis, no Blackshirts, just a band of men getting back to one with nature.

A yell from the river bank, snapped the young man back to reality from his dream world.

"Vito! Sal is looking for you".

He found the partisan leader, Salvatore, waiting for him back in the giant woodland camp; it had become busier by this time. More rebel troops were milling around, greasing and polishing their weapons, there was a large pot of porridge, bubbling away over a fire stove and men were going off checking snares and collecting fire wood.

"Ah, Vito. We will be going to a small village, just south of here, we have friends and family there. They help us with supplies and they also hide weapons for us. The village is far enough from any other major settlement that the Axis forces mostly ignore them," said Sal. "Giuseppe, give the kid a gun," he called to a short, stubby, unshaven comrade, who passed Vito a sawn down double-barrelled shotgun.

The young man did not take the weapon but gave a small smile and lifted the front of his shirt to reveal the Luger revolver that he had kept tucked in the front of his trousers. Sal gave a small laugh.

"You are full of surprises, you truly belong with us, but do take the shotgun. You can never have too much fire-power." Vito dropped his shirt and took the shotgun.

"You know how to shoot it lad?" Giuseppe asked in a tone that had no hint of curiosity. Vito broke open the gun, checked the barrels which were loaded and snapped it back shut. Salvatore laughed out loud, joined by Giuseppe.

"Give him a belt," Sal ordered. Giuseppe passed Vito a thick leather belt, filled with shotgun cartridges; it was too long to go around his waist and instead strapped it from his right shoulder, crossing across his torso.

"Are we expecting some trouble?" asked Vito.

"No, but it is better to be safe than sorry," mentioned Salvatore. "Come."

He led the new partisan through some trees, where a beautiful brown filly, was hitched to a rickety wooden wagon. Sal clambered onto the front and looked down at Vito who was stood watching him, unsure that he had to do.

"Come, you are the guard."

Vito walked around the front of the wagon and climbed up beside his new leader. The ride was not designed for comfort, Vito had always had what could be called a 'boney derrière' and could feel every bump through the hard-wooden seat.

As they were clearing the woodland, Sal began to speak.

"Do not ever go into the woodland alone," he advised his young newbie. "There are only two safe ways, to get in or out of the forest and they are both heavily guarded." Vito looked at him with curiosity, he hadn't seen any guards.

Sal chuckled at his partner's expression, "look up," he suggested. Vito looked up into the trees, where some wooden platforms, camouflaged, with armed resistance soldiers watching them.

"The forest is covered in booby traps. We have spiked, spring traps. If someone triggers a tripwire, they get stuck with sharpened spikes, they shoot forward impaling them, it will also send up a flare to warn us of intruders."

This man was beginning to scare Vito, he seemed to talk about death so calmly, as if he was selling that camp at market.

"We also have Punji traps; they were invented by the Japanese." These were a trap where a man could place his foot on a false floor, with a spike filled side and bottom, trapping the foot and when removed it would slash it, making it useless, "the cries of the man would be enough to warn us of his presence." He gave a small laugh.

“What if they attack with armour?” queried Vito.

“It is not very likely, the forest is too dense, but it is true, it does not mean it is impossible. Did you notice the sloped boulders around the camp?” Vito had to confess he had not, “they are all slanted, to become a natural makeshift, dragon’s teeth, that are used so fondly by the Germans.”

The dragon’s teeth were used on borders of the Nazi conquered lands. They were reinforced concrete pillars, designed to raise the front of the tank, which would reveal the unprotected underbelly, so it could be demobilised by an anti-tank weapon. Vito could not deny that he was impressed by the defences; the camp was more secure than he had at first assumed.

They travelled over some open grassland, Vito held his new sawn down shotgun, upright and pulled out his pipe, with his freehand, then whilst holding it in his mouth, he struck a Vesta match against the side of the wagon and began puffing rapidly as he scanned the open horizon, they were out in the open here, yet Salvatore seemed quite calm as he whistled a cheery tune. He pointed out a quaint settlement before them, it was a blissful, small limestone-built village, built up against the mountainside, with a massive rectangular building standing proudly, overlooking it. As they approached the picturesque foundation, it was not long before they were traversing up the tight, cracked paving into the village, those who were strolling the streets waved to the newcomers, greeting them fondly.

Chapter 10

In the centre of the large, grey stone, town square, courtyard, stood a water fountain. Before the two men had a chance to disembark the wooden horse-drawn wagon, villagers began loading the back with wooden crates of varied sizes, full of vegetables, crates full with loafs of bread, fruit and other food wares. The two men jumped down and received pats on the back by the men and kisses on the unshaven cheeks by the young girls and women, along with small bunches of flowers from the growing crowd congregating around them, it made Vito feel like some sort of superstar.

The two resistance soldiers stood together at the rear of the wagon as more and more things were donated to the rebel cause. Salvatore greeted one man who loaded two large jars of olives and a jar of clear honey, Vito looked at the honey and then to Sal with a quizzical look, not sure why they would use honey.

"He keeps bees," explained the partisan leader, "we use it in the porridge," this explanation was good enough for Vito. He was absolutely astounded by the generosity of the civilians.

"Come we must meet my good friend, Luca, he is a butcher," commanded Sal leading Vito to a butcher's shop with an imitation pig in the shop window. As they entered the shop they were greeted by large, heavy-set man, wearing the traditional, white butcher's apron, hanging over his oversized belly.

"Salvatore, my good pal!" the man roared, in a tone that only could be explained as over exaggerated, yet sincere.

"Luca, may I introduce you to Vito Giordano."

Vito gave a polite nod but something else had caught his attention, behind the counter, stacking jars of home-made marmalade onto a shelf, was a ravishing Italian beauty with flowing black hair plaited in a ponytail, light brown eyes, deep olive skin and a slim shapely body. She gave a lush smile which lit up the room to the young resistance fighter, making the young man who was looking at her agog blush. She was the most gorgeous female that he had ever laid his eyes upon.

"Ah, that is my daughter, Elvera," said the overweight boisterous man.

The young beauty had taken Vito's breath away, even her name sounded heavenly to him, he was so swept away he could only force out a single word, "Buongiorno."

The young girl burst into giggles at his accent as it was clear the young man had been hypnotised by her radiance.

"Vito!" Sal's voice brought the young partisan back down to earth, like a rock. "Vito, take the box out to the cart," ordered Salvatore, embarrassed by his young associate's reaction toward his good friend's daughter.

The young man had hardly even noticed the large wooden crate on the counter, filled with whole chickens, a couple of lamb shanks, a good two dozen sirloin steaks and a couple racks of ribs, it was more meat than Vito had ever seen in his life before, only having ever known the food rations. Even though he would have loved to have a char-grilled steak, but as he would soon learn that this was not the case when it came to his new comrades, apart from the fish and the occasional rodent, which they cooked over an open fire on a spit, large meat produce they would be cut up and put it into a pot with an assortment of vegetables, a few shavings of truffle and make a stew from it, so the entire camp could enjoy the flavours. As he left the store, he saw the young maiden, Elvera whisper into Salvatore's ear, whilst keeping her eyes on her new admirer.

Vito loaded the meat crate onto the wooden cart and examined the selection of cuisine that the people had bequeathed to them, whilst they were inside the butchers. There were bowls of assorted nuts, bottles of Italian home-made wine, three terracotta jars of olives, sun-dried tomatoes, wool quilts, animal pelts, three brown paper sacks of flour, a basket of wild mushrooms and even a large truckle of Mozzarella cheese. A man came out of the local fishmongers with some salted cods, a couple of whole trout's and five metallic pots which said Calvisius White Sturgeon Caviar.

The benevolence of the locals was overwhelming.

Salvatore soon exited after, as if he had not seen the charitable contributions, he said, "We must now go up to the monastery to collect weapons and ammunition." This did make Vito wonder if he had misheard, weapons, at a monastery? "We will be staying there for the night and this evening you will be taking the lovely Elvera out on a date."

Vito was dumbstruck, that must have been what, the maiden had whispered to Sal when he was leaving.

"A date? What will I use for money?" Vito spoke without thinking as he joined Salvatore at the front of the cart, the rebel leader chuckled at his comrade's naive attitude.

"You are a Partisan now, do you not see, they will not accept your money, the people here support our cause and if they know that they cannot reward us for doing our patriotic duty. So, they will never ask us for money." This whole series of circumstances was surreal.

The trek up to the home of the religious order was steep and uneven, the young horse stumbled a few times on loose rock, as it ascended the narrow route, the duo still received waves, cheers and clapping from the few residences that they passed on route.

Reaching the monastery walls, with the middle eastern style towers in each corner. They could tell that the ancient religious construction had been more artistically made than the rest of the settlement it overlooked, as the walls were decorated with the fleur-de-lis. They entered the monastery grounds though a slender archway which stated the Latin line 'Da cor tuum ad Deum', 'Give your heart to God', into a decorative mosaic floored plaza, the rectangular property was full of beautiful architecture, with historic paintings of saints and Christian icons carved on the walls. In the centre of the plaza was a giant Pagan obelisk with a metallic cross fitted on the top point, the entire area seemed deserted.

The duo scanned their surroundings for any sign of life. There was a small chapel on the east side of the complex, candle light could be seen flickering through the flamboyant designed, stain glass window.

"Maybe they are at prayers?" Vito suggested, looking around the deserted area.

Salvatore, rose to his feet and shouted, "Ciao? Anyone here?"

There were a couple minutes of further silence, when a brown robed elderly man with silvery white hair, emerged from the chapel, he wore a set of white coral rosary beads hanging from his robes, which he fingered with his skeleton like fingers.

"Salvatore, keep your voice down," said the monk in a clear comfortable voice.

"Brother Angelino," Sal greeted him. "We have come to collect some of our supplies that you have hidden for us and we will need a bed for the night." The

Italian freedom fighter seemed to be telling the monk, rather than requesting, yet the welcoming monk did not seem deterred by the partisan's demeanour.

"Of course, all who are in need of refuge or salvation are welcomed here. Come, come." The man of God urged them into the main property of the religious order.

The spacious appearance of the front was a total misconception, compared to the inside. Which even though it was beautiful with carved rosewood skirting and pillars along the walls with lavish paintings, depicting the story of Christ, with gold leaf decoration, the hallways were narrow and confined, making Vito feel mildly claustrophobic. Gothic style doorways led off the narrow hallway, to various rooms.

They followed the monk into a small room, which looked like a small private chapel, with nothing but some velvet prayer cushions and a silk covered alter table, with a silver cross, communion goblet, a gold-plated platter and a pair of elaborating engraved candle stick holders. The monk carefully closed and bolted the door behind them, so they could not be disturbed.

With the help of Salvatore the man of God moved the makeshift altar aside with relative ease. The table was in fact just a couple of crates, covered with the cloth on top. There was nothing but the floorboards beneath or so it seemed.

"Do you have the key?" Sal asked turning to Brother Angelino, who fumbled through his robes, before producing a small brass key, the kind you expected to see used for a children's music box and handed it to the partisan.

Vito scanned the floor, he could not see any sign of a keyhole, it looked like ordinary floorboards, but he had also learnt that nothing in the partisan world was as simple as it seemed at first glance. To the young partisan soldiers utter surprise Salvatore went to a small black knick in the wood and slipped the key inside, with a sharp turn of the key a distinct click could be heard.

Vito was in shock, no one would have expected there to be a trap door, not in a million years. Salvatore yanked at the panel and four of the wooden planks lifted together, revealing a hidden compartment beneath. It was full of British Enfield rifles, boxes of ammunition, rolls of dynamite and detonators, which could be triggered either on a timer or by contact when a wire was pulled or retracted, it was the perfect item for a booby-trap. The trio carried as much as each could muster and bundled them into the back of the wooden cart, covering them with a horsehair blanket, to obscure the carts illegal contents from view.

“We must get the cart under cover and get your horse fed,” advised Brother Angelino.

“You are right, of course,” replied Sal, Vito got the impression that this was the usual procedure when Sal visited.

“Francesco!” The monk called out, a mere seconds later, a young man, no more than sixteen years of age, trotted from the property that they had just exited and ran to the three men.

“Sí signore?” He asked keenly.

“Take this cart and hide it, then feed this young horse some of our best straw and oats,” commanded the holy man.

“Sí signore,” the young lad said obediently, giving a small bow before leading the horse and its full load into a wooden outbuilding.

“Shall we go in to eat?” The brother invited them with a smile. “I believe Brother Lorenzo is making a lovely beef stew,” there was a glint in his eye as he mentioned the tasty dish being prepared.

“I would love to join you as always. But unfortunately, Vito here has a date with the beautiful Elvera,” chuckled the partisan leader, in a teasing tone.

“Elvera? The butcher’s daughter?” The brother asked, receiving a single nod from Salvatore, “she is only seventeen, so you do take good care of her.”

“I will do my best,” Vito promised, but from the short time he had met her, he was sure she could handle herself. After all it was her who had suggested the date.

***

After a clean-up and a swift shave, with some smarter clothes that the brother had had mothballed in a wardrobe, the rebel armband looked out of place with this old suit but Sal insisted he wear it, claiming it made the Italian females wild with desire, so with this information he agreed to proudly. Vito walked alone down the steep path into the small township. Due to him wearing his tricoloured resistance armband, got him greetings from passing residents, a small group of youths gave the partisan a salute, he was a hero to these people, Vito returns the salute humouring them. He finally found himself outside the butcher’s shop as the church bells tolled the stroke of seven o’clock.

The sun was setting in the west and the evening sky turned into an indescribable fluorescent colour of pink and orange, like no painting by the great masters could justify. After admiring the dazzling afternoon sky, he turned his attention back to the narrow quiet town streets. Illuminated by the evening light, like an angel appearing out of the heavenly sky, wearing an emerald green dress, down the main street of the small town floated the unmistakeable physique of Elvera. Vito made a quick check of his clothing, before standing straight as he waited to be graced with her presence, his mind racing through what he would say, so that he did not act like the gormless fool as he had done the first time they had met.

"Hello. You…you look amazing" he could never remember ever being so scared, with the exception of saving Jean Moulin in his past life, but this was a totally different type of fear. The Italian maiden looked so alluring that Vito struggled not to stare in awe.

"Well you wash up well yourself," she smiled. She had a sweet, angelic voice. "So where are we going to go?"

Vito was afraid that she may ask this question.

"I unfortunately do not know this town, where would you recommend?" he received a small giggle for this remark.

"Well, there is a nice little restaurant just down the street," she suggested innocently.

"Well, my dear, please lead on," she gave a small smile, slipped a slender arm between his and together they walked down the bleak, quiet streets, arm in arm.

The restaurant was quiet, apart from a few local couples, the maître d' took one glance at Vito's partisan armband and ushered the couple directly to a quiet little table and before they had a chance to order a drink, they were served a carafe of red Italian wine, with two glasses. Vito looked around the beautiful establishment, it was the ideal place for a date, each table had a small candle, giving it a warm romantic atmosphere, the tables were far enough apart from one another, so as not to cause discomfort to the love-struck patrons to express themselves.

Elvera fired continuous questions towards Vito, many which he had to fabricate, with the imaginary facts. He used the information about Naples from the few bits that his mother had told him about her home town. Showing her the picture of his mother, which Elvera commented on how attractive his mother was and showed him an oval, turquoise stone pendant, encased in silver. She claimed it had belonged to her mother who had died when Elvera had been just a child, apparently, she always wore it.

Questions he had to answers about Dresden caused him no trouble having grown up there, yet the journey he supposedly took to France with the refugees was total fiction. Yet, the Italian beauty was in consternation of him. She had never left this small neighbourhood and had often dreamed of travelling. Before Vito knew what he was saying he had promised that after the war, he would take her travelling. That evening the couple enjoyed the traditional Mediterranean meals of Veal Alla Milanese and Pollo Alla Diavola. The waiters served them carafe after carafe of the sweet wine.

Vito's blood ran cold when he was presented with the bill; Salvatore had informed him that the meal would be free. He carefully picked it up; it was blank apart from the words, 'Long live our brave partisans!'

Vito could feel himself blush with pride and walked his date back home along the quiet streets, yet this time she had slipped her hand into his. It was as if they had known each other for a lifetime. Outside her front door, before another word could pass between them, their lips connected in a long passionate kiss, making his head swim in desire, for that blissful minute there was nothing but her, no war, no partisans, just this ravishing beauty. It was at that very moment Vito knew it. This would be the girl he would marry.

Chapter 11

Vito awoke late, with a spring in his step, the following morning and ate some home-made bread and jam that were grown on the grounds and made by the monks. Vito had wondered if he had dreamt his escapades of the previous night, which also happened to be the happiest, he could recall ever being, yet he prayed it had not.

After the two partisans had eaten their fill, they mounted the fully laden wagon and started the treacherous journey down the steep narrow streets through the small town. Salvatore pulled the wagon to stop in the town's plaza, where the men received small bunches of wild flowers from the fair maidens and Elvera handed her new man a silk white handkerchief with her initial 'E' embroidered on one corner, as a keepsake. Vito slipped this gift into his coats top pocket, if the wind blew in the right direction, he could get a whiff of his beloved's fragrant aroma. After a couple of minutes, after Vito had leant down and brushed his lips with his lady friends, Salvatore started up the cart once again and they headed back over the open space to the hidden forest fortress.

Back at the resistance woodland realm, they were welcomed back like conquering heroes and the resistance soldiers began unloading the charitable wares, before the wagon had even come to a stop. Vito felt full of vigour and life, he had found the love of his life, it had filled him with hope for the future, there was no longer a dark thought in his mind and even his comrades noticed their new happier associate and after Sal had told them of the reason, they all understood, love had the power to change all men.

As much time as they had spent away from the encampment, the men that had been left behind had not been relaxing, far from it. Salvatore had given orders before they had disembarked. Making sure that all knives, machetes and bayonets were sharpened on a grinding wheel and all other weapons were to be greased, assembled and loaded. The camp no longer looked like a luxury paradise, but like a fortress ready for war. The duo did not have time to rest, Vito was immediately handed an Italian Mitra MAB modello 1938A rifle and had to set out again for the ambush on the German convoy. The protected military transport was expected the next day, so Vito could not understand why they were moving out so soon.

"Where we will be staging the attack, is high up in the mountains, where the snow is deep, if we go up there tomorrow, they may see our tracks which may spark some alarm bells and then they would be on guard and ready for a possible ambush. But if we go today, our tracks will become covered and obscured by the falling snow and wind."

This made sense to the young patriot, but he did not fancy the thought of sleeping in the freezing snow, as if reading his mind Sal said, "There is an abandoned Alpine hotel which used to be popular with the skiing tourists, but since the war there is no longer any business, so we will make camp there. After all it is directly beside the road they will be taking." This made the newcomer, somewhat happier.

Twenty of the camps inhabitants, armed to the teeth with an abundance of weapons, bundled into the rear of an old baker's delivery van. The back of the truck was stuffy and uncomfortable with the stench of the unwashed body odour of the Italian freedom fighters. Vito was glad when they had arrived at their destination, but when the back doors swung open, there was a dry chill and the whole terrain was blanketed in white, it was not the first time he had seen snow but never this vast, it was like a winter wonderland he had half expected to see a jolly fat man with twelve reindeer to come over the hill.

Behind them like giant pyramids reaching for the heavens were the famous Alp Mountain range which flowed into eight of Europe's neighbouring countries. As well as Italy this mountain range adorned France, Switzerland, Monaco, Liechtenstein, Austria, Germany and Slovenia, stretching a massive one thousand, two hundred kilometres across. Vito had never seen such a beautiful display of Mother Nature.

They had parked behind a miraculous, pine wood built, Alpine châlet, the carved, exterior decoration was breath-taking. Once the civilian army had disembarked, Salvatore led the troop to the back of the building and with a crowbar, cracked open the back door. The inside had an unsettling stillness, the air was stale and it had a sense of dereliction about it. All the furniture had been covered with dust covers, which the partisans roughly tore off to show the luxury seating beneath, revealing that this was not an inexpensive lodge where students may have taken a vacation but a top-quality establishment, as they sank into the leather settees, putting their feet up on the lacquered tables, with no respect for the absent proprietors of the property.

"Vito, come over here, my friend," called Salvatore. He was stood by the bar with two other rebels, all looking grave and serious. "We will need your bilingual skills tomorrow. The military envoy is due tomorrow around mid-day, so we are going to have a checkpoint, a Blackshirt controlled check point, more precisely you three dressed to look like those fascist scum. You must delay them long enough for us to get into positions and launch the ambush."

He made it sound all too easy, thought Vito, except for impersonating Blackshirts, stopping a Nazi convoy, delaying them and surviving the onslaught, otherwise it was simple. But as usual he had no choice in the situation and put on a determined face as he was handed the uniform of the damned squadristi or Blackshirt, consisting of a black Norgi shirt, matching trousers and the black fez with the faeces insignia, the universal symbol of fascism. As Vito got dressed into his black jet, oppressive disguise, he was rather pleasantly surprised by the comfort of it, it was lighter and warmer than the heavy, itchy uniform of the German Wehrmacht that he was accustomed to.

He entered the main reception area, dressed in the full black uniform and received a sarcastic jeering and booing from his fellow freedom fighters. Salvatore approached the disguised lad.

"Keep the partisan armband in your pocket, you will need to put it on when we strike to identify friend from foe." Vito gave a nod of understanding "Do you know how to make the fascist salute?"

In any other circumstances this would have been a weird question, but of course his Italian resistance comrades had no knowledge of Vito's past life. The young man stood to attention and raised his right arm diagonally in front of him, it was identical to the Nazi salute. The partisan leader then took his newest recruit to one side and began to discuss the plan in detail with him, he would be out in the open with only two other partisans for support and if they were discovered before the rest could act. Then the trio would be the first to die at the hand of the Nazis.

***

It was an early morning start, a simple hand operated barrier had been set up on the road, painted with red and white stripes, along with a simple constructed sentry box. All the items had already been painted and were ready to be used, giving the impression that this was not the first time this civilian army had used this ploy.

That night's snow had done its desired effect, covering any of the revealing footprints left by the arriving partisans or the soldiers who had been on guard duty during that night. Vito's two comrades, also disguised as the Italian goons were, Alessandro originally from Milan and Pietro who came from the Italian capital, Rome and had been training to become a priest before the outbreak of the second European war, he would often be seen praying before meals and gave a small Sunday service in the woodland hideout.

Along with the matching uniforms they all wore regimental cotton gloves; rubbing their hands together and stomping their feet, to try and keep the blood flowing through their veins and warm themselves up. Only a couple of civilian cars passed through their checkpoint but the three men had to act their part, checking the identification papers and giving the oppressive salute when allowing them to pass.

It had gone midday by the time that they heard the low rumbling of the Nazi convoy coming down the road. The three men stood in the road in front of the barrier, Vito could not deny that he was anxious and his adrenaline was running through his body at an exaggerated rate. Yet his comrades seemed quite calm by the situation, they must have done this kind of operation before. Two bikes, followed by a military transportation lorry, an armoured Jeep with a vicious MG34 mounted on the back, followed by two more motorcycles, came into view from over the ridge.

Vito raised a hand, motioning the convoy to stop, the lead bikes slowed to a stop, scowling at the Italians. Alessandro ignored the bikers and strode directly over to the driver's side window of the lorry and spoke to the driver, after a quick exchange of words Alessandro turned to Vito, in a laugh he says, "He doesn't talk Italian!"

This was Vito's cue; he approached the lorry and in quite a casual tone in German he started his diversionary tactics.

"Where are you headed?"

"Berchtesgaden," replied the man, handing over his military identification papers.

“Berchtesgaden? A real Nazi,” laughed Vito opening the documentation and scanning through it carefully.

“Look here, you bloody Eyetie,” the driver growled, becoming more agitated by the second, “we are on a mission to deliver medical supplies from your chief and commander to our great Führer! Let us through!”

Vito nearly scoffed, either this driver had been lied to about what he was truly transporting or had been instructed not to inform anyone of his real cargo, but Vito stayed quite calm.

“There is no need to be rude. So tell me, why would that place need medical supplies? From what I have heard the allies have ignored it and not bombed it,” he stated returning the man’s identification papers, the driver hesitated, he had clearly not been prepared for this line of questioning, it could not have helped having this pair of Italian Blackshirts staring at him suspiciously.

“Well…well the supplies are brought together there before being sent to the front,” he tried to bluff nervously. “You can see we are in the German army! Allow us to pass!”

The driver said becoming aggressive once again.

“We have been ordered to check all vehicles, the rebels are disguising themselves as all sorts, Nazis, civilians,” a shot rang out and the passenger of the lorry sprayed blood over the drivers face as he received a bullet to the head “or Blackshirts,” Vito said loudly pulling his Luger and fired a single shot at naught point range, beneath the man’s chin, removing half the Nazi driver’s head, spraying Vito’s face with the driver’s blood. But the young partisan did not have time to care about his bloodied face.

Everyone acted swiftly Alessandro and Pietro took out the first two motorcycle drivers. The heavy cannon, on the back of the armoured Jeep, began firing rapidly into the wooden built building, sending out splinters like fireworks as it ploughed its thirty-three millimetre rounds into the pine wood walls. Vito and his two associates were crouched behind the lorries’ wheels, slipping their resistance armband onto their left arm and disregarding their Blackshirt hats. Vito couldn’t deny that he felt more comfortable with his Luger than the Mitra MAB modello 1938A rifle he had been given.

The young rebel took careful aim at the Jeeps driver, who was looking around in panic, not sure what he should do. Vito squeezed on the trigger and the bullet hit its mark, directly in the man’s temple. One of the rear bikers had been shot and dropped his bike, the second was turning his bike around, preparing to make his retreat. Without thinking, Vito in a crouch ran forward, dodging his allies' bullets as they tried to take out the Jeeps powerful weapon that had been keeping them pinned down.

The biker was now in full retreat. The young partisan picked up the bike from the fallen escort biker, revved it up and took off at full power after the retreating Nazi biker. The German motorcycle escort was driving away at full speed, but Vito would not give up this chase, then the inevitable happened. The German rider hit a patch of black ice; he skidded before toppling from his transport vehicle. Seeing the man fall Vito stopped sharp before the slick ice, the previous man was lying on the road writhing in pain, his leg was twisted in an unnatural way. Salvatore's words rang in the young patriot's ears.

"We hang Nazis, but Blackshirts are our countrymen so we shoot them."

This man was a German, Vito was a German, this fallen biker was his countryman, so without a second thought, he took aim at the man with his pistol, calmly squeezed the trigger, firing a single shot, killing him instantly. Vito had felt a coldness come over him, like never before, he had now seen his first action. That was when it happened, Vito buckled over and brought up his stomach's contents, right there in the centre of the road.

Chapter 12

Returning to the scene of the ambush, it had all become quiet and the partisan army had congregated around the two vehicles, "Vito? Where is the one that got away?" questioned Flavio.

"Dead," the man gave him an acceptable nod.

"Buona, well done." Vito went over to some undisturbed snow and rubbed the frozen water into his face, cleaning off the blood, the cold solid liquid was a nice release and refreshed him.

"Come, let us see our prize," commanded Salvatore gleefully.

Alessandro and Pietro pulled open the back flaps of the lorry, automatic weapons fire broke out from the rear of the vehicle, riddling the torso of Alessandro with bullets, tearing his chest open, as a hidden Nazi soldier in the back of the truck opened fire on the intruders, Vito did not hesitate, swung the Mitra MAB modello 1938A rifle from his back and returned fire, killing the lone soldier.

His associates looked at their young comrade with surprise and admiration; this was a new side of the young partisan that they had not seen before. As Pietro read his dying comrades last rights, before the man passed away. He then helped to carry his deceased comrade's body away.

"Sons of bitches!" roared Salvatore infuriated, kicking the head of one of a dead Nazi soldier, turning it into a red pulp. "Vito, check that that fucker was alone," ordered the leader.

The young resistance fighter slung the rifle back over his shoulder and removed his revolver, which would be easier to use in close quarters and nimbly jumped into the back. The truck was full of wooden crates and an enemy combatant could be concealing himself behind any of them.

Vito moved cautiously, checking behind every box or crevice. After an extensive search, he breathed a huge sigh of relief and replaced his Luger into his belt, there was no one else there. He looked around the rear of the transport, on one side was a stack of rectangular items packaged and tied in brown paper, along with approximately fifty wooden crates. Sal passed up a crowbar to his young friend, the newest resistance member knew what he had to do without Salvatore saying a word. He went to work prying open one of the crates, once he had extracted the lid, he took a step back in utter disbelief.

The inside was full to the top with solid gold coins, each one was double the size of an ordinary coin, on one side was the universal symbol of fascism, the faeces and on the other was the face of a strong jawed man, wearing the helmet of the Italian military, it was the face of the dictator of the fascist Italian state Benito Mussolini.

Seeing Vito's shocked expression Sal questioned him, "What is it lad?"

Vito looked to the leader and then back to the treasure he had just uncovered. The young fellow picked up one of the coins and flicked it to his partisan brother.

After a brief examination Salvatore confirmed in surprise, "solid gold Lire, these must cost at least hundreds each!"

His fellow comrades huddled around their leader to get a glimpse of the valuable currency. Vito looked into the box of precious metal discs, then instinct took over, without checking, he grabbed a handful of the coinage and stuffed them into his pocket, if he was going to take Elvera as his bride and take her travelling the world, he would need some capital to make it possible.

"Vito!" the former German took a short intake of breath; had he just been caught in the act?

"What is wrapped in that brown paper?" Sal called to him.

Vito gave a subtle sigh of relief and tore off the brown covering paper to reveal immaculate pieces of art work, by some of the greatest art masters. Vito instantly recognised some of the master's paintings, a Rembrandt, a Da Vinci and even a Picasso, this was no minor tribute, but a haul worth millions, Vito was astounded beyond words.

Sal jumped into the rear of the Jeep, avoiding the German corpse, "my good friends, today we have had a major victory, but with the great sacrifice of eight of our fellow comrades. This is a great defeat against our fascist dictator and terror counterpart Adolf Hitler," there were cheers in response to this statement. "We will keep these treasures and return them to the rightful owners on the glorious day of our countries liberation."

The partisan army mounted the requisitioned vehicles; Vito grabbed one of the bikes, happy not to be travelling with the corpses in the rear of the baker's van where the bodies of his fallen comrades had been laid. They drove the vehicles back to the hidden camp and concealed them beneath cut off branches and a camouflage netting. Before coming together to bury their dead and toast their great sacrifice to the cause and drank the home brewed alcohol, as was usual, late into the night.

Chapter 13

Over the following months, Vito would take a motorcycle and go down to the nearby village, parking it outside down by the entrance, so as not to disturb the locals, rent a room at a small boarding house, his armband getting it rent free and would spend the night in bed together with Elvera. Both leaving in the early morning before daybreak, the young maiden did not want her father, Luca, to notice her absence and then interrogate her about her whereabouts and who she had spent the night with. Not to mention Vito had to get back to his woodland headquarters, giving three long flashes of his headlight to signify to the camp guards that it was himself approaching and not a Nazi dispatch rider.

One warm autumn day the resistance soldiers were sitting around a wireless radio set, stolen from a Blackshirt control post, listening to a news broadcast on the international BBC channel, which was made in English and then translated into every language of the counties occupied by the Axis forces.

"The Italian island of Sicily has been invaded by the American forces, a majority of the Italian army have surrendered and the majority of the Germans and their allies are in full retreat to the mainland." There was a celebrating roar around the camp as they cheered the arrival of the approaching allied forces. Vito looked over to Salvatore who was sat with a cold stone expression on his face.

"Sal, what the hell is wrong? The Allies are coming, the war is coming to an end!" Vito said, feeling the excitement grow inside him, the partisan leader looked up at his associate.

"At what cost? How many of our Italian soldiers and civilians will die before our final victory is reached?"

"Well it is the soldier's choice whether to fight or surrender," Vito tried to reassure him.

"And what will become of us, Vito? Look around, we are soldiers of Italy, living off our fair land. What will we do? Can you really see us packing bags down at a corner shop? All we know how to do is fight!"

The former German looked around at his Italian comrades, Sal was right, cleanliness was not high on the list of the brutish men, whose idea of having fun was having a bare knuckle fight or hanging a couple of Nazis, to such an extent that some of the men would even go out hunting for loan Nazis, just so they can string them up. This thought struck Vito like a thunderbolt, what would he do? He couldn't go back to Germany, he had not thought much about the end of the war, except for his dreams of marriage and travels with Elvera.

These worries were short lived when a couple of the guys got out a fiddle and homemade pipe whistle and played along with one guy who sang, the famous Italian song, Balocchi e profumi. Flagons of the strong concoctions were passed around and as usual the camp turned into a drunken party full of celebration.

The following morning Salvatore had called for a camp meeting, the hungover partisans gathered around their leader, to hear what had to be said.

"Yesterday we heard the great news of the Allied forces invading our Italian island of Sicily, but this does not mean the end of our duty to Italy or the end of Mussolini's reign, not to mention the Nazi goons that harassed our countrymen at every turn. But if the Americans are coming from the South, then we must step up our attacks in the North to keep their attention away from the invaders.

This means that we must cause so much trouble for the fascist forces, that they need to send as many troops as possible to hold us back, which means that there will be less soldiers defending the South, helping the Americans. But this will mean that it will make our life harder", he paused to look at his comrades faces, yet everyone was too hungover to show any reaction. "If we are to do this, we must start our battle plans, today."

There was a moment's hesitant silence, as the civilian army absorbed what was being said, before an eruption of applauding and cheering. After what Salvatore had said to Vito the day before, the young Partisan just hoped that this was not some sort of suicidal mission.

Over the next few weeks Vito had no free time for leisure, the whole camp was in full alert, whilst plans for the attacks were being drawn up, they had to cause as much disruption and chaos, to warrant the enemy troops to be deployed away from the front line in the south, to counter attack them in the North, but with as little loss of civilian life as possible. The easiest to attack were Blackshirt controlled checkpoints, these were normally manned by only between two to five troops, the Nazi checkpoints usually had more, heavily armed men with a small tank or armoured vehicle of some sort, harder to attack but a bigger final prize.

Outposts were also a good choice, such as communication buildings or ammunition dumps, the destruction of one of these would not only cripple the communication of the enemy forces, but also supply the resistance forces with weapons and ammunition that could be used against their oppressive commander, not to mention that they also only had very few guards. But such attacks would not persuade the Axis forces to pull men off the front line.

The whole camp became busy, with rebel soldiers priming grenades, greasing rifle parts, sharpening a large array on knives and machetes on a hand operated grindstone and one man would reconstruct bullets from spent cartridge cases, whilst another cut down shotguns and filed off the barrels. On Sundays, Pietro would hold a full service, which everyone paid attention to, unlike usually, the whole atmosphere of the camp had changed, even the evenings were more quiet and reserved than they had previously been, the men were entertaining themselves, fearing what was to come in the future, a couple were playing a silent game of draughts and another few played craps. Vito would often sit back, smoking his pipe and think how his life would be after the war and how he would actually be free to do as he wished.

A long fortnight passed when there was a cry for Vito from the tree top guards at the camps front entrance. The youngest partisan wandered round to the entrance, where to his utter surprise and pleasure he saw, holding a tattered push bike with one hand and a basket of fresh fruit in the other, stood Elvera. She wore a vibrant red, cashmere wool coat and a jet-black beret on her head. Vito walked straight up to her and ignoring the ever-watching eyes in the sky, embrace her and shared his love in a passionate kiss, which she returned.

"What are you doing here? If we are being watched, you could be—" Vito could not even force out the final word. Elvera seemed quite hurt by this.

"I came to bring you some fruit! I thought it would be a nice surprise! I think next time I will not even bother!"

Vito cringed, realising that she had taken what he had said in the wrong way.

"It is…I just mean," the correct words would not come from his mouth. A voice came out of the brush behind them.

"He just means to say, in his own sweet way, that it could be too dangerous for you to be seen here. If the Germans or the Blackshirts were to see you, then you would be putting yourself and the whole village at risk."

The young couple turned to see Sal leaning, very casually against a tree, puffing on a hand rolled cigarette. Elvera turned to Vito for confirmation, who thought that this explanation would suffice; he just gave a gentle nod. Sal looked up into the pale sky, the sun was setting in the west and the bright slither of the new moon was shining in the darkening sky, a gaggle of geese flew in uniform over their heads, breaking the stillness that had engulfed them.

"I think you should stay here until it is dark, it could be risky if you were seen out at this time. Vito will take you back on his motorbike. We will deliver your bicycle back to you in a few days when we do our next supply run. It could be our last one for a few weeks," Sal remarked with concern.

The trio walked back into camp, some of the partisans looked at the young, beautiful Elvera, in a way that made Vito feel uncomfortable, so he slipped his hand into hers and gave it an affectionate squeeze. Elvera was Vito's girl.

Chapter 14

Vito gradually awoke the next morning and it took him a couple of minutes for him to recall where he was, the elegant arm of a young Italian women lay on his chest and brought back what had happened, the previous night. Contrary to Salvatore's explicit order for him to return to camp directly after dropping off Elvera, back to her home, yet the young couple were too easily swayed by temptation, so spent that night, for possibly the last time for many more months, in pure passion, in each other's affectionate arms. Having enjoyed most of the night in ecstasy together, they had stayed later than usual.

The morning sun was rising and light streamed through the thin moth-eaten curtains, flooding the small quaint, mundane room in light. When they rose from the bed, it then dawned on the two young lovers; Vito had disobeyed the order of his commander and chief, when Elvera had not returned home to her waiting father.

The couple agreed on a story that she had spent the night at the resistance camp, it being too dangerous, so could not return until morning, this would save her any embarrassment and would not put Vito in a dim light in the eyes of Luca. But he was not looking forward to the wrath he would have to surely incur from the Italian partisan leader. After a very fond farewell, Vito returned to the forest fortress on the former German, stolen motorcycle.

"Where the hell have you been?" Sal questioned, obviously fuming as he spoke, "We had feared that you had been captured by the Blackshirts or even the Nazi soldiers!"

Vito could not escape the trouble he was in; he had no excuse.

"I am truly sorry," he said solemnly. "I know you ordered me back after I dropped Elvera off, but as you said I may not be able to see her or spend time with her for many months, so that is why—" Sal interrupted him.

"That's why nothing! You are not the only partisan in a relationship!" Vito looked to the floor disheartened, of course, he was right and he had never wanted to disappoint, his leader and friend, Salvatore, this man had put his faith in him and he had betrayed that trust.

"I know, I *am* truly sorry," pleaded Vito, not taking his eyes from the leaf littered forest floor. Sal nodded understanding that the young fighter was aware of his disappointment.

"Every man is allowed *one* mistake," Sal said bluntly, "but no more! As you have disobeyed me, you will *not* be coming on the easy supply run, to the village, with me, but you will be remaining here and become familiar with the maps for the attacks we had organised last night, Giuseppe will take you through the plans."

Vito was not happy about his chief's decision but accepted this as his punishment. Salvatore turned to walk away when he froze, the low drone of a plane above their heads made them look up. There was nothing strange about planes flying over the woodland fort, but this one sounded different, it was travelling lower than most and one of the flying crafts engines was making an unusual coughing and spluttering sound.

They saw a twin propeller engine plane, flying just above the tree line making the partisans duck instinctively, it had a large tail of dark smoke streaking from one of its wing engines.

"Bloody hell!" Blurted Sal. "Did anyone see any markings?"

The camps residents shook their heads, when a deaf defying crash was heard in the distance woodland. The resistance leader ran to a giant oak tree beneath one of the lookout posts.

"Tommaso, what do you see?"

"The plane has gone down in the forest, just past the swampland," Tommaso called back down from his high lookout post.

"Did you see what type of plane it was?" Vito enquired.

"Too busy keeping my bloody head down!" came the reply, Vito looked to Salvatore for orders, it was clear the man was deep in thought. Eventually, the leader began to quietly nod as he came to a decision.

"Okay," he spoke to his comrades loudly, "I will need eight men, Vito you will be one of them, these could be krauts and you are the only one of us who can speak any German that means I need seven more volunteers," he announced loudly.

Hands of volunteers began rising up around the camp. Sal walked around picking men he was sure could make the treacherous trek through the woodland with enough energy, if they needed to, fight at the end. Two of the men he chose were two of 'the best trackers in all of Italy', in case any of the surviving planes occupants decided to run then these men could track them easily and would know how far ahead of them the running flying men were. After all this was the partisan's forest and the guests were uninvited. Salvatore took point of this expedition and led the nine-man army off into the dead wild forest.

As the squad approached the crash site, they would have to first cross through a wet, bog infested swamp land, this was a precarious obstetrical. Sal slowed his pace and raised his hand to halt the group, he crouched to the ground and looked down at some tracks in the muddy ground.

"She's here and she has some kids with her," he mumbled, the partisans raised their weapons and scanned the horizon, "she could be hiding anywhere."

"Who is she?" Vito asked, looking down at what looked like canine prints, following beside were some identical prints, yet five times smaller than the larger one. Sal still in a crouch followed the tracks with his eyes.

"She is a Eurasian lynx, she is docile enough and has even come to us for scraps of meat, but when she has kittens, she can become vicious. A couple of years ago, she tore up the face of a good friend of mine, blinding him in one eye and he is now covered in scars," he explained.

Vito scanned the swampland, he had never seen a lynx before, but he knew that they were a large cat of sorts and could be savage when cornered or with a litter. They stayed static for a few minutes, scanning the surrounding area before continuing on, they jumped into stagnate, waist high, murky, bleak, near black, cold water and waded on. They had to wave aside the swarms of mosquitoes that were after their fresh blood. The water was icy cold and stank of decomposing corpses or worse. They continued to scan their surrounding in case the lynx, Nazis or even something worse, there were more dangerous creatures that could be lurking anywhere nearby.

It wasn't too long after that they helped one another out of the forest wetland, their feet were covered in the aquatic vegetation and their water-logged boots made a squelching sound with every step.

As they roamed through the woodland, on the other side of the swamp, they were on full alert; they still did not know the nationality of the downed aircraft. They could hear some faint voices up ahead, they were not Italian, Vito strained his ears, nor were they German. The men emerged out of the brush, before them was a twinned engine aircraft, it looked totally wrecked, it must have come down hard, it had the noticeable insignia of a star in a blue circle, with the red and white striped bars on either side, identifying that this plane was an American aircraft.

This plane was a United State Air Force de Havilland DH.98 Mosquito reconnaissance plane. One of the engines had been obliterated by flak rounds, standing in a small group of four were the occupants of the aeroplane. Seeing the resistance soldiers appear from the dense woodland, the men fell silent. The freedom fighters did not lower their weapons but continued to aim them towards the American airmen, it was not unheard of for Nazi agents to pretend to be allied troops, so as to capture resistance fighters and collaborators, this fact was known by all who fought the Axis powers and Vito had been warned of this by both the Maquis and Partisans.

No partisan force could have lasted this long, if the patriots acted without being cautious. There was also a chance that the plane going down could have been seen by the Axis forces and they would be on their way to investigate, if they were not here already.

"Are you lost? This is partisan land."

Sal greeted the visitors, still aiming his rifle directly at the four men. A tall man sporting a Lord Kitchener style, thick, handle bar moustache, which did not suit him in the slightest, wearing a chocolate leather, wool lined jacket stepped forward and produced his hand.

"Hi, I am American flyer."

Vito smirked at the man's bad, broken Italian. Sal ignored the man's hand and took his bilingual associate to one side and whispered to him quietly.

"I want you to say something to these guys in German. I want to provoke some kind of reaction." Vito hesitated.

"Like what?" he questioned confused, his mind had gone blank.

"I don't know! Tell them you shagged his fat whore of a mother," the leader suggested.

Vito felt uncomfortable, doing this but he did as he was bid. He clearly knew why Sal wanted him to say such an insult, if these were Germans, they would not be able to hide their anger or disgust, even Jerries cared for their mothers, apparently. The partisans studied the blank faces of American pilots. Salvatore seemed a bit disappointed that he had not received some sort of evidence, so began his interrogation of the allied airmen.

"Who is in charge?"

The same man replied, "It being Major Hawkes, be he dead. I be co-pilot, lieutenant Hanson, this is sergeant Taylor, that be Gibbs and James" the man introduced his comrades, once again produced a welcoming hand, which Sal once again ignored.

Turning to a pair of resistance counter parts he ordered, "Check the plane."

The two freedom fighters rushed forwards and began to investigate the belly of the aircraft. After a couple of minutes a cry came from inside the metallic machine.

"One pilot, he's dead! There is a K24 reconnaissance camera"

Sal lowered his weapon, this was enough proof for him, his fellow fighters followed suit, yet still keeping their guns at the ready.

"Take out the cameras film," the partisan leader commanded.

The two men went to work unscrewing the necessary components to remove the nine-inch-wide photograph film from the giant camera. Upon exiting the flying machine, the lieutenant, seeing the film canister, stepped forward making the seven partisans raise their weapons, forcing him to raise his hands and in instantly improved Italian said directly.

"That is the property of the US military!"

"We will develop them for you." Salvatore said calmly, "we cannot allow you to have any photos of our camp."

"We have not taken any, I swear it!"

"Well, it is lucky that we do not need to take your word for that." Vito interjected, getting a stern look from Sal for his interruption. The American pilot backed down and the partisans once again lowered their malicious arms.

"Now, we will be taking your weapons, you will get them back when you leave. Until then you will be our guests."

Sal gave a nod to his comrades, who stepped up to the men, frisked each of the crashed airmen, removing their side arms and knives. All of a sudden, the partisans swung round with their weapons raised, when they heard a loud, rustling in the bushes behind them.

This could be the anticipated Nazi patrol, but they held their fire, when an enormous brown bear wandering past their position. The group watched with bated breath as the large beast walked by. They could see the creature's immense muscular form, moving through the forest with relative ease, as if it had not noticed the men, one false sound or quick movement could startle the great beast and it could compel the animal to attack, one swipe from one of its giant paws would be fatal. Only once it had dissipated into the dense woodland did Salvatore motion for the group to make their long trek back to their hidden resistance base.

Chapter 15

It was mid-evening by the time the group had struggled their way back to the woodland camp, with the partisans remaining on high alert. The hidden fortress residents were full of curiosity and interest of who the new visitors were. There were some disappointed faces, when they found that the new people were not Germans, but allies, as there had not been many hangings of late. The lieutenant, who they had all believed, at first, only spoke very little Italian, had begun speaking fluently, after he had explained his reason for giving the impression that he could not speak their language was in case they were axis forces posing as rebels, translated for his fellow comrades, who could only speak the one language.

As instructed by Sal, Vito listened carefully in case any of the visitors let slip German or for any accent that they had been trying to hide, as he burnt off a couple of leeches, which had attached themselves to his waist from the swamp, with a half-smoked cigarette he had taken from Sal. The black bloodsucking, slug like creature shrivelled up as it was burnt, giving the partisan the opportunity to pull it off. That evening, despite some strong objection from the American pilot, they refused to discuss the plans for their guests over the next few days or even come to a decision of what they may do with the United State soldiers, but instead, as with every night, they drank their home-made beverages until early morning, except that this night's inebriated jolliment did not involve Vito smoking, after going to fill his pipe he found that he had run out of tobacco.

Vito did not wake, the following day, until late and the camp was already in full swing. Before he could say a word Salvatore handed him a bar of shaving soap and a straight razor.

"You need to shave, you are going into the city today," he informed Vito bluntly, before walking off.

Vito just put his friend's acrimony down to him being stressed and ignoring it he made his way down to the quiet stream. The stream was already full of rebels, taking their morning swim. Looking at his reflection in the tranquil water, he was shocked to see a stranger looking directly back at him, it had been multiple months since he had last shaved and no longer looked like the inexperienced, junior partisan that he had been when he had first joined.

He had joined the partisans almost eighteen months by this time and no longer saw himself as the newbie but a fully-fledged resistance member of the Italian partisans. Salvatore had said that he would be going into the city, but what city? And why? He guessed that this was part of his punishment for disobeying the leader's orders, but he had not, had the time to find out. Crouching on the soggy bank and using the bar of soap, along with the razor he began trimming his tangly, matt facial hair. Before he shaved his upper lip he stalled and looked at his reflection in the clear water, he did not look like the same person with a moustache. Instead of shaving it off, he trimmed it and kept a 'painter brush moustache'.

He calmly walked back to the camp feeling rejuvenated, his chin was red raw, his upper lip felt strange yet he was sure he would soon get used to it. He saw Salvatore lighting an unfiltered cigarette as he observed the goings-on in his secret forest dwelling. He had to do a double take when he saw his friend approaching, the Italian rebel leader chuckled.

"You look like a new man," he remarked. "Go down into the back room and pick yourself out a suit, no city folk would be seen in our rags." Vito could not bear the suspense of mystery any longer.

"What city? Where, the hell, am I going?" He asked.

"Torino, there is a photographic shop there, the owner will develop the photos for a small wedge of money, with no questions asked. He supports our cause but cannot be trusted."

Vito could not deny that he was pleased not to have to remain in the camp but he had heard about the abundance of enemy troops in the larger settlements and that the major cities had been mostly obliterated by the allied bombing raids, also after Sal commenting that the business owner who he would be dealing with could not be trusted, did not fill him with a great amount of confidence. Yet, Vito was still skating on thin ice after his escapades with Elvera previously, so he dared not protest the new mission.

The youngest member of the rebel army went down into the fortified, underground bunker and walked down the narrow subterranean corridor, passing by the rooms of bunks and cots, the small armoury, the 'War room' filled with maps of Italy marking Nazi positions and strong points. To the end of the passageway, where a room, much like a walk-in wardrobe, that was filled with various clothes hanging from railings, the range of clothing was eminence, from high class hand tailored three-piece suits to military uniforms from an assortment of countries and nationalities from the jet-black Nazi Schutzstaffel to British or Canadian uniforms. On metallic pegs along the wall hung a massive variety of hats, from bowler hats to military hats to tartan flat caps and on a wooden rack along the floor were footwear from steel capped boots to loafers.

Vito took his time, flicking through each uniform before choosing a black and white pin striped two-piece suit, a silk white shirt, a matching wide rimmed fedora hat and a pair of handmade black 'Salvatore Ferragamo' Oxford brogue shoes. There was a tray of an assortment of accessories which included signet rings, wrist watches, pocket watches, cigarette holders and many other bits, which were not the normal attire worn by partisans and could be used to assist in a disguise. After a brief rummage, Vito chose an engraved silver pocket watch and a matching Albert.

"Very impressive," approved Sal as Vito eventually emerged from the sub-terrestrial living quarters. "You are no longer the new young lad, you look like a new man, no one would even imagine you could be a member of the resistance." Vito scoffed; he never knew that a moment's praise could become an insult in such few words. "Put this on," said the leader handing him a cotton, olive green tie. Vito was at a loss; he had never worn a tie before and did not have the faintest idea of how to tie the knot.

Sal gave a sly smile seeing his friend's expression and fitted it beneath his comrade's collar. Salvatore took a cautionary glanced around assuring that he would not be overheard, he lowered his voice to a near whisper, as he tied the knot for Vito.

"There will be a contact waiting for you at Torino station, he is a good man, he is an underground market trader who assists us partisans. He will recognise you by this tie, you can identify him by a white rose, which he will wear in his button hole. But you must be careful in the city, it is under the total fascist regime, the only person that you can trust out there is your contact, Alfredo."

Salvatore took a second brief scan of the area, before he continued:

"I will take you to the station by cart, from there you must go by train, up north, on your own." Vito withdrew his luger from the back of his trousers, checked the magazine was full and cocked it before replacing it under his suit jacket. “Make sure you have your identification papers and a good excuse for your reason for going into the city, in case you are questioned.”

Vito thought for a moment.

“How about I say that I am going to visit family?”

“Perfetto!” exclaimed Sal in agreement.

The ‘knitting partisan’, Eliseo approached the duo.

“Vito, you are going to the city? Are you not?” He asked, he was a stubby man, had a gruff yet soothing voice, Vito looked towards Salvatore, unsure how secret this operation was to be.

“What the hell do you want, Eliseo?” Sal asked sternly, in response the short man produced a small tanned briefcase.

“I was hoping he could take the clothes to the orphanage on my behalf. I just haven’t made any deliveries to them for a while,” quaked Eliseo nervously.

***

It had taken around forty-five minutes to an hour for Salvatore to take Vito down to the small urban train station, in the rickety horse-drawn cart with Vito carrying Eliseo’s case of wool clothing on his lap. They sat still behind the station house for a couple of minutes, they had no fear of being seen, as these small rural railway stations were rarely guarded, the partisan leader handed his young associate the salvaged camera film, retrieved from the downed air force reconnaissance plane.

“Keep it safe. Buona fortuna.” Sal wished his young friend well. Vito had to force himself from his bench, it felt as if he was glued to his seat and his legs did not want to work.

Sal watched as Vito nervously entered into the station house and joined the short line to the ticket kiosk, which consisted of a middle-aged love-struck couple and what appeared to be an elderly businessman, aged in his mid-sixties. Vito had to use all his strength not to tremble as he asked for a ticket to the city of Torino and paid for it with some of the money Salvatore had given to him previously.

He looked along the station platform, it was very sparse, yet every time someone looked in his direction, he felt that they knew exactly who he was and what he was doing there, his paranoia was at peaks, he checked his pocket watch and compared it to the clock on the platform *any minute now,* he thought to himself.

The high pitch whistle signalled the arrival of the train, even though he had seen many trains pass through Dresden, this would be Vito's first ever train journey and his fear turned to excitement as the giant, matt black steam locomotive screeched to a standstill. Unsure of what he had to do next, Vito watched the other travellers open the carriage doors and load onto the transport, before the partisan did the same.

He took a vacant seat on an empty wooden bench, which neighboured a pair of grey uniformed Nazi officers, with the hope that this would deter any possible suspicion from him, surely someone who wanted to hide from the Axis powers would not sit so close to enemy commanders. He huddled up to the suitcase, full of the children's woollen attire. He felt a sense of achievement as the train jerked forwards to deliver its customers to their desired destination.

Chapter 16

A round, plump man wearing a navy blue, rigid, gold-rimmed hat with the universally hated golden faeces in the centre, with a matching navy, gold trimmed uniform, travelled through the carriages, checking the tickets. Vito used all his powers, not to shake, as he handed over the small snippet of paper that the man clipped with his machine and handed the ticket back with a "Grazi", Vito gave what he hoped was a confident smile back.

His expression soon vanished when he saw who was following the conductor. A pair of Wehrmacht soldiers, asking for the passengers' identification cards, they were now standing to attention in front of the German officers opposite from where Vito was seated. The partisan stayed stock still, fixing his eyes to the blur of the grassy verge that was passing them at an alarming pace, hoping that the two soldiers would just pass him by.

"Ausweiss papers, please," said an Italian voice, with an unmistakeable German accent. Vito ignored it, hoping and praying that if he had ignored them, they might be convinced to leave him be. But to no avail, he could see in the reflection of the window as one of the Nazi rail guards removed a revolver.

"Papers," he replied in a louder, harsher voice. Vito took a deep intake of breath and turned putting on a surprised face as if he had not realised that it was he that was being addressed.

"I am sorry. What?" he said politely, wondering how Sal was able to keep so cool and calm when being confronted.

"Identification papers! Now!" ordered the Nazi soldier severely, Vito went into an inside jacket pocket and quite casually handed over the brown covered, imitation identification booklet. The German examined it carefully.

"Naples? Why do you go to Torino?"

"I am visiting my sister" Vito lied so well by this time, his whole new life was based on a lie.

“What is in the case?” The soldier spat, handing back the ID papers and pointed to Vito’s suitcase.

“Clothes for my sister’s children.”

“Open!”

The undercover partisan did as he was bid by the axis trooper, the German rummaged through the hand knitted clothing. Then without another word the soldiers continued on their way, harassing other passengers for their identification papers. The covert partisan had to hide his small sigh of relief and sat back, giving a confident smile to the pair of Nazi officers, who were looking at him with disgust.

Vito could feel every bump on the hard train bench and was relieved when they ultimately came to a stop at the Torino train station. Vito remained seated as he watched the other patrons collect their baggage, standing aside to allow the two officers to depart first and leave the transport. The partisan finally rose from his seat and carrying his case in his left-hand, he disembarked from the locomotive, stepping onto the platform; the extensive size of the station took Vito’s breath away. He had never seen such a large, elaborate building, since he had left Paris.

He walked to the station’s archway entrance, admiring the engineering of this impressive structure, only after a couple minutes admiration, did he remember that this was where he was to meet his black-market contact. Looking around him he saw the huge amount of Axis troops, both Italian and German. He checked every man’s button hole for any sign of the white rose, there was none, his paranoia was rising again, he looked at the giant elaborate clock, embedded in a pillar in the centre of the building, he confirmed the time with his pocket watch.

He was on time, but not his contact. Had he been arrested? Had he told the enemy about his arrival? Were the large amount of military presence for him? He saw a tall man leaning against a steel pillar, with his eyes glued on the partisan, the man had a thick, long, black overcoat and matching fedora that hid his face. The man was wearing the similar clothing to the Gestapo, which was not an uncommon site when he had lived in Germany, they possibly had a portfolio of him, labelled as a traitor and deserter. The man approached Vito and reached into his inside jacket. Well Vito would rather die, than to be arrested by the vicious Gestapo and sent to one of their evil, underground, torture chambers, especially after what Jean Moulin had told him, before being put up against a wall, to be executed like a common criminal.

The partisan carefully motioned his right hand around his back, not wanting to make any quick moves, he reached beneath is suit jacket and took hold of the revolvers grip. The tall man slowly withdrew his hand, it was as if Vito was seeing what was happening in slow motion, revealing a white rose which he slipped into his button hole. Vito let his hand drop back to his side.

"Vito?" he asked calmly, the junior partisan gave a relived laugh as he presented a hand. "Sal radioed me, I know why you are here and your mission. I am Alfredo."

Vito didn't even know that Sal had a radio set but he was far from surprised, he was beginning to feel that there was a lot about Sal that he was unaware of. The men shook hands, Alfredo's hand was rough and dirty, implying that this man did hard manual work. The black-marketer looked round at the abundance of enemy troops.

"Are you armed?"

"Yes, I have a luger," confirmed the partisan in a whisper, his associate gave a mocking shake of his head and opened the left side of his coat to reveal a concealed sawn down shotgun connected to the inside of the overcoat, quickly closing it again to hide it from view.

"We must go, rapido," urged Alfredo. They walked down the city's main cobbled street and Alfredo began to get to know his new counterpart.

"Where are you from?"

"Naples."

"Ah, Naples, I do not know how comfortable I would feel living by a volcano," he said jollily.

"Volcano?"

"Sí, Somma-Vesuvio."

"Oh, of course," he had heard of Mount Vesuvius before but did not even consider it when talking about his city.

"Anyhow, our city is not as grand as yours but our city has been spared the allied air raids that have obliterated your Naples." The tall man suddenly cringed, realising what he had just said. "Do you have family there?"

His voice had changed and was now one of care and consideration.

Vito continued his charade and said solemnly.

"My mother."

“I am sure she is okay.”

Vito nodded in response, keeping his eyes to the floor, they stayed silent as a couple of German sentries walked past, ignoring the two men, chatting away in their native tongue. From what the partisan could overhear they were talking about some Italian beauty they had procured the services of at a local brothel. Once again out of earshot Alfredo continued his interrogation.

“Does she know that you are a partisan?”

Vito did not want to speak in case he gave something away, he just shook his head, in his mind’s eye he envisioned his own real mother back home in Dresden.

“I have some contacts in Naples, rebels, if you wish we could get a message to her and let her know that you are safe. I am sure she must be worried about you.” Vito had never expected this and had to think of an excuse quickly.

“No, no, I don’t think my mother would still be there, she has probably moved to her sister’s farmhouse on the city outskirts when the bombing started.” Alfredo nodded in understanding.

“And here we are.”

The partisan looked up, they were standing directly outside what looked like a family-owned photography shop, with five old cameras in the dust filled window, showing that the display had not been cleaned since before the war. There was an A4 sign in the window and written in bold writing said ‘We develop camera films and do portraits inside’.

“Go in, tell him that I sent you and discreetly give him the money. Do not tell him where you got the film, he is an Italian but he cannot be trusted,” he instructed his new friend explicitly.

“I will wait out here.”

The black-market dealer removed a silver cigarette case, removed an unnaturally thin cigarette and lit it with a match from a match book.

Vito walked up to the shops door and scanned the streets as he decided how he was to play this. Deciding on the ‘strong silent approach’, Alfredo had been the second person who had told him that the shopkeeper could not be trusted and hoped that this reaction would put enough fear into the man, so he would obey the partisan’s orders, he entered the establishment. A small bell above the door rang, informing the working staff of his presence. The shelves around the shop were full of various cameras and framed black and white portraits of babies and families.

"Buongiorno, how may I be of help?" said a man in his fifties appearing from a back room, behind a curtain. There was nothing notable about the man, except for the circular glasses perched on the end of his nose which looked like they had been designed to resemble the ones worn by the Reichsführer of the Schutzstaffel, Heinrich Himmler. He had a broad smile on his face. Vito did not return the smile but with a stern face, strode directly over to the counter the shops proprietor was stood behind.

He bluntly said, "Alfredo sent me," and slid the wad of notes over the counter towards the man. The ageing proprietor held up a skinny hand, took the bank notes, which he slipped into a pocket of his charcoal grey waistcoat. He walked calmly but deliberately from around the counter and flipped the open sign to closed, before returning back to his side of the counter. Vito got out the film canister and put it on the counter without saying a word. The elderly shop keeper opened the canister and examined the negative film roll.

"Well, my word, a nine-inch-wide film, I have not seen one of these for a long time. Where on earth did you find this?"

Vito remained silent with a stern look and just stared at the shop keeper, who ignored his customer's silence.

"It will take me a couple of hours to get these developed for you," he said motioning to leave into the back of the property.

Vito grasped the elderly man by the wrist and held it in an iron tight grip.

"No copies and I will take back the negatives," the partisan said harshly showing the man that he meant business. "I will be back in two hours," with that Vito turned and left the property.

He stood beside the waiting Alfredo and took a deep in hail of the cool outside air and slowly exhaled. He had never acted like that before and could not deny that he had slightly scared himself.

"So where to next my friend?" questioned the tall man. Vito took a few minutes in quiet thought before replying.

"I need some pipe tobacco and then we must go to the orphanage."

"There is a nice little tobacconist on the next street down," informed the underground dealer. "They can get you any tobacco you would like."

Vito allowed Alfredo to lead the way and after a minute's leisurely stroll they were standing outside a quaint Italian tobacconist's shop. Upon entering Vito was mystified, along three of the walls were glass cabinets, where inside was a massive assortment of tobacco products, such as cigars, many brands of cigarettes, cigar cutters, pipe cleaners, cigarette cases, lighters and a large selection of pipes from standard rustic designs to elaborately decorated meerschaum pipes. There were three round tables where men were sat, talking in low voices, smoking their newly obtained tobacco products, leaving a low cloud of smoke above their heads. Along the fourth wall, behind the counter were four long shelves, filled with large glass jars, each full of various brown tobacco types with an array of exotic names.

"Alfredo! Your usual?" said a slender, pale faced lady in her late thirties.

"Not today, my dear, Maria. We are here for my good friend here. He desires some pipe tobacco."

"Of course, what type would you like? Our best is the 'Dark Mist' from India, it has a deep strong earthy flavour." Vito was at a loss, he did not have a clue, he looked at the assortment of jars and re-read the names for some kind of clue, but he was none the wiser.

"I…I do not know," he said bewildered. "I do not want anything too brutal," Vito explained embarrassed for his naive perspective, the female gave a knowing smile.

"You are a new smoker?"

Vito confessed that he had not been smoking long.

"We'll let me recommend this one," Maria said removing a glass jar from the shelf. "It has a smooth flavour with a hint of pine. It is ideal for a new smoker," she recommended. Before Vito could reply, Alfredo interjected and replied in his stead.

"He will take a pouch of that and put it on my account, my dear." Vito was in shock; the two men had only just met but this man was already buying Vito his tobacco. The lady gave the two men a fetching smile, took a scoop of tobacco from the jar, put it in a small cloth pouch, tied it shut and passed it over the counter to the partisan.

Chapter 17

Once they had left the quaint tobacconist, the bracing fresh air gave them a joyful sense of freedom from the smoke-filled establishment. They began to make their way down to the orphanage, passing the abundance of Axis soldiers. They passed an alleyway where they saw three Blackshirts, laughing and jeering as they kicked and shouted obscenities at a downed youth. Vito looked to Alfredo, who as if reading his associates mind shook his head, the partisan understood, if they tried to intervene then they could draw unwanted attention to themselves.

The Nazi presence here was shocking and put Vito on edge, yet his counterpart seemed to be rather relaxed and even nodded welcome to some of the Jerries as they walked by. They wandered along a brick, ten-foot-high wall and through a giant pair of iron gates with the word 'Orfanotrofio', Orphanage, above their heads. The brick encased courtyard was vast, but bare, except for a couple of a pair of long wooden tables with benches situated alongside, this must be where the parent less children would enjoy their meals on a warm summers day, Vito could almost visualise them laughing and chatting playfully as they gauged on their food.

On the concrete floor, there was chalked numbered squares, to play the game of hopscotch and other chalk drawings, indicating that children did reside here, though the entire place seemed deserted. The two men stood in the open mundane court area, unsure of what they should do next, Vito was about to suggest entering the school like building before them, when a door to the large building opened and out walked a nun. The two men removed their hats out of respect. She was wearing her black and white habit uniform, but what took the two men aback was that carrying in her right hand, she was welding a malicious looking meat cleaver.

"Who are you? What do you want here?" She cried pointing at them with the blade as she approached the pair. Vito was too taken back to speak, by the knife brandishing 'women of god', so Alfredo took charge of the introductions.

"Easy sister, we are friends, we have come bearing gifts for your poor castaway children."

He motioned her to calm, the nun looked at the two men with curiosity. Vito flipped up the suitcase and put it on top of one of the wooden tabletops, opened the latches and flipped up the lid, to show the knit wear to their aggressor.

"Gifts from Eliseo of the partisans," explained Vito nervously, still eyeing up the lethal looking cleaver. Seeing thc clothing the sister lowered her weapon and her serious face cracked a small smile, which did not suit her in the least.

"Eliseo is a good man, my apologise for my aggressive behaviour," she said closing the case. "A week ago some soldiers came over and molested one of our young girls, she used to be such a lovely child with such a joyful nature, but now she is quiet and secluded."

There was a sadness in the ladies' eyes. "Please thank Eliseo for the children. We were just about to eat; would you care to join us?" Vito had been taught to never refuse an offer from a nun but Alfredo had obviously been taught differently.

"My thanks to you sister but we have plans," he gracefully declined.

"Well may god go with you both," she blessed the duo, taking the wool laden suitcase.

As the two men walked out of the courtyard, Alfredo whispered.

"Well that's it, if we die now, then we die in the grace of god," he jested. Clearly, he was not very religious and found it all a great joke. The two men stepped outside the giant gate onto the street's pavement; there was a sense of peacefulness out here.

"Can you believe that? She would have killed us, if she thought we had posed any type of threat," Vito said in disbelief.

"It is war, my friend, people will go to any lengths to protect the people they love and care for," said Alfredo calmly.

Vito thought about this sobering fact for a minute, his new friend was right, he wondered to what extent he would go to protect his mother or even his first true love, Elvera, he would stop at nothing to keep them safe.

"You said, we had some kind of plans?" inquired Vito, looking at the tall black-market trader, who continued to stare straight ahead of himself, as if he was looking through the stone walls of the buildings opposite.

“Yes, indeed, we do. I intend to take you to a lovely Argentinian restaurant; the owner is a good friend of mine. He will cook us the best, most succulent steak fillet you will have ever had in your life, in an amazing peppercorn sauce.”

This would not be a hard challenge as Vito had never had a cooked steak, except for the stew that the partisans made back in their woodland fortress. Alfredo was almost salivating as he spoke about the special meal.

“He also has a beautiful, expensive Rioja. That I had actually helped procure for him from a Spanish transportation vessel.”

This sounded like a luxury meal to the partisan, when he was given this mission, by Salvatore, he had never imagined to receive such an amazing feast.

The restaurant looked like a high-class establishment, with linen table cloths and polished cutlery which glistened in the sunlight. Above the entrance in elaborate golden text were the words ‘Ristorante argentino di Alfredo’.

The duo took a seat on a street side table. But Alfredo rose when a round man with long dark brown hair which went down to the nape of his neck, wearing a white apron on a mud brown tartan suit.

“Joaquin, my dear friend,” said the black-market dealer.

The large man gave a jolly smile.

“Alfredo, what a pleasant surprise. What can we do for you?” Cried the restaurateur, embracing his friend.

“Meet Vito, he comes from our friends in the east,” Alfredo introduced Vito who just gave a nod of welcome, without raising from his seat. “We were hoping you could cook us a couple of your extraordinary steaks in peppercorn sauce.”

“Of course.”

“And a bottle of Rioja.”

“Naturally! I only serve it to my special guests,” confirmed Joaquin, as if he was overjoyed by the request and wobbled (as that is the best way to describe the action) off to place the order as Alfredo retook his seat at the table.

“Tell me,” started Vito intrigued, “How did you acquire the Rioja?” Vito enquired innocently. Alfredo smiled.

“Well, that was a matter of genius, even if I do say so myself. We heard about a transportation operation from the Spanish dictator Franco to Mussolini. So we took a fishing vessel,” he cut off as a SS officer walked passed them before he continued. “We set off at last light and checked its location and stormed it at dark. We killed all on board and took anything that we could sell or use to fight the tyrannical Italian forces.”

“You killed them? Why are you not a partisan? You certainly have the courage to be one of us,” quizzed Vito.

“I am a partisan,” Vito looked at his counterpart shocked. “Just me and some of my colleagues thought that the war could make us some money on the side, we do not sell to the enemy and take up arms when we need to,” said Alfredo sitting back in his chair calmly, as the restaurant proprietor put down a bottle of the expensive Spanish red wine and filled two glasses for the gentlemen.

Vito took a sip of the wine, he was pleasantly surprised, the flavour was like nothing he could compare to, it was amazing. The two members continued to chat, about Alfredo’s other black-market supplies, Vito quickly learnt that Rioja was the least of his stores.

“So how do you get your orders?” inquired the partisan.

“Many of my customers are cautious, due to the enemy presence here so they often use dead drops, usually a house which has an upturned flower pot, they put their order, date and place and will leave the money there, so we need not meet face to face.”

Vito was bewildered by the man’s chosen trade and the complexity of his illicit operations. He began firing questions towards his newly found friend. “How easy is it to smuggle the goods?”, “How easy is it too hot wire cars?”, “How do you know if a policeman will accept a bribe?”, “How do you conduct a trade?”

Alfredo did his best to answer the young partisan’s questions in as much detail and as truthful as possible, only pausing when an enemy agent got too close for comfort.

Eventually, their meals arrived, it was a large juicy steak, covered in a flavoursome peppercorn sauce, herb and garlic boiled baby potatoes, a large garlic roasted Portobello mushroom, with some beautifully caramelised onions, The pink medium cooked meat literally melted in his mouth, the herb potatoes were cooked to perfection and the garlic mushroom was not over seasoned but enough to enjoy the flavour of the food, with enjoyable sweet caramelised onions. Vito had never tasted anything like this in his life and now understood why his new friend’s mouth watered every time he spoke of it.

He looked around the small restaurant where the few patrons looked at their meal jealously, as they ate their own small moderate meals. They ended with a shared, slate board of cheese, which was quiet disappointing compared with the main courses, there were three cheeses, which were all bland and as flavourless as each other, so unlike the cheese Vito had enjoyed back in Paris, the biscuits were soggy and had a horrible nutty after taste. Yet the hand ground coffee they had with it helped wash down the banal dessert.

Vito then began once again interrogating his associate about his underhand dealings, when Alfredo said, "How about I just show you?"

The duo reluctantly left the restaurant, Vito followed his new friend and a sense of excitement grew inside him. Alfredo led the young partisan down a small row of residential properties, on one windowsill was a clay upturned plant pot, with a quick look around, the black-market trader lifted it and removed a small scrap of paper, he unrolled it with a small smile. Without a word he led his young comrade down a small dark alleyway.

"Watch for anyone approaching." He whispered and began unscrewing a small grating in a wall, this seemed so simple, yet this is what the black-marketeers did every day. Alfredo removed a small paper wrapped block and slipped it onto his pocket before, refitting the grate. The duo did not speak, every time a soldier, Blackshirt or Italian police man passed them, Vito could feel his adrenaline rise.

The partisans stopped by an outside laundrette.

"Stay here and keep a watch for enemy troops or the law," he ordered in a whisper. Vito gave a short discreet nod and Alfredo peeled from his associate; Vito watched Alfredo through the corner of his eye. Quite coolly the man walked up to a pile of freshly laundered sheets and lifted the fifth one, he removed a small wad of money and replaced it with the small block of rare commodities, concealing them beneath the sheet and casually returning to Vito.

The two men stood looking out to the street. Alfredo gave a pleasant nod as a pair of Blackshirts walked past. "And that is my business," he told the young partisan proudly. "Now I think it is time the photos should be ready," suggested the Torino partisan

"I think so," Vito replied and they made their way back to the photographic shop. Once again Alfredo stood outside the establishment as Vito reverted back into his stern silent facade.

"Be sure he has no copies; he cannot be trusted!" urged Alfredo as Vito entered the place of business. The proprietor tried to ignore the entering partisan, as he finished serving a Nazi trooper, who left the shop, with hardly even noticing Vito. Only once the door closed behind the soldier, did Vito approach the counter. The elderly shop keeper handed over a brown envelope and film canister, the partisan opened the envelope and flipped through the developed observation photographs.

"Do you have any copies?" Vito questioned gruffly; the man looked nervous before replying.

"No, of course not."

Vito could hear a hint of deception in the proprietor's voice, this was enough to rouse his suspicion, he removed his pistol from its secluded place. He gave the man an evil glare.

"Well, you don't mind if I have a look then," and without waiting, he strode directly behind the counter and through the open doorway hidden beneath the curtain. The older man made some objections as he followed the partisan, that Vito ignored completely, the back of the room was like a small home with a kitchen and a living area, with an open fire place. Vito scanned each room as he passed through and entered through a metallic door.

Upon he entered into a red lit room and hanging, like clothes on a washing line, from string hung a selection of photos, the partisan looked closer and switched on the rooms light, he knew this would destroy any photo developing but that didn't bother him, his eyes were fixed on the hanging pictures. In this new light he could see them clearly, he recognised them, they were the photos that he had just received in the envelope, that 'son of a bitch' had made some copies.

He turned to confront the man, but as he turned, he felt a sting across his cheek and a small trickle of blood ran from a cut. The old Photoshop keeper had a malicious glare in his eyes, he had just swiped at Vito with a razor-sharp Stanley knife, from the workbench, the man took another swipe at the rebel soldier, who took a step back, he tried again, every time missing Vito by millimetres. The partisan could not keep dodging the constant blade attacks; he raised his German revolver and fired a single shot into the elderly shopkeeper, who fell with a surprised look on his face. The partisan did not hesitate for a second, re-holstered his weapon and hastily began tearing down the copies of the reconnaissance pictures.

A mere seconds later, Alfredo burst through the door with his shotgun drawn, the first thing he saw was the old shopkeeper collapsed on the floor before him, he gave Vito a stern look, asking for an explanation.

"The son of a bitch, tried to shank me!" elucidated Vito, "he took copies!"

He continued tearing down the pictures. Accepting his young associate's explanation, he re-concealed his weapon. The two men threw the torn down photos into a waste paper bin, before Alfredo grabbed a bottle of PEC12 developing liquid, which was highly flammable, from the side table and began sprinkling it over the body, dumping the remainder of the bottle in the trash bin. He then removed his match book, lit the matches and also dropped it into the bin, which blew up like a firework.

The duo hastily left the property, Vito quickly picking up the envelope from the counter as he passed. The two men stood on the opposite side of road, observing the shop as the flames spread. They could hear the high pitched, electronic wailing of a military police siren. Thirty seconds later a Nazi Sturmwagen screeched to a halt outside the photographic shop. Five heavily armed soldiers jumped from their armoured transport and entered the building.

Alfredo took a small look around and whispered to his comrade "Wait here." With that he casually walked over to the military vehicle, removed a black box from his pocket and stuck it to the side of the axis mechanism, he then hastily crossed the street and without stopping said, "We must go".

Vito was taken aback but turn to keep up with his black-market associate. Behind them, there was an ear shattering explosion, Vito looked around to see the armoured transportation erupt into an inferno, fireball. Alfredo did not turn, but a small discreet smile emerged on his face.

It took them a good while to get to what Alfredo called a 'safe-house', it was a room above a café, where all patrons were apparently resistance rebels and partisans. In the cafe below it was not what Vito had expected in the slightest, nearly every table in the quaint bistro, was packed with men and women of all ages and sizes, it looked just like a popular establishment. As the two men entered the coffee shop Alfredo was welcomed by the abundance of people. Without offering he walked to the bar and was given two cold beers for himself and his acquaintance. This was no normal cafeteria. He then led Vito to a group of five men who were standing in a small cluster, talking quietly among themselves.

"Vito, my friend, this is Giorgio," he said introducing a lean man, who wore a brown and white striped shirt and a tartan waistcoat. "He is the head of the partisan movement in Torino. Giorgio this is Vito Giordano, from our friends in the east." the man scanned over the young partisan.

“Vito? One of the Salvatore’s men? The forest dwellers,” Giorgio’s voice did not match his build, he had a large bellowing voice that vibrated around the room. A rather good-looking man with wavy blonde hair turned to the group.

“Did I hear that you are in a different resistance group? He asked curiously.

“Yes, in the east” replied Vito boldly.

“Who is your contact?” the man asked.

“Contact?”

“This man is the British SOE, Captain Michael Lees, who is teaching us guerrilla warfare,” said Giorgio.

“I don’t know if we have a contact,” Vito replied, yet this could just be another thing that Salvatore had objected to tell him. He had heard of these special operations executives, they were fearless men who would volunteer to be dropped behind enemy lines, train resistance groups, organise attacks on enemy posts and arrange sabotage jobs. They also had a knack for recognising accents and Vito was hoping the man had not heard Vito’s German twang, which had become all the more subtle than it had when had first joined the resistance. Giorgio ignored the Englishman’s interruption.

“You are leaving tomorrow?”

“Well that is the plan at least.” Confirmed Vito, Giorgio gave a smirk at the man’s uncertainty.

“Well, you will not be going alone, this man, is Colonel Valerio, he will be going with you.”

A man turned to face them, there was nothing very noticeable about the man except for his balding head and thinning moustache.

“Colonel Valerio, is my resistance name, for the Nazis you understand.” Laughed the man, his voice was the opposite of the resistance leader it was quieter and reserved, “my real name is Walter Audisio.” He produced a slim well-manicured hand, Vito shook it, the hand was soft, so unlike that of a resistance freedom fighter.

“You will be joining us then?” Vito said cheerily, realising that he would no longer be the newest member of the forest dwelling partisans.

“No, I will not. I will be coming with you on the train but I will be continuing further eastwards.”

“Walter, here is an expert at living off the wilderness,” explained Giorgio, “we call him the lone partisan,” he laughed. Alfredo interrupted them, before he had to save Vito from boredom.

“Come, Vito, I have a couple more people I must introduce you to,” he said leading him to a corner table where three young girls were sitting, they were very pretty, yet could not have been over thirteen or fourteen years of age, drinking what looked like milkshakes. “These three lovely young ladies are some of the bravest members of the partisan army”.

Vito looked at his friend and then back to the table where the girls were smiling sweetly, how could these innocent looking schoolgirls be partisan soldiers?

Seeing Vito’s puzzled expression Alfredo explained, “These young ladies dress themselves attractively and then go into a bar, that are frequent by Nazis, they seduce them, then they ask if they wanted to ‘go for a stroll’ in the forest, where, as they say, they would ‘liquidate’ them.”

Vito was shocked he would never have suspected that these harmless looking girls could be such ruthless killers. Just then the whole café fell utterly quiet, not one person uttered a word, everyone’s attention had turned to the bar. Vito turned to see what had attracted the partisan’s attention, to shock them into silence. Standing at the bar were two men, one supporting a Hitler style toothbrush moustache, both wore slick oil black overcoats and black fedoras, there was no mistaking them this time, these were Gestapo agents.

Vito pulled this own hat down lower to hide as much of his face as he could and kept his head down to the ground, he knew that his picture would have been circulated through the ranks of the secret police. His true identity could not be revealed, only his new moustache could help hide who he truly was.

“Two men murdered a shopkeeper and then attacked the responding Reich’s police. You will point out the culprits and we will deal with them,” said the man with the moustache.

“We will then leave you in peace and whoever informs us will be rewarded,” the second man added. Not one person made a sound, until a totally bald elderly man, sitting with an elderly lady at a corner window table said loud enough for everyone to hear.

“Like hell you kraut bastards!” The crowd smile at the man’s distinct disrespect. Yet the two agents did not seem the least bit amused, the German with the moustache took a couple of steps forward before speaking.

“You know who these criminal terrorist are. Who are they?” The resisting man stayed silent. “Very well, you will be coming with us and we will be taking you back at Gestapo headquarters!”

Giorgio stepped up and said sternly.

"I don't think Domenico is going anywhere!" then every patron, young and old, male and female, drew an assortment of weapons aiming them directly at the two men. Vito had never seen such a range of firearms, they had sawn of shotguns, German MP45s, British Enfield rifles and even an American Thompson sub-machine gun, as well as Lugers, Colt pistols and even a couple of Walther PPKs. Vito drew his own pistol and joined the Italian aggressors. The Gestapo agents hesitated as they observed the situation they were confronted with. They cautiously shuffled back towards the door, but it was blocked off by a couple of armed partisans.

"Mauro, check the car," the Torino rebel leader ordered, one of the men blocking the exit gave a nod and walked out. "Now gentlemen, you will not be taking any of us to be tortured in your lair!"

The second German then spoke he was looking more nervous than his colleague and stuttered as he addressed the aggressors.

"Okay, okay, we will go." Giorgio shook his head sarcastically.

"I am afraid that will not work you see; you leave and then return in a couple of days with a SS extermination squad and slaughter us. You will not be leaving here…alive." His voice had turned menacing and there was an obvious tone of maliciousness as he spoke. The man who had left previously, Mauro, returned.

"It's a two-seater, boss, no driver!" he reported.

"Okay then, Mauro and Roberto, disarm them and take them down into the cellar." He then looked around the room, to choose a couple of men, "Alfredo you get rid of the car, take Vito there with you."

Chapter 18

Once Alfredo and Vito had taken the powerful two seated Mercedes, that was jet-black with an eagle adorning a swastika in grey on each door. The windows were blacked out making it easier for the two men to drive it to the opposite end of town, without being recognised, before setting it alight, burning it to a cinder, down a secluded alleyway. With great regret Vito decide that he should leave Torino that evening, before things got too precarious for him to leave. So, he and Walter Audisio wished their comrades farewell and left on the next eastbound train.

Vito had no time to relax once he had returned to the woodland fortress. "Vito, my young comrade, I need you to take these Yank pilots to the border for me". The Italian leader led his young recruit over to a hollow tree disguised with overgrowing, climbing ivy, there was a radio set hidden beneath, Vito gave a smirk, 'so Sal did have a radio'.

After the Italian civilian resistance had a quick chat over the radio in French, Salvatore turned back to his young partisan.

"Okay, Vito, you will take the Americans to the Maginot Line, to be picked up by the Maquis. In the same place we picked you up. Do you remember the way?"

"I think so, but I don't speak any French," commented Vito.

"That shouldn't be a problem, they will probably send that bloody kraut, Yosef. I will not be going with you."

Vito did not like the way his counterpart spoke about his old friend but knew only too well what his partisans thought of Germans and he now considered himself as an Italian. But Vito did feel a jolt of excitement to see his fellow countryman again. He knew that Salvatore thought of this as part of his punishment, yet Vito felt rather proud to be trusted with this mission, this was the first time he had been put in charge of a team and he must be trusted by Salvatore to be given such an important mission.

Salvatore examined the developed reconnaissance photographs and seeing no pictures of their woodland camp, but he made detailed notes on German strongholds and positions, which could assist them with attacks orchestrated at a later date.

Before they knew it, an eight-man strong resistance team left the camp, with the four downed American airmen and headed for the French boarder, Sal instructed Vito on protocol. He would have to wait and watch the Maquis, assuring that they did not have a radio and were not accompanied by Nazi troops; this had to be done even if he recognised them.

"He may be a Jew but he is still a German, so cannot be trusted!" warned Salvatore, this offended Vito, not because he was German but that Yosef had always had faith in Vito since they had first met, in Paris. The resistance leader then handed his associate a small brown paper bag, the younger partisan looked inside, it was full of green olives. He took one out and popped it in his mouth, it had a lovely strong flavour.

"They are good, no?"

"Amazing!" agreed Vito.

"But they are not for you, my young friend; you must give them to Yosef, only after he has given you some of the French treasures, which will be yours to do as you will." Vito dared to imagine what rare French 'treasures' he may be receiving from his old Maquis comrade.

The journey was hard going and the men continued to watch the horizon for any enemy troop movement as they crossed the open land. The grass was knee high and the ground uneven. The men were quiet, except one of the American airman who was whistling cheerfully as they walked along, Vito heard a faint rumbling sound, which grew louder by the second.

Out of the blue one of the Americans named Gibbs said loudly in English "Panzer!"

Lieutenant Hanson said in Italian, "Get down quick," without hesitation the men dropped to the ground, hiding in the long grass.

The low rumbling turned into a roar, along with the metallic sound of caterpillar tracks and the sound and heavy mobile artillery began to vibrate the ground, as a giant panzer tank rolled past the men, they watched it nervously as it passed them by. They remained down on their stomachs until the sound of the armoured vehicles engine turned faint. Checking around for any infantry, that would be following the tank before rising and nervously continued their journey. This had been a close call but they had an appointment to keep.

As they approached the French fortifications the Italian resistance members disappeared out of sight, hiding themselves, but still able to keep their eyes on the position where they would be meeting the French resistance, until it was just Vito, another resistance member Emiliano who was the second youngest partisan soldier only two years Vito's senior, they had spent a lot of time together and had become good close friends, along with the four foreign airmen.

The six men walked into the underground fortifications, Emiliano and Vito switched on their torches as they walked deeper into the concrete fortress. There were names, dates, what looked like French poems and anti-German slogans, etched into the walls. They walked into a bleak barren room, with only a metallic bucket in the centre, with ash in the bottom, identifying it as a small fire bucket.

Emiliano collected some kindling from the room's dark corner and lit the small fire, illuminating the room. Vito sat against one of the cold concrete walls and lit his pipe, the tobacconist had been correct his new tobacco was lovely and smooth, Emiliano followed suit with a hand rolled cigarette. The American men just remained standing, looking at the two men, unsure what was happening. "Please, sit. We may be here for a while," invited Vito.

"Well, this is pleasant," said the Italian speaking American in complete sarcasm as the men joined the partisans on the dirty concrete floor. Still inquisitive about the allied airmen and their country they continued to fire questions in their direction, the Americans did not seem annoyed by these two young Italians curiosity and answered happily. As the sun began to set in the distance, they heard sounds from outside the previously used military fort and a moments later saw a camp fire crackling outside, the men inside did not make themselves known to the people, but decided to wait until morning, when they were sure who these people were and could see them clearer in the daylight.

At sunrise, the men decided to complete the transaction with the other European resistance group. Whilst Emiliano remained in the room with their American associates as Vito stood in the shade of the dark tunnels.

He hesitated for a moment before saying loudly "Good morning! Are you lost? This is Free Italian territory." He could see movement from outside as the men scrambled for their firearms, alarmed by the mystery voice.

"FFI," came the reply, "I am Yosef! Who are you?" Vito stepped into the light with a wide smile. Yosef squinted to see the man beneath the moustache "Vito? Is that you?"

"Sí," the two men embraced. It had been so long since they had last seen each other, Yosef had noticeably aged, making Vito wonder if he had changed as much. The partisan looked around to see a group of three other Maquis members and he was disturbed to see one of the men, was the very same man who had accosted him those many months ago, after he had rescued the prominent French resistance leader, Jean Moulin. The man had also aged but his features were unmistakeable, it was the same man. The duo reverted to speaking in German together.

"How are they treating you? Have they found out who you really are?"

"No, I am fine, they trust me, yet Sal is not too happy with me right now."

"Why what happened?" Yosef inquired concerned.

"I disobeyed his orders. I have fallen in love and spent the night with her when I should have returned to the base." Yosef laughed loudly.

"Well, you are only human," he commented. "When I saw you for the first time you were just a lost young man without a country or cause. But now you have changed my friend, you are now a true Italian partisan and have grown into a confident man." Vito looked down, blushing, "Shall we get this done?"

Vito gave a nod and handed his friend the small paper bag, in turn the German Jew handed his associate a wicker basket, as Vito checked the goods, he was overjoyed to see a bottle of thirty-year-old port, a wooden circular box of Camembert, a generous wedge of blue pungent cheese and mini baguettes.

"Emiliano, bring out our guests!" Vito called behind his shoulder. The five men exited the concrete room and out to meet Yosef and his French resistance comrades. Yosef greeted the airmen in English and introduced himself to them. The two resistance parties parted ways and travelled back to their headquarters.

Seeing his good friend again had cheered Vito up no end and as the two youngest members of the Committal id Liberation of National Liberation returned, their fellow freedom fighters re-joined them.

That night Vito opened the port and shared it among his friends, he had never tasted something like this, it had a sweet, smooth flavour and they spent the remainder of the night, finishing half of the bottle of beautifully aged port, which ended in alcohol infused sleep.

Chapter 19

After the downfall of the fascist dictator Mussolini with the Allied forces successful invasion of the Southern Italian island of Sicily, to Adolf Hitler's dismay. Mussolini's fascist government deposed him from his position of power and placed him under arrest, he was imprisoned at Gran Sasso, which was an Alpine Mountain massif, guarded by over two hundred Carabinieri, Italian police.

With the Italian forces surrendering in droves, the Nazi forces, retreated from the Italian island back to the mainland and took command of Italy under Generalfeldmarschall Albert Kesselring. The presence of the vicious Italian Blackshirts, had dissipated to non-existence but was replaced by the worse Nazi troops. The Italian resistance had decided to celebrate, the removal of Mussolini, with a week of festive occasion, which combined with a time to remember those who died for the patriotic cause, both which consisted on a large amount of alcohol consumption, the once aggressive guerrilla fighting force swiftly became an alcohol fuelled rabble.

It was the fourth afternoon of inebriated partying, the newest and youngest recruit of the partisans, was sat against a felled tree, smoking his pipe as he and his comrades watched and laughed at a drunken comrade doing a hysterical comedy impersonating the tyrannical dictator, Adolf Hitler, making his fellow resistance fighters roll around and cry in laughter, when over their heads they heard the low drone of German planes flying low, this was not unusual. But what they heard after was far from normal, much like a swarm of butterflies had been disturbed, a fluttering kind of sound as if someone was trying to straighten out a crumbled newspaper. The partisans looked above them to see, raining down from the heavens, like leaves falling from the trees in a mid-autumn breeze, thousands of white pamphlets fluttered down.

"What the hell is going on?" yelled Salvatore.

“They are peppering the entire valley!” replied a lookout from his tree top perch. Vito picked up one of the distributed flyers, it was all in German.

“What does it say?” questioned Sal, picking up his own. Vito had to give his head a violent shake so he could read the pamphlet clearly. In thick red Fraktur writing was the title ‘Der Rote Tag’. “The Red Day” Vito translated and continued to read the remaining text that was now written in black.

“Since the treacherous act by the Italian army against their great leader Benito Amilcare Andrea Mussolini, the Nazi powers have claimed Italy as a country under the Reich and by the order of our great führer Adolf Hitler, Generalfeldmarschall Albert Kesselring will be in control of Nazi Italy.”

Vito could hardly believe what he was reading, “Our first quest in the new land is to rid us of the terrorists, known as the Italian resistance, we have started our grand quest by cutting off their supply lines, starting with the execution of all who aid them. On the day named ‘The Red Day’ we have begun with the elimination in the north with a village, who supplies these terrorists with food, arms and shelter. This settlement is called—” Vito dropped the pamphlet in shock horror as a deathly chill ran up his spine.

Before anyone could say a word, the young civilian soldier had mounted a Nazi motorcycle, ignoring the cries from his fellow fighters, who called after him and unable to stop him, jumped into the other stolen vehicles, to chase down their comrade and friend. As he approached the township, he could see plumes of black smoke erupting from the monastery on the hilltop. On closer inspection you would see that the holy historic structure, which had once been looking down on the small town for over one-hundred years, no longer stood and was replaced with a pile of charred brick and timber, along with a smouldering rubble were the corpses of deceased monks, who had at one time called this place their home and anyone else who had fled up here with the hope of refuge.

As always Vito came to a sharp, abrupt stop and dismounted the bike at the foot of the steep slope that led up to the small town, leaving it leaning up against the village wall, the same place where he had always left it, on his previous visits. He removed the Luger from his trousers and carefully ascended, he had not totally dismissed what his associates had said, ‘it *could* be a trap’, this was not unheard of, a way to flush out resistance groups. Down these narrow sandstone paths, with a well-placed machine gun, such as a MG13, they could take down a whole battalion of men travelling up here.

Soon the reality of what had happened hit him, the walls were pockmarked with bullet holes from small weapons fire, accompanied with blood splatter and on the side of the road lay the dead bodies of the former residents of this small community, surrounded by empty cartridge cases. He recognised some of the dead, who had welcomed him upon his first visit. The streets were eerily quiet, except for a black and white cat which came up to the partisan and nuzzled up to his leg purring. Vito had been here on an almost weekly basis over the last few months, yet he had nearly always heard something, whether it was children playing, a mother scolding, intoxicated men joking and laughing or even an uncontrollable dog barking, but there was nothing.

Even upon entering the square, which was always buzzing with activity, but instead there were more dead bodies of residents littering the ground, among the deceased were the corpses of a pair of hounds and even a horse who had been slaughtered along with their previous owners, even the trickling fountain sounded fainter as if mourning the tortured soles of the dead.

Vito looked around; it was worse than he had expected. Then he saw something that made his blood run cold, the door to the butcher's shop was ajar, hanging off its hinges. The young man pulled himself together, preparing himself for the scene he my witness inside and with his pistol at the ready he cautiously entered the fresh meat establishment. The first thing that met him, apart from the shop being in disarray, was hanging from a meat hook he saw a limp hanging body of the overweight owner Luca, he had a number of bullet holes in a tight pattern around his chest as if he had been used for target practise. Lying on the white tiled floor by his feet was the thing the young resistance fighter had most feared the young slender body of the proprietor's daughter, Elvera.

Vito rushed over to her corpse, turned her over and nestled her head on his lap, her black hair was matted with blood and she just stared back at him with cold, dead eyes. Around her delicate neck, where her mother's pendant once hung, was a red mark where the pendant had been torn from her body. Then the young man's emotions took over as he broke down in tears over the girl he loved, this was the girl he was going to marry, the only girl he had ever loved. He was sure, if he had informed her about his previous life in the Wehrmacht, he was sure, she would not have forsaken him. He began to shake as tears ran down his cheeks uncontrollably as he looked down at her slain body. A sound made Vito look up with a start, to see Sal and Flavio looking down at the overwhelming display.

“Why? What did she ever do? Why?” Vito asked distraught, his voice was shaky and high pitched.

“It’s war, kid” said Flavio showing a heartless side “That’s what happens. You think you are Christ or something? You going to raise her from the dead or something cradling her head like that?” Salvatore gave his associate a hard stern glare, before signalling him to leave and placed a comforting hand on the young man’s shoulder who had gone back looking at his fallen love.

“Come, we must bury her, bury them all, as the true heroes they are.” Vito wiped the tears from his eyes, with a sleeve and looked up at his comrade.

“Heroes?”

“They did not reveal where we were, they said nothing about us. They saved our lives.”

This did not comfort Vito in the slightest. But what the leader had said was the truth, if they had informed the Axis forces of the location of the rebel base, they may have spared their lives and the partisans would know by now if that had been the case.

The rest of the day the partisans halted their merry making and dug eighty-seven graves, in the soft grassland outside the small settlement, with makeshift crosses, made by splinters of wooden planks, nailed together and the names of the deceased, etched into each of the wooden crosses.

Vito had not been the only one to lose a loved one, many of his fellow resistance fighters, had had family living here, who had also fallen victim to the Nazis and their so called ‘Rote Tag’. Pietro gave a small service in Latin for the fallen settlers. Vito tied the silk handkerchief, she had gifted to him after their first date, onto the cross with her name and that night, as all the families and loved ones of the lost, slept on the soft ground beside the graves of their fallen. A tradition that dated back to the ancient Roman times.

Vito had a restless sleep, dreaming, as if in a never-ending loop, of the execution of the young man he had witnessed, in Mont Valérien, France, yet the face he saw, when the body was turned over, was that of the beautiful, Elvera, making him wake in a start. Meanwhile, most of the other members had returned back to the woodland base to plan a retaliation against the National Socialist forces. Yet, the grieving people that remained behind, were not abandoned undefended, for heavily armed resistance soldiers were patrolling the perimeter for the whole night.

That night a dark, coldness enveloped in Vito's heart, no one who wore a Nazi uniform or swore allegiance to that satanic cult would be spared by his hand.

Chapter 20

The reprisals for the Rote Tag massacres started almost immediately. Eight separate small squads of six people were arranged, to make small single attacks, against Nazi outposts. After seeing a distinct change in Vito's demeanour and a much harsher, almost ruthless reaction towards the enemy forces, Salvatore came to the decision to make him the head of one of these teams. The entire task was to harass and hinder the German invaders to the best of their ability.

Vito's team consisted of his friend Emiliano, a lean older rebel who had been a long-term member of the partisans who had joined at the very beginning when Salvatore had first formed the resistance, called Matteo, the other three men Vito had chosen were from his team who had helped returned the Americans Giulio, Samuel and Nicolo', because they were all well-built, fast and had experience in sabotage.

His first mission was to disable one of the small communication hubs, these were small wooden huts, to avoid local suspicion and dotted around north of the Gustav line. These were far enough away from the line so if the heavily fortified Nazi defences were overrun then the Nazis would still have a communication network running to call in reinforcements. These posts were guarded by only one or two men with usually one more person inside to decode and relay messages, this was an operation that had been initiated by rebel forces across Italy. This communication line had been set up long before the German occupation, when the country was still under the tyrannical rule of Mussolini.

For Vito's first mission as a group leader was to take out one of these communication depots, simultaneously the other partisan groups would run similar operations on other communication posts. Vito and his associates, were laid flat on the damp, dew covered grass watching one of these standard looking sheds, it looked no different to any normal garden shed, there was no light around it except for a small crack at the bottom of the door.

There was a pair of Nazi Wehrmacht guards walking back and forth outside, since the takeover there was a curfew imposed on the Italian civilians, so if they were spotted then they would be shot on sight. Vito peered through the darkness and watched the two patrolling soldiers; one soldier lit the others cigarette before they continued their duties. After studying them for a further few minutes, he turned to his fellow counterparts.

"We should go around the back of the building. They never seem to go past the back wall, if we can get there, whilst their backs are turned, they won't see us." He suggested, Emiliano interrupted.

"Why don't we just shoot them?"

"In case you have forgotten, that is a communication post, one shot and they could sound the alarm, then this entire place would be swarming with those sons of bitches in a matter minutes," warned Vito, not taking his eyes off the guards "no, we will have to use stealth".

Being sure they kept low to the ground the troop moved around to where they could focus on the back of the shed and then one at a time, as the sentries turned away, they darted to the hind wall and waited, for their comrades to join them, hardly daring to breath in case their condensing breath was seen by the eagle-eyed German sentries.

Vito stealthily looked around the side, the guards had just turned, so he gave a nod to Emiliano and another partisan Nicolo', who were both the most skilled with a knife, who ran round, Nicolo' with a machete and Emiliano with a bayonet, sneaked up behind the two Nazis and cut the man's throats, spraying blood over the dew-covered grass. The remaining resistance fighters walked around to the front of the structure; Vito removed his Luger that he had always kept close to hand.

He looked around to his comrades, who had all their own firearms out. The youngest partisan without hesitation kicked open the door and before the radio operator knew what was happening, Vito fired a single shot into the back of the man's head, the Nazi communications engineer fell forwards, dead.

Whilst three of the men kept watch outside, Vito removed the radio set that was linked into the German signal, so that the rebel army could covertly listen in on the German radio whilst Emiliano set timed devices around the wooden outpost and Matteo searched through the tabletops full of intelligence, removing any papers, maps or code books that could be used to aid the resistance army.

Only then did the men retreat to a safe distance and watch the building erupt into a cloud of smoke and debris.

The following weeks Vito hardly slept, he would listen to the stolen radio, he being the only one who understood the German language, continuously flipping through one of the booklets to decipher any codes and during the night he would go on other operations which consisted of felling down large trees across roads used popularly by the Axis force, climbing up telegraph poles to cut communication wires, destruction on Nazi vehicles, blowing up fuel or ammunition dumps.

Thanks to the radios they had stolen from the communication hut, Vito was able to intercept a message, stating that a train was to be expected, with a carriage of men, weapons, ammunition and fuel. Such transports would be strongly defended, which would include metal foxholes in the top of the carriages that would have approximately eight heavily armed men with four Italian made Cannone-Mitragliera, better known as a 'Scotti', it was lethal twenty-millimetre anti-aircraft gun, aiming in all directions. There would be approximately one to three men, per carriage, on the gangways fitted to the top of the freights, not to mention the five or ten men who would be protecting the ammunition and weapons cache on the flat bed carriage. But such an opportunity to cause a major blow against the Nazis power was too good to miss. Vito told Salvatore that this was his mission, he did not request it, but demanded it.

That night the six-man squad left the camp at the dead of night and headed directly to the railway tracks.

The men chose a spot with secluded ridges and small woodland beside the train tracks. As Vito supervised Giulio, Samuel and Nicolo using a giant pry bar the team removed three metal rail tracks and half a dozen wooden ties, with the intention to derail the train whilst and the hope that the fuel would then erupt and blow the whole transport, killing the Axis troops. Whilst Matteo dug a foxhole, a ditch for the men to hide and protect them from any possible gunfire or shrapnel, Emiliano kept watch for any patrolling soldiers, who may be examining the tracks for any possible sabotage and the approaching train, it was not due for a couple of hours, but this was not a normal train so they did not stick to standard timetables. Once the sabotage was completed the men reclined into the hand dug foxhole.

Vito had brought, in a brown burlap bag that he always carried, with him a couple of the prêt baguettes and a wedge of the Roquefort blue cheese, that he had received, as the sign of respect, from Yosef and shared it with his comrades, wishing he had brought the port, the small meal was a small piece of ecstasy in this damp, black surroundings. The men began smoking their tobacco wares, that night was jolly with much laughing and joking, you could almost forget that they were there for a darker deed.

"The train is coming!" whispered Samuel harshly as he crawled back from the track, being of a cautious disposition he had nominated to remain at the track to warn the men of the locomotive's arrival. The men put out their tobacco wares. They could hear the tracks rattle and the chugging of a train and giving a high-pitched air whistle as it approached, the men hunkered down waiting for the crash and explosion which would follow. Another sound came to their ears; a piercing screech that made the partisans freeze and look to each other in urgency, the train was breaking, hard.

Vito peered over the ridge of their hidden crater, the single light on the front of the train. Above the swastika flag, which lit the path before it, had seen the dismantled track. The partisans disappointedly witnessed as the train stopped just three meters short of the disassembled railroad; the squad leader slumped back into their hole in dismay, his counterparts looking at him, what were they going to do? As spotlights from the top bunker scanned the woodland for any sign of the saboteurs.

Vito dared another glimpse of the train, two passenger carriages, followed by a flat freight rail car, with crates covered in tarpaulins guarded by between eight to twelve men, at this distance Vito could not make a solid head count, after this were two colossal fuel tankers with a single soldier on top of each, who were now scanning the woodland with their torches, each passenger carriage had one of the metallic bunkers on top with each manning their deadly Cannone-Mitragliera or the massive spotlights.

The squad leader hunkered back down and went into his burlap bag, he had not wanted to consider this eventuality, but he was prepared for the possibility. He removed two black boxes, connected to five sticks of dynamite each, these devices had two ways of detonation, one was a simple timer and the second was a wire which could be extended and fixed to a solid structure, so then any movement, whether it was pulled or retracted, on the wire would detonate the explosives. He looked at his comrades, who looked back at him with a nervous look on their faces. Vito gave a smile, though in this light his comrades could not see it.

“Stay here and get ready to move,” he whispered, knowing he may not survive he finished with two words “good luck!” Before his friends could reply the youngest partisan had rolled out of their defensive position and had ducked behind a tree.

Vito darted from tree to tree, dodging the scanning lights, he travelled parallel with the train until he had reached the rear of the locomotive, he was levelled with the final petroleum tanker. He could see the guard on top who was scanning the opposite woodland with his hand torch, the partisan edged forwards, dropping flat to the ground as a spotlight travelled over him, he froze and dared not move as the light scanned past him, as the beams moved on, Vito did not hesitate and bolted for the back of the tanker, he stood with his back tight against the metallic container, he breathed a couple of deep breath to regain his composure.

“Vito what the hell are you doing you bloody idiot?” he murmured to himself. He slipped to the floor and crawled over the tracks beneath the first tanker, he continued to the end of the container and fitted the first explosive device beneath it, fixing it onto the bottom with a zip tie, he then took the wire of the black boxed detonation device and looking to the woodland to assure the guards attention was still fixed on the woodland, he continued beneath the second vessel and fixed the second device. Hooking the wire onto the second device, if the first detonation did not set of the second device, then the retracting wire would, he set the timer on this second device for ten minutes that should give him enough time to get away.

Vito crawled back the way he had come and once again straining his back against the barrel like tank, he checked around the side and cautiously looked down the track, some of the soldiers had exited the carriage and were walking along the tracks, Vito bound straight into the woodland and raced towards the bunkers where his compatriots were hidden, he was only six feet from the foxhole when a stream of light flooded over him, he had been caught in a spotlight, Vito could not freeze, if he did he would die, he turned at a right angle and ran into the forest as behind him Nazi shouts were heard.

“Run you bastards run!” he shouted to his fellow rebels as gunfire broke out. Rounds from the menacing Cannone-Mitragliera guns crashed through the brush, ripping through the smaller trees causing them to disintegrate into clouds of sawdust. The other five civilian soldiers had left the safety of their bunker and were also running through the woodland. As they entered deeper into the Italian jungle the timber became thicker and they were hidden from the soldiers on the carriages, who were now firing their giant weapons blindly. The men took positions behind large trees. Checking from around the tree they could see approximately seven Wehrmacht troops were fast approaching.

There was a sudden cry from Vito's right, he looked over to see his friend Emiliano on the ground with a giant twelve-inch splinter embedded in his leg, as one of the Cannone-Mitragliera twenty-millimetre rounds had hit the side of the tree he had been hiding behind. He looked to Matteo with his back flat against a neighbouring tree, with his German StG 45 assault rifle at the ready, Vito removed his Luger.

The gunfire was then blotted out as an ear shattering explosion erupted sending up a cataclysmic ball of fire as the explosives, Vito had set, had detonated, igniting the petroleum and ammunition, maximising the blast, engulfing the train's entire carriages in an inferno. Only then did the men reveal themselves from their hiding places, the pursuing soldiers had ducked and turned to see what had just happened, making them clear targets, the men fired at the German troops, felling them in quick succession. But this did not mean they were safe yet; they did not know how many of the transporting Wehrmacht had survived the colossal blast. The squad leader ran to his fallen friend and lifted him onto his shoulder, in a fireman's lift, as the small group continued through to the other end of the woodland.

Vito lowered his friend to the floor; they were safe and the mission was a success. "I am sorry, boss," blubbered Emiliano, in agony as Matteo examined his wound.

"You have nothing to be sorry about," Vito said comfortingly. "Can he make it back to camp?" he asked Matteo.

"He will need some help, but he should be okay," said the partisan veteran.

Though these disruptions and attacks were fulfilling, Vito still felt an emptiness, the attacks did not feed his desire to avenge his one true love, the loss the invading forces may be feeling at this time did not compare to the deep loss he had felt since the fateful 'Rote Tag' massacre.

Chapter 21

Vito spoke to his small team of operators about suspending any further operations until Emiliano recovered from his injury "We are a team and I don't think that we should do anything without Emiliano."

"I agree, out there we have to have each other's back and trust each other totally." Matteo added they looked at each other and the men nodded in agreement.

This wouldn't take too long as Emiliano was already getting better at an extraordinary rate, thanks to a German concoction called Schwedenkäuter, made from a selection of six herbs and strong alcohol. It could be digested to help with liver and kidney problems or put on stings, burns and cuts to heal them.

Over the following few months, in between the occasional minor attacks which had been fewer and further in between, Vito would listen to the Nazi communication, over the stolen Nazi radio set. He eavesdropped on many contacts and messages being exchanged, some were more direct than others, but nothing that was much use or help to the rebel cause. That was until one late evening, when Vito was laid back, half asleep, on bedding that he had made from bits of moss, smoking his pipe, when a message aroused him from his docile state and he had no choice but to convey this message to his chief, Sal, immediately.

He rose from his moist bedding to seek out Salvatore. He found his friend and leader, where he had suspected, in the centre of the camp, half way through a flagon of home brewed alcohol. Seeing his most junior member of his partisan band appear, he greeted him, slurring his words as he spoke.

"Ah Vito, where on earth have you been? Come we have some Eurasian wren on the spit." Over the roaring open fire, Vito saw six of the small birds browning nicely on two spits with three on each. But as tempting as this morsel was, it was a personal favourite of Vito's since he had lived in Italy, it could not distract enough to stop him relaying this most important message to Salvatore, what he was about to say could make a decisive blow against the Axis forces.

"Sal, there is an SS regiment, headed to Rome," Vito spoke fast, but this news seemed to sober up the partisan leader in an instant. The Schutzstaffel was not a rare sight in Italy, though an entire regiment, which could consist of more than one-thousand men, was almost unheard of.

"What? When?" he interrogated his comrade.

"On the day after tomorrow, they are meant to be entering the city at eighteen hundred hours," Salvatore stayed silent as he contemplated what they must do. "We cannot just let an SS regiment enter the capital unhindered!" urged Vito, Sal nodded in agreement as his head cleared.

"Okay," he looked around at his drunken men, who all seemed worse than he did. "Vito, meet me by the maps, give me a moment to wash this alcohol from my face in the river and we will discuss what our next move should be," Sal said struggling to his feet.

Whilst Salvatore disappeared to splash some cold, stream water in his face to try and sober himself up, Vito wondered over to the makeshift table, which consisted of a plank of wood resting on a pair of tree stumps. He began to observe the many routes in and out of the historic capital city, Rome. *All roads truly do lead to Rome*, he thought to himself, slightly overwhelmed by the huge amount of ways you could enter the immense city. It was a couple of minutes before Sal joined him at the table with a steaming mug of black coffee.

"Did you hear what route they would be travelling on?" he queried. Vito had not heard any mentioning of an exact route, but he had overheard enough to make an educated assumption.

"No, but it is a regiment, so I think we can ignore these smaller entrances and they said they would be entering from the North, which leaves these three roads, which are all connected about thirty-three kilometres away from the city, so it makes sense that they would travel along this road," he informed his friend, proud of the deduction. Sal wiped his eyes and gave his head a quick shake, to try a clear his blurred vision and focus clearly on the map before him.

"That would make sense." Vito took another look of the Italian map, he had seen it multiple times before, but this time he noticed something, that he could hardly believe he had missed. Going from east to west there were twenty thick red lines, splitting the country into sections and one was splitting the northern sector of Italy from the rest, blocking their route to Rome.

"What is that obstruction?" he questioned his leader.

"Those red lines are the Nazi fortifications, stretching the entire width of our land. They are defensive lines to try and hold back the Allied advance. The only one we would need to worry about is this one," said Sal pointing to the most northerly line. "The krauts call it 'The Gothic Line'. I doubt it will be much of a challenge, its construction is behind schedule, so there are many gaps and it is lightly guarded. The chance of being seen is low, especially at night."

"Do you know a safe route?"

"No. But I know someone who could help us get across. He is a smuggler." Sal said confidently.

Of course you do, thought Vito, Sal knew someone for every eventuality.

"We will prepare to leave tomorrow night, when my head is a little clearer," laughed Sal. The duo decided to close their plan making and joined their comrades for the remainder of the night. They ate the freshly cooked meat and continued to drink to the early hours, as was common practise in this rebel hideout.

Vito awoke the next morning vibrant and alert, following his normal routine he went down to the stream for his normal morning swim, before returning into the camp for a warm porridge with the remaining honey that had been donated to them before the village had been brutally obliterated by the Nazi regime.

After breakfast he went to seek out Salvatore who was pouring intently over maps, oblivious to what was going on around him. Other resistance fighters were loading their weapons, whilst others were reinforcing the camps defences with long sharpened poles sticking diagonally out from the ground, as well as digging a spike filled dyke around the camp.

"Why all the extra fortifications?"

"Well, you know we can never be too safe," Sal said, he did not sound at all convincing. Vito gave his boss a stern look. "Okay, Vito, if we do this, we could bring a lot of trouble our way, so some extra defensive cannot hurt," he explained quietly.

"How many people are we taking with us?" asked Vito looking around at the camps inhabitants.

"There will be forty of us. Thirty-two for the initial attack and eight with heavy machine guns to assist our retreat."

Forty against over one thousand was not favourable odds that Vito particularly liked, these were not ordinary soldiers but SS, the elite, but they had no choice and Salvatore knew what was best; he had been doing this a lot longer than Vito. He was handed a British Lanchester Sub Machine Gun, which had two magazines which would be loaded into the side of the weapon. With Sal informing him, that he would need the fire power and extra ammunition for this particular mission, if they were to have any chance of success.

"You said that they are expected in the city by six in the afternoon?"

"That is what they said."

"Right, well if the information is correct, we will set up our attack here," said Sal pointing to a point on the road, approximately an equal distance between the Gothic line and the Italian capital, Rome. "They will be there around ten in the morning."

Other members of the camp were making Molotov cocktails out of old milk bottles. Molotov cocktails had first been used in Finland and had worked so well, that they had kept the Russian forces from a full invasion. It was a crude incendiary device typically consisting of a bottle filled with flammable liquid and a rag wick, set to ignite when the bottle smashed or the wick ran down.

Vito was apprehensive about this mission; this was going to be a conceivable fatal task and the odds would be certainly against them. He spent the following few hours, stripping down and greasing the guns mechanisms, to make sure it worked freely and did not jam when he needed it the most. The support team each had a German MG34, it was an efficient and manoeuvrable gun that could be mounted on a bi-pod, many had been abandoned at Nazi weapon dumps when the German military got the new faster and lighter MG42.

Chapter 22

As the sun began to set, the small forty strong army left the safety of their camp and headed south. The men travelled through ditches on the sides of the road, the stagnant, knee-deep water made it harder for them to walk through but gave them good enough cover to hide, if it was called for, if an Axis transport were to come along, they could duck down and hide out of view, without the enemy being any the wiser. By the time night had fallen, it turned dark as they arrived at a crossroads, where a ten-foot-tall granite cross stood tall and proud.

"We must wait here, our contact, Piero, will be along shortly." Salvatore commanded. The partisan soldiers sat around the giant cross and began snacking on the small food they had brought with them; they had not eaten since they were back at base. They all lit some tobacco products, as this would be the last time they could have a smoke until they had passed out of view of the Nazi fortifications.

Half an hour later a voice from the darkness called out to them, making them jump up with their weapons ready to fire.`

"I could see your cigarettes five miles away." Sal held up a hand to stop the men from shooting, this could be their contact. "Salvatore?" asked the voice.

"Sí."

"I am Piero." The voice said stepping into the moonlight so he could be seen by all. He looked nothing like they had expected. He was a stumpy, tubby man with a balding head, wearing a loose blue and white pin striped shirt with green and brown combat style trousers. The man seemed unaffected by the large amount of firearms pointed in his direction. The men cautiously lowered their weapons, this man was clearly not a German.

"If you want me to get you over the Gothic Line, then you must all do what I say, when I say. No talking, it could rouse suspicion and no smoking, you can see the cigarette light for miles. So now we should move. Presto!" said the man calmly, it was clear that the men did not like being told what to do by a stranger and looked to their leader for commands.

Sal looked back at his men, gave a small shrug and turning to the guide said bluntly, "Lead the way."

The men grudgingly followed their new contact, surveying the blackness around them. Out of the bleakness before them a giant concrete structure, loomed, it appeared like a massive wall, with anti-aircraft weapon placements and spotlights scanning the surrounding area. Vito had seen similar structures, before the war when he was a German civilian and he would go to the cinema. The newsreels, which Vito had now learnt were full of lies and propaganda, showed a colossal reinforced structure, it was an extensive system of coastal defence and fortifications built by Nazi Germany that travelled from the northern most point of Norway, down to the French/Spanish border, they called this complex of barricades and bunkers 'The Atlantic Wall'.

From this distance the rebel freedom fighters could not see any way that they could pass this obstacle undetected by the guarding German troops. Piero led the resistance members along the ditch by the roadside. As they approached the fortress the murky water here smelt stronger and worse than further down, the vile odour made the men wretch. As they continued down the route, they noticed that their eyes had been deceived, the reinforced concrete barricade was larger as it had first seemed, the men ducked neck deep into the sewage, to avoid the continuously scanning spotlights. A gutter led to a tunnel beneath the structure, the stench was unmistakeable, it was clearly sewage waste. Their path was blocked by a thick metal grating, the partisans gave an unenthusiastic grumble.

"Shhh," motioned Piero harshly and with a sharp tug the grating gave way, it had been cut, the smugglers had made it into a trap door, it was an ingenious contraption, at first glance it seemed as secure as the structure above it. The men rushed through, eager to clear the nasal singeing fumes. This side of the wall was less well defended, after all this was still Nazi controlled. To the rebel fighters delight, after a brief whisper to Salvatore, this is where Piero left them, the partisans kept quiet and continued along the ravine, until they had escaped from the eagle eyes sentries of the Gothic line, before Giuseppe broke the deafening silence.

"That bloody stank!" he complained in his gruff manner.

"Well, what did you think we would be doing? Walking through the front gate?" said Vito sarcastically.

"Well, I did not expect to be wading through Kraut shit!" he complained.

"Giuseppe shut it!" said Salvatore bluntly; their leader was clearly feeling the pressure. He pulled out small silk map, a gift he had received from the American Airmen; it was thin, flimsy, light and easily concealed. He lit a Zippo lighter and studied it.

"Okay, gather round!" he called in a hushed voice, the troops huddled towards their leader. "Down this road there is a crossroads it will take us a good twenty minutes to reach it. The road crossing it is the main road heading into the north end of the city that is where we will set up our ambush!" He commanded; they had now passed the point of no return.

***

The journey to their defensive position was uneventful; they set up three kilometres along the main road. Thirty-five men armed with automatic sub-machine guns and petrol bombs, hunkered down into a man dug trench, beside the tarmac road, approximately twenty feet from the road where the support team, were setting themselves up on a ridge behind their comrades with their MG34 machine guns and the expressed orders not to fire until they heard Salvatore blow on his brass whistle.

The sky was turning blue as the sun began to rise, the men had been trying to get whatever sleep they could before the mornings ambush and prepared their weapons, each of the attack team had a Zippo cigarette lighter to light the wicks of the petrol bombs, which were now lined along the trench wall, down by their feet. No one spoke much. The situation was tense and the wait almost unbearable.

It was almost a relief when they heard the unmistakeable sound of a Nazi motorcycle. The men held their breath, this was either a German courier or a scout, the bike seemed to have come to a standstill on the road before them. The hidden men stealthily observed him from their hidden position as the motorcyclist waved a triangular flag above his head, along the road they saw an alarming mass of SS soldiers, along with a couple of jeeps and a 'Schützenpanzerwagen' half-track armoured vehicle, which made the ground shake as they approached.

The Axis troops seemed rather relaxed and in a carefree mood, as they sang boisterously the 'Devils Song' SS Marschiert in Feindesland, translated as 'The SS marches in enemy territory', this was their victory song, that they commonly sang when they entered a newly occupied country. The sound of this song in the air, made Vito feel sick to the pit of his stomach. They watched their leader for a signal to attack, he looked as if he had frozen at the sight of the German troops, as he peered over the side of the embankment.

Sal dropped back into the trench and picked up his Molotov cocktail, his comrades followed suit and removed their lighters, Sal lit the wick of the projectile and paused until his men had done the same. All at once the men then hurled their cocktails out of the trench towards the road, peaking up to see where they had landed. Many had shot short of the targets, gleefully Vito saw that his missile had landed directly into the back of the half-track, setting the ten occupants ablaze, they were spilling out of the back wailing, another petrol bomb hit a small group of infantrymen lighting them up like moving bonfires. The other projectiles had erupted onto the roads, making a barrier of flames.

The attack team opened fire on the enemy forces, Vito founded it hard to keep his powerful weapon level and he found it rising high, wasting much of his ammunition. Reloading a second magazine, he decided to fire lower down and take out the enemies' legs, as he fired, he saw the SS soldiers fall, crying in pain, as he obliterated the men's calves. Vito's gun run out of ammunition for the second time, this was his last magazine, he threw his weapon aside and drew his Luger side arm, he began shooting with his pistol, as many of his comrades had also had to resort to. He looked to his leader, Salvatore, who was looking along his men.

"Blow the god damn whistle!" Vito shouted over the din, not that his boss could hear over the gunfire. Vito signalled to Sal, with a wave of his hand that they should retreat. The partisan looked along the line and nodded and keeping low to the ground the attackers retreated, Sal blew his whistle nearly instantly and gunfire from their support team flew over their heads to hold back the German forces advance.

As the attack team ran to the top of the knoll, the support team continued to hold back the Axis powers. One at a time, the heavy weapon gunners followed their comrades down the other side. Vito helped Emiliano from his position.

Hidden behind a hedge row, on a mud road, was a large open back truck, with approximately twelve bales of straw in the rear. Salvatore removed a pair of bales to reveal a metal box.

"Put you weapons in here and then cover it back up. Vito come with me in the cab, we may need your linguistic skills."

Vito could tell that his leader was stressed and he could totally understand the reason why. They were in occupied territory and they had just made a massive attack against an SS regiment and they still had to get past the German fortified line. With the weapons hidden the men piled into the back with some lying back on the straw. Sal took the steering wheel and drove down the dirt road; Vito could not help but scan the area, in case the attack had raised an alarm.

It had not taken them long before the giant Nazi barricade came into view, it all seemed unnaturally quiet and made the approach even more eerie. They approached the defensive walls gargantuan reinforced gates. Spotlights lit the vehicle up, under the overcast sky and they could see a large array of enemy weapons pointing in their direction. Eight German guards motioned them to come to a stop. Salvatore crawled the truck to a stop, "Ciao," he said casually as he wound down the window.

"Papers," ordered the soldier, in very good Italian, Vito and Sal passed over their identification documents to the German, who examined them, comparing the photos with the cab's occupants. "Where are you going?" the man was very abrupt, Vito had no idea how his friend could act so calmly, when being accosted in such a way.

"We are farm hands, we have just finished on the farms and been moved to the farms in the north," explained Salvatore. The soldier walked around back and observed the men in the back.

"There are a lot of you," he commented returning to the front.

"There is a lot of work," replied the partisan, the German judged the man before accepting his story.

"Okay. Öffne das Tor!" he called out. The concrete gate began to slide open and Sal drove past the Gothic wall. Vito gave a nervous laugh, he could hardly believe that they had been allowed to pass so easily, but something he had seen preoccupied his mind.

"Did you see that?" he asked his leader; Sal gave him a questioning glance.

"What did you see?" he questioned the younger partisan.

"There was a sign back there, it said 'Gefängnis', prison." Sal did not seem surprised.

"I told you, the wall is behind schedule. That is probably where they are keeping their slave labour force."

"Slave labour?"

“Yes. Jews, partisans, communists and even possibly some prisoners of war. They are made to work on the German construction until they collapse from exhaustion.”

“What happens when they finish?” asked Vito, realising how deceived the German population had been and wondered how many more lies they had been told.

“They get sent to labour or execution, concentration camps.” Sal said glumly. Vito could feel his eyes well up slightly, the cruelty of the Nazi powers seemed without restrictions.

Chapter 23

It was mid-evening by the time the troop had finally returned to the hidden base and contrary to their normal boozy sessions, the men were exhausted, from a lack of sleep and the waning adrenaline had left them fatigued and muscles sore from the morning's event. So the mass of the men retired to the underground beds and slept deeply until late the following morning.

After Vito's normal morning swim, shave, he gauged on a hearty breakfast, since the demise of the townsfolk who had supplied them with the small luxuries, which had soon run out, the breakfast now consisted of nuts, berries and other woodland fruits, he went in search of his good friend and comrade Emiliano. After his wounded leg, he had not been among the assault squad, but his constant insistence to join the attack, Salvatore had made him a support gunner, the duo had not spoken much since their previous day's exploits. He found him in a quiet corner of the woodland headquarters, re-bandaging his leg wound.

"How many do you think we killed?" he asked Vito, seeing his friend approach.

"At least twenty, enough to make them think twice before they decide to cross open land in an occupied territory again."

"Good, that is good" said Emiliano glumly, Vito looked at his friend with concern, this was meant to be a time of rejoice, the whole operation had been a great success, but Emiliano was being so out of character, so morbid.

"What the hell is the matter? We destroyed those satanic sons of bitches; the German moral would be shattered!" exclaimed Vito happily.

"Well, that is exactly it," commented the wounded man. "I don't think I hit even one of them," he seemed quite tearful as he spoke, this had been his first real action. Apart from the men who had burst into flames from his petrol bomb, in all the chaos, Vito could not be sure of how, many confirmed kills he had under his own belt.

"Don't be so bloody ridiculous! Of course, you got someone, no one can tell who shot what, in that shit back there. It was madness!" Vito said gleefully, trying to encourage his friend.

"Do you really think so?"

"Of course!"

A loud cry came from one of the treetop lookout post caught their attention, without considering his friends limited mobility, Vito ran to the north bound tree where the alert had been called, with Emiliano hobbling along behind. A crowd of the forest partisans had already summoned at the foot of the giant shrub, where the lookout was monitoring some object through on old pair of World War One binoculars.

"What do you see?" Sal called up to the lookout.

"A beige Citroen, it is heading this way fast, it is kicking up a huge amount of dust," the guard called back, still following the approaching vehicle with his field glasses.

"It's got to be guards from the Gothic line!" said one of men in a panic.

"That's impossible," Vito interjected. "The Gothic line is south of here and that cars coming from the north-west". Sal was deep in thought.

"Do not worry, that will be Alfredo, he is coming to let us know, the Boche's reaction to our attack," Salvatore called back and then as if he was rethinking he added, "but keep an eye on it, just in case I am wrong." The rebel leader had not fully recovered from the escapades from the previous day. This second comment surprised Vito making him smirk, Sal hardly ever admitted that he was wrong.

Their visitor was indeed, Alfredo who after fond greetings, he spoke to the rebel band leader. "Your attack is all over the radio, it is all the Jerries are talking about." The resistance fighters, who were listening intently, gave a shriek of joy.

"I hope Adolf shat himself," yelled out one of the men cheerily, which received a small laugh from his comrades, Alfredo did not seem amused.

"Apparently, you killed thirty-three SS soldiers and wounded another one hundred and ten, they are calling it the Ardeatine massacre."

"That is good news," added Vito.

"Not really," Said Alfredo, feeling put out by his young comrade's interruption, "as you can imagine, Hitler was furious and he ordered a man called SS Obersturmbahnführer Herbert Kappler, head of the Sicherheitpolizie in Rome, to execute thirty Italian citizens for every one soldier killed."

Vito attempted to do some quick maths in his head, with no success, mathematics had never been his strong point.

"That is nine hundred and ninety civilians to be slaughtered, they have already started." Sal fell to the ground in disbelief, the entire camp of freedom fighters was dumbfounded, not one of them spoke, you could have heard the burrowing of a mole beneath their feet.

"Nine hundred and ninety innocent civilians," Sal finally stammered.

"They are just pulling people off the street at random. Men women and children," confirmed Alfredo, Salvatore was almost in tears, their whole attack was intended to help the civilian people from the malicious Nazi regime, but they had just resulted in more deaths of the Italian residents.

"And I am afraid that is not all the bad news I have my friends," Vito had no idea how this could get much worse. "Yesterday Hitler sent a special SS paratroop unit to break Mussolini out of prison. They killed all of the Carabinieri guards and he fled to Germany. Now, there are rumours that he is back in Italy in communication with Kesselring."

"Wait! Mussolini's back here?" Questioned Sal raising to his feet.

"As I said it is just a rumour, it is most likely just some Nazi scaremongering. But you know how these things come around," explained Alfredo.

"It is probably rubbish anyway." Sal gave a mutter.

"In my experience every rumour has an element of truth."

***

"We cannot just lie down and accept this outrage! We need to interrogate some soldiers and find out the key location to attack," recommended Alfredo.

Since they had recovered from the depressing news of the executions made by the occupying forces. They had all agreed to orchestrate reprisals to an extent that would be impossible to avenge, an attack so large that it could end the war in Italy. Around the planning makeshift table stood Salvatore, Vito, Alfredo and other squad captains, who all were silent in concentration.

Eventually, Vito spoke up. "What about those Gestapo agents that we captured in Torino? Could they be any help?"

Alfredo smiled like a parent humouring a child.

"They are gone, my friend, you cannot hold people like that forever, they are now at the bottom of the Po River."

Giuseppe who was the leader of one the most ruthless teams, who did not just kill Nazi soldiers but mutilated them, the Germans had even begun calling this squad 'The Butchers', spoke up.

"Why can't we just attack another fuelling station? We got good information from them before."

"How?" Questioned Sal, "we have destroyed nearly all of the Nazi outposts this side of the Gothic line!"

"What about Walter, the Colonel?" suggested Alfredo. "He may be able to suggest something. He is not one of the most wanted partisans in Italy for no reason."

The group stayed silent, all eyes were on Salvatore, whose eyes were fixed on the map before them.

"Do you know where he is?" Vito eventuality asked his black-market friend.

"Well I think I know the approximate area that he is in. He will find us once we enter his area, I am sure. You know how he likes to be in control," said Alfredo, getting out one of his cigarettes.

"Okay, take Giuseppe with you, in case you run into trouble."

"No you know how suspicious Colonel Valerio can be. No if I take anyone, it should be someone he knows, like yourself or Vito there." Sal nodded.

"Vito it is". Vito was not too happy to be nominated without being asked, even though he would have been more than glad to volunteer himself.

"We should leave soon," suggested Alfredo to his young friend. Vito gave a sharp nod and went to a fellow partisan who was known as the 'armourer', he was the man in charge of the distribution of weapons and ammunition.

"Amerigo, I need some more ammunition for my Luger," the stocky man gave a cringe.

"I am out of the German bullets," he said apolitically.

"Damn it!" Vito cursed, handing his side arm to the man. "Let me know if you get some more. What else do you have?"

The armour walked to a hidden hatch on the outskirts of the camp, unlocked it with a key from his wool lined coat pocket and pulled up the large door that was hidden beneath leaves and fern. The two men climbed down a rustic ladder appearing in a massive underground vault like structure. Amerigo lit a lantern and held it up. Vito took a step back, there were enough firearms in here to supply a dozen army's, from all parts of the world, Russian, French, German, British, American, Chinese, from small side-arms to cannon like artillery.

“Try this,” Amerigo said passing Vito a M1917 revolver. “It is light, easy to conceal, American and we have a huge amount of .45 calibre rounds for it.”

One thing to be said about the stocky armourer was that he was deeply passionate about his job. Vito examined the firearm; Amerigo was correct it was light and easy to handle.

“How many rounds does it take?”

“Only six rounds, but each hit will kill.”

“I don’t usually need that many.” smiled Vito, it accidentally came out like a boast. Amerigo, a bit offended by Vito’s last comment, remained silent and handed the young partisan a handful of bullets, which he tucked into a pocket before joining back up with Alfredo.

“Now, listen carefully my young friend, Walter is a good partisan and a strong soldier, but he will not like his current residents being discovered. He is a very solitary man, so be on your guard, we will have to step carefully,” advised Alfredo. “He will be around Lago d’Iseo. The lake is massive but I think I know where he will be. We will have to take the train to the town of Villongo and then head north from there. We should arrive in the town around nightfall, we will stop at a small boarding house I know and head up to find Walter’s camp in the morning.”

Vito accepted this plan, it seemed nicely simple and that is what he wanted and needed right now. He had hardly had time to let his adrenaline wane.

Chapter 24

The duo waited for the arrival of the public train, at the same station that Vito had gone to, before travelling to Torino. As what seemed his usual attire, Alfredo was still wearing his giant overcoat, concealing his sawn-down shotgun and fedora.

"So do you know anyone in Villongo?" questioned Vito, trying to act natural and not to look like a couple of partisans on the way to make contact with other rebels.

"Not, well, but there is a nice small bed and breakfast which I stay at, when I go fishing at the lake."

Vito got the impression that 'fishing' was code. "I caught some nice perch that they kindly cooked for me" Alfredo continued, so fishing was not code. Vito was surprised that between Alfredo's black-market business and partisan operations that he had time to go fishing, but then again people did what they could to forget about the war, even if it was only for a brief time, otherwise it could drive you insane.

Eventually, the matt, jet, black, steam locomotive arrived at the platform. Unlike his previous journey, these were compartment carriages and the pair of partisans waited for everyone to board, before they chose an empty compartment. Where they could speak freely.

"How did you know where Colonel Valerio would be?" Alfredo looked around the empty compartment cautiously in case of any eavesdroppers outside the door, listening into their conversation.

"Walter! Remember he is only known to the krauts as Colonel Valerio. We only use his code name in partisan circles, if we think it is best to be cautious, but if we know him and are alone it is Walter," informed Alfredo sternly.

"Okay. But how do you know that Walter would be hiding out by this lake?" Vito persisted, taking note of his black-market friend's command.

"He will be somewhere by the water. The lake is fresh water and teaming with fish, there is also a lot of woodland, for him to take shelter and the forest is also full of food, berries and root vegetables. He could live out there for months, without needing to make contact with anybody else." The faith Alfredo had in this man, was astonishing.

"How big is this lake?"

"Around one thousand three hundred and fifty square kilometres, give or take a little." Alfredo said calmly, as if this daunting fact of the size did not bother him.

"But you do know where he is, so we can measure down the searching distance" asked Vito hopefully.

"Well, we can assume he will be on the western bank and I would guess about half way up the lake, from my memory that is the denser forest, giving him the most protection and food source. But that is only a guess."

***

It took them a couple of hours to arrive at the small town of Villongo, as the duo exited the train they froze. The entire station was crawling with Nazi troops.

"Is it always like this?" muttered Vito to his counterpart.

"No," replied Alfredo looking around at the huge abundance of Axis soldiers, "it seems we have a garrison in town. Stay alert." This did not fill the forest partisan with much confidence. The duo tried to act as natural as possible, as they exited the train station.

Vito followed his black-market friend through the streets, there were no fewer of these enemy troops on the outside of the station. The town of Villongo was full of apartments, villas and farmhouses. They continued through the town to the outskirts until they arrived at a, surrounded by magnificent vineyards was a beautifully rustic, flint-built church, it seemed quite isolated. Alfredo turned and walked between the trellises towards a three-story farm building at the other end.

"They are the vineyard keepers," explained Alfredo knocking on the door. "But they run a bed and breakfast without any questions asked. It is popular with fishermen and cross-country hikers." The blue painted door opened and a man in his forties, wearing a fishnet vest answered the door.

“Can I help?” he asked. He had a pleasant voice, but did not open the door to its full extent.

“Good morning,” Alfredo smiled reassuringly. “We are looking for a couple of rooms, just for one night.” The grape farms caretaker eyed up his two visitors suspiciously.

“It will be five Lire each,” he replied, Alfredo got out a small wad of notes, making the middle-aged owner crack a wide smile. His voice suddenly turned inviting and pulled open the door wide. “Welcome. We have many two rooms which are neighbouring each other, would you prefer ground floor rooms or first floor.”

Vito could see advantages for either, they wanted to avoid any Nazi patrols which may come knocking and from the amount of troops they had just seen that was a high possibility. On the ground floor they could make a quick escape and on the first floor they could see, if any troops were to approach the farmhouse. Alfredo requested a couple of ground floor rooms and the couple congregated in the black-marketers room. The bedrooms were small, but comfortable, with white washed walls, a single wardrobe, a small wooden table with a single chair and a soft double bed. Vito sat on a chair, whilst Alfredo sat on his bed.

“We will leave at first light, we do not want to be noticed, so we meet in my room and we make our getaway through the window.”

“You make it sound so simple, this is going to be the first time I have had a chance to sleep in a soft bed,” complained the partisan.

“Well get as much sleep as you can my young friend. Tomorrow is going to be a long trek to look for our comrade.”

With that Vito retired to his own room which was identical to his associates. Vito did not need any more persuasion and took to the bed like a bee to a flower. He sank into the soft goose feather mattress, still fully dressed in case they needed a fast escape, it was like sleeping on a cloud, heavenly and he soon fell into a peaceful restful sleep.

He was rudely awoken, from a pleasant dream involving his fallen love, Elvera and his mother as they lived happily together in an Italian villa, cooking fish over an open barbecue on the back patio, as the baking hot sun shone down on them, he had an overpowering sense of contentment, until he was rudely awoken by a rapid tapping at his room's door.

It had been more than two years since he had slept so well, without waking from a nightmare or in a cold sweat. Before he could register where he was, he grabbed his pistol from the bedside table and with his back flat against the wall, aimed the gun at head height as the door handle slowly turned, the door crept opened and creeping in from the hallway emerged Alfredo, seeing the side arm pointing at his head, he raised his hands.

"Easy, my friend, easy. Did I wake you?"

"Jesus Christ!" Vito exclaimed relived, lowering his gun "I nearly bloody shot you! What the hell do you want?"

"The sun is rising, we must go" urged Alfredo, Vito looked to the window, the sky was most certainly brightening up and a few streams of morning sun was beginning to show over the horizon.

"And I was just having such a nice dream!"

Chapter 25

Vito had not properly woken up, it felt strange waking up without his normal morning swim, it is what he had grown accustom to and anything different to his normal regime made him feel tired and awkward. But even with those reservations the two rebels made good time and they were eventually walking north along the banks of Lago d'Iseo, the water on the lake glistened in the sunlight. The pair of men took a minute to splash the cool water in their faces' and refill their canteens. As they observed the surrounding area, it was bare to say the least, they were in open grass land with the giant lake on one side and shrub land all around except for a small forest in the north. They could see a small island in the middle of the lake, it looked tranquil, almost picturesque.

"We will take a break here, that forest is probably where our friend is residing." Alfredo commented, sitting down on the damp earth, "I would be surprised if Walter was not watching us right now."

Vito settled down beside his friend, keeping his eyes on the woodland, he did not like the idea of someone watching them without his knowledge, even if it was another partisan, who was observing them. As Vito began puffing on his pipe, which he always carried on him and Alfredo was smoking one of his abnormally skinny cigarettes. When the sound of a boat engine caught the men's attention and from the opposite side of the island came a grey motor boat, with a MG42 light machine gun on the front and it had the bold, black Balkanize on the side, identifying itself as a Nazi raft. The duo watched as the boat passed them by, straining for their own weapons. In case, it turned in their direction.

Yet, the craft seemed to ignore the two men and continued to the most southerly end of the waterway and out of sight, allowing the two men to relax again. They then heard the faint sound of a motorcycle revving off and disappearing off into the distance. Vito did feel a bit uncomfortable, knowing that the Axis forces were still in force even up here. The men agreed to continue on to meet up with their loan patriotic comrade, as soon as possible.

They eventually reached the edge of the forest, unlike Vito's headquarters, there was not a sound, no birds singing, no rustling of rodents, not a single sound of any type of animal and no sign of human life, this made the dense woodland all the more eerie. Feeling uneasy Vito reached for his gun, but Alfredo grabbed his arm stopping him with a shake of his head.

"You won't need that lad," said a voice from a tree above them. The two men looked above them and like Tarzan, the lone rebel fighter, Colonel Valerio, swung down, before them. Looking at the pair before him with a grim look, before he eventually spoke again "What the fuck are you two doing here? I have been watching you for the last half hour." Vito decided to let Alfredo make the explanation, as he was unsure how best to respond.

"Walter, we have come to find you, we need your help."

Walter looked at the two men carefully, examining every aspect of their faces for any indication of an alternative agenda. Before he gave them a wave, directing them to follow him deeper into the heavy woodland. They came to a small camp, with a shelter, only tall enough to lie down in, with open sides and a roof made with moss and leaves and a small camp fire. The three men sat down around the small log fire. Hanging from a tree was a line of trout. Walter did not speak for a little while longer but just scanned the duo; the silence was becoming nearly unbearable.

"So what the hell do you want?" He finally questioned gruffly; he was clearly not pleased that he had been searched out.

"Nazi powers have started executing civilians. We need to capture and interrogate some German soldiers and find out the key location to attack, an attack which could end their occupation of our country. We were hoping you could assist," Alfredo insisted. The partisan studied his associates, Vito felt like he was in court.

"A brave task," the man said in thought. "How serious are you about this mission of yours?"

Vito interjected, getting irritated by Walter's light-handed attitude, he was beginning to wonder if this man actually did anything, perhaps he disappears on his own to escape conflict and claims other people's work to gain his reputation.

"Without boundaries. Innocent civilians are being murdered!" The single partisan closed his eyes in thought. Alfredo and Vito just looked at each other. Then without opening his eyes Walter spoke.

"Have you heard the rumours?"

"Which rumours?" Alfredo questioned "There are so many," Walter smiled.

"About Mussolini" then he slowly opened his eyes and looked directly at the men, "They are all true. Come with me."

In utter disbelief the two counterparts followed the man to the river's edge. There were a couple of rustic fishing rods hanging into the water beside a pair of binoculars, directly in front of them was the small island in the centre of the lake.

"He is there."

"What?" blurted Vito, this man must be insane, how and why would the previous leader of Italy be staying on a remote island, which was only accessible by water?

"I have been watching the island since I heard rumours about constant German activity here. It is called San Paolo Island. Boats are coming and going at all hours, messages to that Generalfeldmarschall Kesselring."

"Who told you about this constant German activity?" Questioned Vito, this could be a Nazi trick.

"You see that house up their?" he pointed to a mountain looming over Pistolke, he could see a speck of a house in the distance. "There is an old man living there in his sixties. He lost an arm in the Great War. He is a partisan at heart, but feels he is too old to participate in partisan activities. He watches the Germans activity and reports back to the Allies. But when he saw this, he contacted me." He handed the binoculars to Vito, "look," he directed pointing out to the island.

The partisan did as he was bid, scanning the horizon with the binoculars. He didn't see anything a first, except for white picket signs, every five feet which in red German fraktur writing said the German words 'Sperrgebiet. Treten Sie unter dem Schmerz des Todes ein', translates as 'Restricted area. Enter under the pain of death', but then against the island forest, he could see some movement and then something else, there were soldiers, Nazi soldiers patrolling the small water locked landmass, wearing camouflaged mosquito netting over their faces. Vito's jaw dropped he was agog. The longer he looked the more and more soldiers appeared, he counted around eight-armed Axis forces, without a word the partisan passed the binocular device to his black-market comrade.

"My god!" he exclaimed, seeing what his comrade had seen. "How many troops over there?" he questioned.

"I have counted about fifteen, there could be around five or ten more further into the island. Where there is a log bungalow, frequented by the Italian dictator and his mistress." Walter said, his eyes stuck on the small island. Vito was overly curious.

"How can you be so sure Mussolini is over there?"

Walter smiled broadly, showing a mouth of yellow teeth.

"A couple of nights ago I crept ashore with a canoe and dodging the troops, I got to the cabin and took a look through the window. He has grown a thin beard but that face is unmistakable."

"Then why didn't you take him out?" continued Vito, not sure that he could trust every word this man said.

"Too many troops. So you help me take out that monster and then I will help you end the war." Vito looked to Alfredo who was laughing.

"Are you serious?" asked Vito astounded; this was meant to be a simple contact mission.

"No point getting rid of the organ grinder just to have the monkey take charge," said Alfredo, "and with the help of the Nazis that are left here, after we have got rid of Kesselring, then Mussolini could take power again and we will not have changed anything."

Vito just gave a shrug of agreement, he was here to assist the liberation of Italy after all and if this partisan was as good as the stories about his patriotic accomplishments, then he could not deny that they needed his help, so they had little choice.

"Do you have an armband?" he asked his two guests. The duo did not reply, but pulled their CLN tricoloured armbands from their pockets and slipped them onto their upper left arms.

Chapter 26

That night, once darkness had fallen, Walter requisitioned the weapons from his associates and replaced them with a pair of British De Lisle carbine rifles, which each had a suppressor, to muffle the sound of the shot as well as a couple of British Welrod, it was a bulky silenced pistol measuring a thirty-two millimetre cylinder and was three hundred millimetre long. He also armed himself with the same, he grabbed some rope and a couple of machetes, handing one to Alfredo.

"Sorry, I did not expect visitors," he said looking at the youngest of the trio. "I only have two knives."

"Well you seem to have enough guns," said Vito full of sarcasm.

"You can never have too many guns," smiled The Colonel, "special gifts from the British military intelligence."

He pulled out a CLN resistance armband and pulled it onto his upper left arm. "We do not want to be accused as spies," he said

"No, just terrorists," whispered Alfredo making Vito burst into laughter.

Without a second word the lone patriot led them back down to the water bank and began removing a mound of twigs to reveal a wooden paddle craft. After the men had moved the boat into the water, Vito lay on the front of the vessel, pointing his rifle out ahead of them as his two counterparts slowly and quietly paddled towards the heavily guarded island. He stared into the cavernous, pitch blackness for any movement, on the small island. This was the first time Vito had been on water and he rather enjoyed the gentle rocking and lapping of the water.

The youngest of three partisans saw some movement ahead of them, it was a guard and he was looking in their direction. Vito took aim with his silenced rifle and as the partisan slowly exhaled, he gently squeezed the trigger. There was an almost inaudible pop and enemy combatant fell to the floor, he then pulled on the rifle bolt handle, to preparing to fire again, before going back to scanning their target.

It had only taken them a few minutes to reach the small land mass, that had laid before them, as they unmanned the boat, they saw the body that Vito had just assassinated, the bullet had penetrated directly into the man's temple.

"Nice shot!" whispered Alfredo.

"Keep the talking to a minimum," Walter whispered sternly, "Alfredo, help me get the boat hidden, Vito get rid of the body, before he is found."

"What? How the hell am I going to do that?"

"Hide him in the brush."

Walter was quite obviously not much of a people person; this must be why he preferred to work alone. As Walter and Alfredo pulled the canoe up the shingle shore and cut branches with their machetes to obscure it from view, Vito lifted the heavy dead weight of the body over his shoulders and chucked the corpse behind a prickly bush, a place that he hoped, a soldier would not consider looking for his missing comrade.

Once the three men had completed their designated tasks they congregated, in a crouch on the edge of the woodland that covered the small land mass. The partisan then picked up a hand full of shingle and carefully sprinkled it over the blood splattered stones to obscure them from view.

"The hut is in the centre of the island, remember we are not safe, there is anywhere between ten to fifteen enemy guards and the only way to escape is the way we have just come, so stay alert. But if you want a couple of men to interrogate then do *not* shoot at the first thing you see move!" he warned the two men.

Vito did wonder if it would be better to capture Mussolini and interview him, but Walter had gone into a zone of his own, that Vito did not want to interrupt. During hostile operations, many soldiers whether conscripted or civilian would put their mind into a certain state to keep them focused on their objective, this could make them ruthless and, in many cases, so unpleasant that it would border on violent, even to their comrades.

The rebel trio pressed slowly forwards, watching each step so as not to make a sound, until Walter motioned the men to stop and duck down, they saw a Nazi trooper stomping through the woods without a care in the world, he looked bored, Vito guessed that they never had much trouble out here. Alfredo took it upon himself to take out this man, whilst Vito and Walter looked around them to make sure that this was the only man in their vicinity, suddenly, just as he was about to fire Alfredo stopped as a German voice called out to the trooper.

"Hey, hast du ein Feuerzeug?"

The three men watched with baited breath, as another soldier turned up and the first German lit the others cigarette with a lighter, illuminating their faces and the two men then parted ways. Alfredo gave a small sigh of disappointment. Walter waited a couple of minutes before waving the men to continue forward through the dense woodland. They had only walked a few more steps when the men froze, Walter had a German rifle pointing directly at his head, his two associates were unsure what they could do, any movement they made could end their comrade's life.

Yet the lone partisan did not seem rather bothered by the weapon pointing at him and with a swift single movement he had spun round and stuck his machete straight through the man's gut. The Nazi trooper dropped his firearm as he gurgled, unable to catch his breath; Walter twisted the blade, sticking it deeper, until the man collapsed into a lump. Without wiping the blade, he replaced it into his sheath, picked up his own rifle and continued on, followed by his uninvited guests. It did not take them long to reach an open space in the centre of the woodland.

There was a single storey log cabin, with a stone chimney, bellowing out plumes of smoke from a fire heating up the inside of the property, it had two BMW R75 motorcycles, modified to go over the muddy, uneven island terrain and a third with a side-car, to transport their high-profile commander. Outside was a small wood camp-fire, in a stone circle, which had a steel kettle hanging on a spit, with two soldiers sitting by it, talking, laughing and smoking, with their rifles leaning against a large tree at least ten feet from the two seated men and their backs to the intruders. The trio observed the two sentries, for any sign of a third patrolling guard. They could see light flickering through the closed curtained windows and a couple of shadows could be seen moving about inside the cabin.

"There are your prisoners for interrogation," whispered Walter, "We will take them by surprise, gag them and tie them up. Then once Mussolini has been dealt with, we take them back with us, in the boat, along with that bastard's body."

He made it sound so simple, this seemed to be a knack that partisan leaders had. The men dropped to the floor and crept forward, keeping their stomachs to the ground, to be hidden from view as they moved towards the two guards.

The two axis soldiers were utterly oblivious to the approaching aggressors. Before they knew it the trespassers were only a couple of feet from the two men, warming themselves by the open fire. Alfredo and Walter acted in unison and pounced on the two men, giving them each a rifle butt to the head, before an alarm could be raised.

"Vito, check round the other side of the house, to make sure there are not any more of the sons of bitches lurking round there." Walter ordered in a whisper.

Vito gave a nod and ran at a crouch to the back of the residence, he peered around the side, there was nothing, keeping to the wall he ran around to the front of the building. By the time he returned to his comrades, they had stuffed a rag into the sentries' mouths and hog tied them, tying their limbs together, rendering the soldiers immobile and helpless, with their hands tied behind the back and the feet were tied together, with one end of the rope forming a noose around the man's neck.

"It is all clear," Vito whispered to his two compatriots, who were kneeling by the captured Nazis.

"Okay, now it is my turn," murmured Walter, "I need you two to stay alert and make sure that we are not interrupted, until the deed is done." His orders were simple. Alfredo and Vito dragged the pair of bound soldiers with them, who had now fully recovered and were wide awake, taking firing positions on the wooden patio at the front of the house. Colonel Valerio did not hesitate for a moment and kicked in the front door, which swung shut behind him.

There was silence for a few seconds before a shot rang out from the cabin, breaking the blissfulness, it could not have been their comrade, he only had suppressed weapons, they then heard a pair of tapping like sounds, accompanied by a couple of flashes. The two partisans outside could not make sure their counterpart was alright as the first shot would have alerted the whole island to their presence and they would be coming down on them, within the next few minutes.

"Vito, Alfredo, in here!" Came a yell from inside the wood building. The duo entered through the front door, dragging a bound soldier with one hand, whilst keeping their weapons pointing behind them, with their one free hand, for the troops who were drawing in on their position.

It was a Spartan three room hovel with a settee, coffee table and wireless radio set by the open fireplace. The second room was a kitchen/dining area, which had apart from the granite sideboards only had a single rustic dining table, one leg was broken and was replaced with books, with four chairs, there were a couple of plates still at the table with a few crumbs left indicating that the occupants had just finished dinner, the third room had a massive king size bed, the only decoration in the entire house were some Persian style rugs. Hardly the way you would visualise the previous leader of Italy to live.

In the centre of the lounge were two bodies. One of the corpses was clearly that of the infamous dictator Benito Mussolini, in a single hand he was holding a Pistola Automatica Beretta modello 1934 pistol, favoured by the Italian dictator, the other corpse was that of a woman, Clara Petacci, the fascist ruler's mistress.

"Alfredo, guard the window." The black-market trader grabbed a dining chair and dragged it over to the front window, he sat astride it, using the back to steady his weapon.

Walter seeing his younger comrade looking at the young maiden he said, "The god damn coward used her as a human shield, I understand you speak German?" Vito nodded looking up to the partisan "Good, now tell those pigs that if they want to live then they will help us."

Vito did as he was asked, the two men had a horror stricken look in their eyes.

Walter passed Vito his machete "cut them loose and warn them that if they make one false move, they will end up like them" he commanded, pointing to the two corpses. As the young partisan sawed through the ropes binding them, he spat the lone patriots warning, these two soldiers were very unlikely to have had anything to do with the 'Rote Tag' massacre, but they wore the Nazi uniform, so were no more innocent. Scared to their wits the men stood watching their captors. A sudden sound of gunfire alerted the entire group of rebels and helpless prisoners alike.

"I think these bastards know that we're here," cried Alfredo, returning fire. "Colonel Valerio if you have an escape plan, now would be a good time." Alfredo was not one to use aliases, but in a case where Germans can have overheard, they could not give away the partisan's true identity.

"Ask them where the escape hatch is."

"What escape hatch?" Vito questioned bewildered by the proposition.

"They would not house someone this important without an escape plan! Now ask them." The former German did as he was bid and in unison the two Germans pointed to the dictator's bedside table.

Walter roughly pulled it aside to reveal a hatch in the floor beneath. “Tell them krauts to carry the bodies.” Once Vito had given the order to their prisoner the two troopers hesitated and looked to each other.

“Jetzt!” Shouted Vito, pointing at them with the bloodstained blade, making the two detainees jump and scramble to pick up the corpses.

Chapter 27

As the five men jumped down into the stone walled tunnel, Vito found his claustrophobia grow as it had done back in France, yet there was a strong breeze travelling along the straight shaft, helping him keep his fears at bay. Before leaving Walter chucked a handful of bullets onto the open fire to give the illusion of a continuing gun battle, giving the men the chance to escape. It did not take them very long to reach the end of the underground escape route. Hidden behind some hang over vegetation the opening, opened up to the shore line, on the opposite end of the island that they had arrived on, there was a small wooden jetty, with an ash grey, Chris Craft, speedboat docked.

"There is our escape route, Alfredo." directed the operations leader. The three partisans, two prisoners and two corpses were loaded onto the small boat. Whilst Vito guarded their captives, Alfredo untied the boat and Walter sped off, skimming over the clear water at speed. Making the two Nazi soldiers feel ill and vomit over the side, Vito enjoyed the faster speed they were travelling away from the island and found the captured Germans discomfort rather amusing.

Instead of going to the closest shoreline, Walter swung around the island, giving it a wide berth, so as not to draw unwanted attention and landed at the same place they had left earlier that night. The morning was dawning, among the stars the blue sky of day was appearing above them. Little was said among the men, their adrenaline was still at peaks and they were not yet out of danger. Once again on dry land, Walter shot three rounds into the bottom of the boat with his silenced rifle, making it totally ineffective as a boat, scuttling enemy crafts was a common practise and would leave the soldiers on the island stranded until support came to aid them, with a second boat which could take them a great while.

Walter reunited his two comrades with their original weapons and dismantled the ones they had been carrying, making them as inadequate as the enemy craft. He was to carry an American Thomson sub-machine gun, known better as the

Tommy gun or in the United States military as the 'annihilator' for its destructive power and a Walther PPK, favoured by the Nazi elite, each high-ranking member of Hitler's inner circle had a gold-plated version with a mother of pearl grip. He also got out two small lengths of rope and bound their prisoner's hands behind their back. Then tied the two men together with a rope around each of their waists, so they could only move in single file, making them easier to control, even though they had been no trouble to their captors as of yet.

"We can't take these bastards on the train," commented Alfredo. He was right, of course, travelling on public transport with a couple of bound Nazi soldiers could only prompt suspicion, not to mention walking through the heavily patrolled station of Villongo.

"We will be going via the road," the team leader said boldly.

"Well, won't they have road blocks set up?" questioned Vito.

"On the main roads, it is likely, so we will be travelling on the smaller back lanes." It was obvious Walter had thought of everything, "but I assume, because they were using couriers, they do not have a radio set on the island. So I would say we have a twenty-four-hour head start. We have a van parked at Santuario Madonna Della Neve church in San Gregorio."

Alfredo looked back in the direction of the island nervously, "I think we had best get going."

Colonel Valerio led the way, followed by Vito, then the pair of German prisoners and Alfredo brought up the rear with both barrels of his sawn down shotgun aiming at their hostages, who were struggling to walk together forcing one or the other to trip over protruding roots or scratched by a branch pulled back by his leading cohort.

The group walked deeper into the forest only pausing for one or the other of the partisans to take a call of nature. It was a hard trek, with uneven, forest littered ground, the heavy forest canopy above them made it hard to figure which direction they were travelling in, in this dense jungle like woodland, every tree looked like the next. But it seemed that their fearless partisan leader new exactly where he was going, as he did not waver from his fast-paced ambulatory. It took them half the morning to get to the edge of the forest.

They arrived at a secluded building that looked like a lavish villa. The exterior of the structure had a gabled facade, preceded by a portico with three arches. Along the left side, rose a twentieth-century bell tower, with a brown van parked beneath it. Walter opened the back of the van as the two partisans hurled their captured men into the back.

"It will look less suspicious if I travel alone," said Walter.

Vito and Alfredo took the hint and jumped in the back with the prisoners slamming, shut the doors behind them. The back of the van was dark and damp, with a strong smell of rust. They were sat on the cold metallic floor, with their weapons out facing the Germans. It was open enough so Vito was able to hide his claustrophobia, but was happy when, Alfredo got out a torch and sourced out a kerosene lantern and lit it with a match, lighting up the back of the vehicle. The two partisans looked at the Nazi sentries, the soldiers looked scared as the old transportation shot forwards. They could feel every bump in the road as they drove along mud trails and weaved through the small country back roads.

The pair of partisans slept in turns, as the second guarded the men. Three and a half hours later when the van stammered to a halt, Vito woke with a start and the duo got their weapons at the ready, this could be a random Nazi or Blackshirt spot check, there were three bangs on the side of the vehicle. This was Walter's signal that everything was all clear; this was not a military checkpoint.

One of the back doors opened, ignoring the Germans, Walter said "get out and stretch your legs for a couple minutes, it will be another hour before we get back to your home." He looked at the spectacular view from this parking place. "We are just on the outskirts of Pavia. I will grab you a couple of Stromboli from that street vendor, over there."

Stromboli was a type of turnover filled with various Italian cheeses such as mozzarella and cold cuts of Italian meats such as salami, capocollo and bresaola. The partisans took off their armbands and concealed their weapons in the back of their trousers, before jumping out and locking the back doors of the van.

They observed their surroundings; they were parked in a lay-by, on a small side road, overlooking the stunning view of a tranquil valley below. On the side of the road were a collection of five different roadside vendors, selling home-grown fruits, vegetables, homemade wine and like the one that Walter was visiting, selling filled home-baked rolls and sandwiches. The civilian resistance soldiers stayed prepared, with their weapons, as these street marketeers were often armed as they were often the victims of criminal gangs and axis forces who would take advantage, by requisitioning their wares and meagre takings, sometimes with force.

The three partisans congregated outside the back of the van and enjoyed their home-made rolls.

"We will stop off at the town first, I have a good friend living there, I am sure he can lend us a wheelbarrow to cart our dead bodies," said Walter coolly. Alfredo could see Vito's discomfort at the mention of the village and putting an arm around the lone patriot's shoulder led him away, talking to him quietly, Vito knew that the black-marketeer was informing the lone patriot of their partisan associate's loss after a few words they reconvened with the younger patriot. "Well this is an outrage," continued Walter; the people of the town must be avenged.

"They were," said Vito solemnly "we attacked an SS regiment, killed thirty-three of them."

"Great! I bet that upset a few people," Walter smiled.

"Yeah, they were so upset they killed nine hundred and ninety."

"What?"

"When Hitler heard of it, he ordered the execution of thirty civilians for each soldier killed," explained Alfredo. Walter looked dumbstruck; much the same reaction of the resistance members had been at the forest dwellings.

"Nine hundred and ninety? This is infuriating, we cannot allow this!"

"That is why we need you," explained Vito.

"We will let Salvatore, explain it to you," added Alfredo.

"We will have to stop at the village first and then go on to your headquarters on foot," Walter said.

Vito felt his emotions taking over as he thought of his fallen love. The Colonel recognised his young counterparts' feelings, so added, "You need not enter the town, Alfredo and I will go in you can guard those Bosch bastards outside the town walls."

The trio, having finished their enjoyable meal, filled their stomachs, then re-entered the van and set off again.

Chapter 28

Walter had made good time arriving to the small deserted settlement, only taking forty-five minutes before they stalled to a stop outside the town's archway entrance. To the left of the arch was the makeshift cemetery, with the field of wooden crosses that the partisans had made in respect of the former residence of the small town. A small field of white flowers had grown over the cemetery mounds decorating them. On the lime white wall some German goon had painted in black a large swastika, an astonishing symbol of disrespect. It was something that Vito had not noticed on his previous visit, yet his head had been focused on other details.

The group disembarked from the truck and as promised, Vito stayed with the van and allowing the two prisoners out to get a spot of fresh air, as he guarded them, whilst his two comrades entered the township. With his pistol continuously aimed at the hostages, Vito removed his pipe, from his pocket and lit it with a match as he watched the pair of Germans carefully. A mere fifteen minutes later, the Italian guard could hear the rickety sound of wooden wheels coming back down the steep slope, approaching them, from the settlements cobbled streets back to the entrance way. He stole a glance and took a double take; Walter and Alfredo were coming down pulling a wooden cart, with a pile of folded white, sheets and a pot of black paint, on top.

Walter cut the rope bindings from the German soldiers and asked Vito to translate.

The young partisan ordered their prisoners, "Put the bodies onto the cart and cover them with the sheets. Then you will be acting the part of the horses and pulling the cart. We will be returning to our resistance base."

The German men hesitated briefly, why would these men, these terrorists, be showing them the way to their rebel base? But deciding it was futile to argue, they did as they were ordered and lifted the deceased, lifeless bodies of the much hate former dictator and his concubine side by side on the cart and covered the cadavers in the sheets. Before they set off back to the secret rebel camp, Vito took a moment to pay his respects and remember his fallen Italian maiden at the crosses of murdered villagers, whilst Alfredo took the black paint and painted a thick cross over the Nazi symbol; and wrote CLN beside it, indicating that the settlement had been rescued from the Nazi forces.

Then with Alfredo ahead in the lead, followed by the two prisoners pulling the wooden corpse cart and the other two freedom fighters following behind. The rebels, were scanning the surrounding area, the going was slow, the ground was muddy, it stuck to their boots and the wheels of the cart.

After a couple of hours travel, rapid gunfire and bullets riddled the ground before Alfredo's feet, making the group freeze where they stood, as they reached the border of the forest.

"What the fuck are you doing? It's Alfredo," shouted the black-market dealer, up into the tree, where the gunfire had come from. Seconds later, they were confronted by an army of armed resistance fighters, but recognising one of their own men, Vito and ally, Alfredo, they lowered their guns. The youngest of the group cracked a smile as he saw a face, he knew approach them.

"Sal!" He cried overjoyed, shaking his leader's hand warmly, he could have embraced the man; he was so pleased to see him.

"Vito, Alfredo, Wa—" he was cut short as Walter raised a hand.

"I know you, Salvatore, but I do not know your people," he said in a low voice so as not to offend the rebel fighters. But he was right to be cautious, it had been so simple for Vito to join and no one knew his true identity, so it was a possibility that someone without such an honourable agenda had infiltrated the group.

"Of course, I apologise Colonel Valerio, how are you? I am sorry but we had not expected five of you," he said looking at the two Nazis who were watching this civilian resistance army nervously, who had not yet dared let go of the trolley. The partisans greeted their patriotic comrades, with pats on the back and shakes of the hands. Once they had escorted the Germans into the camp, Giuseppe and another partisan dragged the two prisoners into the ravine, where Vito had conducted the interrogation when he had first arrived.

"Giuseppe, don't kill them!" Sal shouted, receiving a malicious glare from his lieutenant. "We need them to talk first," the leader explained.

Vito looked around the camp, not much had changed except for at one end there were between fifteen to twenty small wooden cages, each holding three pigeons.

"Carrier pigeons," said Emiliano appearing beside him, the two men embraced each other as the friends reunited. "It's so we can contact other resistance groups covertly."

"It is so good to see you. How is your leg?" Asked Vito.

"Totally healed, I do not even have a limp anymore," he replied proudly. The two men walked to join their leader, black-marketeer and the lone patriot by the wooden wagon.

"So what have you brought us here?" Salvatore asked looking at the sheet, covered barrow.

"Well, you know the rumours," Vito explained, "about Mussolini, hiding somewhere in Italy, communicating with the Nazis, to make a return."

"Yes."

"Well, he is not anymore," said Alfredo and with that he swung back the sheet to reveal the face of the hated dictator.

Sal took a step back in disbelief, he half laughed and stammered as he spoke, "That is, that is—" unable to get out the words.

"Bloody hell, that's Mussolini!" exclaimed Emiliano, within minutes the whole camp had clustered around like flies around a corpse, to see the body of the man who had at one time been the most powerful person in Italy.

"Those bastards, that your man, Giuseppe, took away were guarding him, so they may able to help us, I hear you want to make an attack to end the war? Well they may have the answer." submitted the loan patriot.

"Well we best interrogate them before Giuseppe gets carried away and we end up interviewing another pair of dead krauts," Sal laughed, the others listening in, chuckled.

As the leader guided their guests, Vito and Emiliano down to the ravine. Walter said "I hope that was a joke."

Emiliano gave a small smile and said, "When it comes to Giuseppe, you never know," his comrades smiled as they saw the two Nazi soldiers on their knees with their hands rebound behind their backs and Giuseppe, cruelly overlooking them. The group took turns looking at the Germans, this was meant as an intimidation tactic, before perching themselves, somewhere around the ravine. Salvatore stood over them.

“Italiana?” he asked them, the two prisoners looked at each other and shook their heads, so Sal turned to Vito, “translate for me,” the young partisan gave a single nod of agreement.

“You are going to die, that is inescapable, but how you answer my next questions will decide how.” With that one of the Nazi soldiers panicked and attempted to flee, he had only got three steps away when Giuseppe opened fire upon him, tearing the man apart. The second man began to shake, terrified about what had just happened to his military brother.

“Giuseppe! For Christ sake!” cried Vito. “Do you know what we had to bloody go through to get him back here?” Giuseppe just gave a disgruntled shrug, making the men around him smirk, he was a savage man, but his attitude was comical.

“Right back to business,” Sal injected. “Where is Generalfeldmarschall Kesselring hiding?”

Vito translated, but the soldier did not reply, but just looked around at the men around him. Impatient Giuseppe urged Vito to continue.

“Say it again,” the younger partisan repeated the question.

“Monte Soratte bunker, near the town of sant’Oreste,” the German soldier blurted out in a panic. Vito translated to his commanders.

“Sant’Oreste?” Sal questioned the answer.

“I bloody knew it; I knew there was something of importance there!” Walter roared, everyone looked in his direction.

“Do you know what he is talking about?” inquired Vito.

“Yes, it is small town, about fifty-three kilometres north of Rome. I passed there a few months back and thought the amount of Germans in that area were a lot, with no known bases nearby.”

“How many troops?” Sal questioned; Vito once again translated.

“Ungefähr dreihundert.”

“Around three-hundred.”

“We should look it up on the map,” said Sal. “Vito, Giuseppe, hang the bugger!” he said leaving the two partisans alone with the Nazi captive.

***

The two partisans grabbed the Axis combatant by an arm each and dragged him off to an area of the woods, that was a grotesque display of executed Nazis, each tree hung at least one but in most cases more. Enemy soldiers of an assortment of ranks and coloured uniforms, in various states of decomposition, the smell protruding off the bodies was the most vile stench, making a man of the toughest constitution gag, the smell singed the nasal hairs and if you tried to breathe through your mouth, you could taste the rotting flesh and no amount of liquid could extinguish it.

Vito and Giuseppe were prepared for this and had cloths fitted over their mouth and nose. This was not the first time Vito had been here, Sal had taken him here a couple of weeks after he had first joined with this army of patriots, yet this would be the first hanging he would witness first hand.

"Vito, grab that stool, buddy," Giuseppe requested.

The junior partisan grabbed a toppled wooden stool from beneath a previously hung German, whilst Giuseppe flung a rope with a noose at one end over a branch and tied it to the trunk. The two men did not communicate with the German at all, except for commanding him up onto the stool and to put the noose over his neck, the German soldier new better than to argue, as the vicious looks from Giuseppe warned him from it, if he made any objections he would be beaten to an inch of his life and then hung.

Without any equivocation, Giuseppe just kicked out the stool from beneath the captured man. The German soldier flayed with his legs as if he was trying to run in mid-air, as the rope tightened around the victim's neck, cutting into his skin. It was a pitiful sight and Vito was not enjoying this display, he did not feel anything for the man after all he was a German but he was viewing a man slowly strangle to death.

The soldier's eyes widened and bulged, appearing as if they were about to pop from the sockets. He couldn't understand why so many members of the camp enjoyed watching this exhibit. Yet, Giuseppe seemed to be getting some amusement and pleasure from witnessing this execution. After a minute the flaying legs died down and changed to small twitches, the body went limp as the air was completely restricted, the soldier's eyes glazed over, his career was over, his life had come to a torturous end.

Chapter 29

The captains summoned around the maps table, as Walter pointed out their target.

"Shit, don't tell me that we are going to have to wade through all that bloody sewage to get through that god damn barricade again!"

Giuseppe groaned, talking about their previous escapades across Gothic line.

"Maybe. There is part of the wall that they have not yet completed, beside the prison, this will be our route, so if you are part of the jail break team, then we can get through that way," replied Walter, Giuseppe backed down. "Now we have two things to consider if this operation is to be a success. First how do you expect to stop any reinforcements arriving once the attack has started? They will most likely come via train."

"Well Vito has already demolished the tracks, isn't that right?" question Sal, Vito shuffled from one foot onto the next.

"Well it was only a small part and I am sure the krauts would have fixed it by now."

"I think we need something a bit more permanent," complained Walter, the men leant forwards to examine the map.

"What is this?" questioned Alfredo, pointing to a stretch of railway expanding over a river.

"It is a wooden beam railway bridge," the whole group perked up.

"How many supporting columns?" queried Vito in thought.

"Eight, four on either side."

"How much 'Bridge killer' do we have?"

The bridge killer was a pack of plastic explosive, it was rare for the partisans as most of the explosives they had was dynamite, but the plastic explosive was received by allied air drops, it was much more stable than any other explosives and water resistant. Plastic explosive was a soft and hand-mouldable solid form of explosive material, plastic explosives was also known as putty explosives. The second part of the pack was a plunger detonator to set off the explosives; the only downside was that you would have to be nearby to detonate them.

"Enough," replied Sal. "Are you suggesting what I think you are?"

"Exactly, as Colonel Valerio said we need a more permanent solution, so if my team goes to the bridge the night before our operation and demolish the bridge, it will stop any reinforcement trains arriving," concluded Vito, making sure to use Walter's alias.

"Buona. It will only be lightly guarded. Cut down a tree on either side of the tracks as well, that will delay the response team," instructed Walter. "We will block the roads once we have passed over the Gothic line."

"You said first thing?" urged Salvatore.

"Yes, the other thing is that it would be easier to get through the kraut defensive line if it was lighter guarded. There is a secret German chemical plant here." The lone patriot pointed to a space a couple of kilometres from the barricade, "If we blow this, they will have to pull men off the line to investigate." Sal gave a small understanding nod.

"Giuseppe…" Walter cut off Salvatore.

"No grazie mio compagno, it is up to me and I will take two men. Two men I know and can trust," he said turning to the two men who had just helped him vanquish the former Italian dictator.

"Well, you will have to count me out. I will have to get back to Torino and deliver the good news to the city's partisans. Not to mention rally the troops," commented Alfredo.

"Va bene, I will take Vito and Salvatore, we will destroy the chemical plant and then move to take the prison," he instructed, Vito could tell he was not going to have much of a break during this ambitious enterprise.

"How many people will you need for the prison break?" questioned Giuseppe, not wanting to have to wade through the sewage beneath the concrete walled structure.

"Four or five more," ignoring the monster partisan and turned to Sal for a decision.

"Okay. Me, Vito, Giuseppe and Matteo."

"Can I suggest Emiliano also," the youngest member of the group requested, he knew he could rely on his friend.

"Okay," agreed Sal, "There is your jail break team."

"Buona. Now we must contact the other partisans. How do you plan to notify them?"

"Let me show you," Salvatore said proudly, leading the men over to the radio tree, which stood beside the cages of pigeons.

"We will make a coded broadcast on the radio and then send out carrier pigeons for those groups that are too far to pick up the broadcast," he boasted.

***

The remainder of the day, after a fond farewell to Alfredo, Vito was sat with a magnifying glass, writing out messages on small pieces of rice papers, so that the messages could be easily destroyed or eaten to hide, stopping the message falling into enemy's hands. The small short but direct notes were delivered to partisan cells, it was a call to assemble their arms for the major attack against the occupying forces, which would be rolled and put in a small cylinder, it would then, in turn, be fitted to the leg of one of the messenger pigeons, it was a fiddly job, which need great care and precision, to be done without wounding the bird. Once he had completed this assignment, he joined up with Salvatore by the radio and listened to the message he was relaying.

"To all fathers, a barbecue at the house of our saviour tomorrow, bring the kids and all the toys." Vito was quizzical, the message did not sound like a call to arms, more like an invite to an evening's fun. But Sal deciphered it for his younger comrade. "The fathers are code for resistant leaders, the barbecue stands for the final attack against the occupiers, the house of our saviour is the large granite cross, by the crossroads, where we took our break on the way to attack the SS, the kids are the partisans and the toys are—"

"I know the guns, right?"

"Correct," smiled Sal. Vito questioned his commander.

"Shouldn't we ask for support from the Maquis?"

"No we do not need them. They have English Special operation executives or American Office of Strategic Services telling them how to fight and where to fight. I am not letting some foreigner tell me how to liberate our country. The resistance cells in the area range from half a dozen men to over one hundred. By the time we arrive at our objective, we will have a great army. Not to forget that they have their own invaders to deal with."

This did make Vito wonder if there was such a great number of rebels in the area, why had it taken up to now before conducting such a large objective. Perhaps the right partisan, just needed the right push.

Chapter 30

As evening fell, Vito summoned his team, to discuss that night's operation. With a stick he drew up a rough map in the dirt.

"This bridge," he said pointing with the branch, "is the main supply line which is the route they will send any reinforcements. It is the fastest way and as soon as the alarm is sounded, they will be coming. Which could be moments after we attack the base."

"Which will be inevitable," added Emiliano.

"Exactly. Our task tonight is to stop that happening, by blowing up this bridge, apparently it is only lightly guarded and we have been ordered to fell a tree either side of the tracks to hold back the repair team, which will delay them as much as possible. And if we are successful with any luck this should hold back any kraut support," the team leader explained.

"What about the roads?" Nicolo queried. Vito replied swiftly.

"We will be dealing with the roads whilst we are on the march. But with the bridge" he said trying to stick to the point "We will have to plant the explosives below the water line; this should hide them from view, from any nosey Bosch, who looks over the side of the bridge. And then once we have blown the bridge, we will have to take out any further guard posts that is if the explosion does not take them out for us, before we cut the trees. Giulio, you used to be a tree doctor, before the war. Correct?"

"Sí."

"Good, you and Samuel will hide by the trees, ready to cut them with a chainsaw. Nicolo, Emiliano and I will plant the explosives, whilst Matteo will hide here," he said pointing to a high point, behind the tree line near the bridge.

"Wait a second," Matteo interjected, "Why don't I just go on the ridge on the other side, it gives me a clear view of the bridge and there are no trees to obscure my vision of fire."

“I have already considered that, but if I know anything about Nazi defence tactics, I would assume that it will be defended with some sort of sandbag bunker, possibly armed with a heavy machine gun like a MG42, overlooking the entire area,” confirmed Vito. “So, Nicolo, Emiliano and me will swim up the river and down to the rail bridge, set the plastic explosives onto each of the bridges support beams, wire them up and then continue down river, where we will hide ourselves and trigger the detonation with the plunger. Does everyone get what they are doing?”

He got his reply by a small sea of nodding of heads. With that Vito rubbed out the roughly dirt drawn sketch and the men went to collect the necessary tools and weapons they need for that night’s exploits.

As evening turned to night the six-man team, clad in complete black and had even darkened their olive-skinned faces with mud, vanished from the camp and began their long trek to their ultimate objective.

The packs of explosives, plunge detonators, fuse wire, a pair of chainsaws and the lightweight M1 carbine rifles, which each man carried, together they were heavy, making the trek slow and hard going, it took them a long hour by the time why were just down river, overlooking the metallic structure. Vito cursed Walter under his breath, this piece of impressive German engineering was anything but lightly guarded.

If he had known it would be this heavily patrolled, he would have prepared some sort of diversion. As anticipated, there was indeed a machine gun bunker, surrounded in sandbags on the ridge, that Matteo had pointed out previously, but there was also a Guard tower on each end of the bridge and ten or twelve guards strutting back and forth along the overpass, with two more on each end to operate handmade barriers. Each column support was wrapped in razor sharp barbed wire. This would be more of a challenge, than they had at first anticipated. Vito took a deep breath and scanned the two river banks, the bright new moon gave the water shimmering silver, blue glow, for a suitable hidden place to set up the blasting, plunger, detonator, where he and his two associates had to feed the fuse wire to.

There was no place that they could exit from the river unseen, they had just had to hope that the guards were not looking in their direction, half of all operations of this type was down to luck. They could not linger as they were wasting the pitch darkness of the night. Vito urged his men to dart through the woodland, with a waving hand signal and like shadows in the midnight air the men ran swiftly and quietly to the ridge from where Matteo was to mount his armed support.

The men stayed motionless as the partisan veteran got into position. They then continued on and stopped on a bend beside the railway tracks, where Giulio and Samuel hunkered down with their mini chainsaw, out of sight. From here they were out of sight from the guards on the railway bridge, but the fortified bunker was directly in front of them, if either of the two guards looked directly down from their high positioned guard post, when the further three men, carrying the 'Bridge Killer' pack and a second mini chainsaw, were crossing the railway tracks, then they could be spotted.

The men looked along the railway tracks, for any lone sentries, they could not see the military soldiers in the bunker above them, which they hoped meant that they could not be seen. Vito crept out onto the track, as far as he could see, it was all clear, he could not see a single agent of the Axis powers, so he gave his associates a sign and they ran into the thicket opposite in a crouched position. The team leader led his counterparts further through the woodland and down to the stream.

The three rebels bound together four lumps of wood for buoyancy, then with the 'bridge killer' pack and the second chainsaw, resting on the wooden craft, the three men entered into the freezing stream. For such a beautiful night the water was intense and brisk, it shocked the men down to their bones. Holding onto the raft, kicking with their legs, the demolition operation was underway. As they got closer to the bridge through the bleakness, they could see the sentries patrolling back and forth, to their right-hand side they could see the sandbag bunker, all that they could do was pray that the Axis troops did not notice them or would mistake them as a piece of floating debris.

It took them ten minutes to reach the enemy structure. They rested the small craft against one of the barbed wire covered pillars, each man took a block of plastic explosives, then one at a time they dived down and strapped a block beneath the barbed wire, under the waterline, obscuring the devices from view. They started with the outside posts and worked their way inwards.

Emiliano fitted the last of his devices and upon surfacing he caught his arm on the razor-sharp barbed wire surrounding the pillars, which shed some deep gashes in his arm. The young partisan gave a small yelp, which Vito cut short by clamping a hand over his mouth, the trio stayed stock still, not daring to move or make a sound, they could hear a couple Nazi goons above them. The Squad leader listened.

"Did you hear something?" said the first soldier.

"Nein," came the reply.

"I am sure I heard something."

"Most likely just some fish." They could hear a pair of heavy jackboots walk away.

"Yes, I guess." The first man grumbled, with that a cigarette butt fell into the water, directly in front of the hidden rebels, they could then hear the second set of boots walk away from the edge. The three resistance saboteurs breathed a bit lighter.

Nicolo took the end of the fuse wire with the detonators and dived down to fit them into the putty explosives. He surfaced and Vito edged out, carefully, looking up, it looked clear, but he could not be positive, this was the point that a diversion could come in useful. The freedom fighters held their breath and holding onto the hand-built craft, with their hands they dived under the dark water and directed it further down the shore, feeding off the fuse wire as they went. The youngest forest partisan, popped his head above water, they were just passing the boulders on their left, where they were to set up the plunger.

Vito signalled to his comrades and they paddled to shore, the men crawled over the sand and rested, catching their breath behind the rocky barricade. The men checked over to the side, they could not believe it, the Jerries had not noticed a thing. Vito and Emiliano crawled onto the grassy knoll, lying flat on the ground, with their weapons pointed towards the bridge and its guards.

Emiliano removed his navy-blue neckerchief from around his neck and wrapped it around his torn-up arm "I think I am jinxed" he whispered, still scanning the horizon before them, doing the same Vito questioned him.

"What are you bloody talking about?"

"This is the second time I have been hurt on an operation. You other guys have not been injured once," the team leader's friend explained.

"Hey, the nights not over yet," said Nicolo as he tested the plunge detonator, by putting his finger on the fuse and pushing down the lever, it gave him an electronic shock, which meant it was working fine, he gave a nod to Vito.

"Okay, give us two minutes to get to the track and then let them have it," he commanded.

“Good luck,” came the reply. Vito and Emiliano were heading to the railway tracks to fell a tree on their side, whilst their comrades, Giulio and Samuel, did the same on the opposite side.

The friends, keeping as low to the ground as possible, until they reached a small ridge beside the railway tracks. Vito looked along the tracks for a suitable tree, it had to be tall enough to fit across the tracks, but also heavy and sturdy enough that it could not be easily moved. Five feet along the embankment stood a giant Stone Pine tree, it was a giant plant with a thick trunk, this was the perfect structure. Vito indicated the timber, to his friend, the duo rushed towards it. Then Vito checked his watch, twenty seconds until the detonation, the friends hunkered down out of sight.

The junior partisan watched as the seconds ticked by, they continued to wait for the ear shattering eruption of detonation. Another thirty seconds passed, then forty, Nicolo was running late. Vito was about to go back down to check on their lone comrade that they had left by the river bank, when the silent night sky exploded as the planted charges received the electronic current from the plunger. The cataclysmic explosion disturbed a swarm of resting Pipistrellus bats from the forest, sending them franticly up into the dark midnight sky. There was a loud splash as the bridge collapsed into the dim water below. There was a cry of the men who had fell into the glassy cold waters, along with the bridge, but they soon fell silent as they got crushed by falling debris.

The sound of gunfire from Matteo attacking the fortified gun placement alerting the Nazis guards of their presence. Vito jumped onto the tracks, the guard tower on the opposite side of the bridge had been demolished in the explosion, but the one on this side was still standing, with a guard scanning the area with a spotlight. It flooded Vito in light, the young partisan fired three shots, the first two took out the light and the final one dropped the man, toppling him from his high lookout post. The high up, sandbag fortified guard post on the opposite side had fallen quiet and now they could hear the faint sound of a chainsaw in the distance.

Emiliano was struggling to pull the cord to rev up their own chainsaw, with his wounded arm. Vito took the mechanical saw from his friend and pulled sharply on the cord, setting the teeth rotating, He went up to the chosen shrub and carefully cut a wedge from one side sending it crashing onto the tracks, splintering the carbon steel railroad tracks in two, a second crash indicated that their comrades had done the same on the other side of the river.

Emiliano and Vito ran back to meet up with Nicolo at the bank of the flowing crisp water where he was waiting for them, the trio swam across the river, doing all they could to dodge the debris from the obliterated bridge, which was flowing along the stream. A large piece of timber smacked into the head of Nicolo, knocking him out cold. Seeing his comrade's collision Vito rushed to his partners aid and turning on his back he grabbed his teammate and pulled him back to the river bed, the squads medic, Matteo, instantly went to work recovering him.

Meeting with their other comrades on the opposite side, without any hesitation and adrenaline running through their veins, the band of Italian partisans fled the area, heading back to their base before any reinforcements could turn up to investigate the commotion.

Chapter 31

They returned as morning dawned to find over two hundred more heavily armed partisans, all wearing the tricoloured resistance armband. Vito looked at all the new people, these could not be the city partisans from Torino, he did not recognise a single one. He had never seen the camp so alive at this time in the morning. This no longer looked like a hidden partisan base, but a military fortress, ready for war. So bewildered the young partisan, squad leader decided to seek out Salvatore.

"What is with all the new faces?" he asked his commander and chief.

"They are mountain partisans from high up in the Alps. They heard the broadcast, they have come down to help us with our final struggle," said Salvatore proudly.

"So was your mission successful?" questioned a voice, the two partisans turned to see Walter approach them with a second man, older that the others and Vito instantly noticed the man only had a single arm, his right arm was missing, from his elbow down. Which identified him as the man who had informed Walter about the constant German activity around the island where they had found and executed Mussolini.

"This is my good old friend Piva, he has decided to help us fight our last battle. Even with one arm he can still shoot a pistol and he wants to have a chance to kill a few Germans before the war is over," Colonel Valerio gave a chuckle.

"Well, he is welcomed," said Sal shaking the newcomer by his one remaining hand, Vito just gave the man a nod of welcome, who gave a courteous version, which seemed more like a bow than a nod in return.

Turning back to his young friend Sal said "You and your team should get as much sleep as you can. We leave in a couple of hours."

Vito agreed, he passed the orders to his men and went to have a nap.

Emiliano shook Vito awake, "Come on Vito, Sal and the colonel want to speak to the troops" he said excitedly. Vito rubbed the sleep from his eyes and wearily rose to his feet. The crowd was already gathering around a felled tree, each man had weapons, hand grenades hooked to their clothing and some even had ammunition belts strapped across their body, the army was ready to move out. The voices died down to a hush as Salvatore and Walter jumped up. Sal spoke up.

"I am only the leader of the partisans who live here. The ones you all call the 'Forest partisans'," there was a small titter around the observers, "but if you have not met him before, the man beside me is someone that I am sure every one of you has heard of Colonel Valerio. I think you will agree that he would be the right person to lead this great crusade."

This was received with a huge applaud and many cheering as Walter took a step forward, he held up a hand to quieten the crowd, he looked around before speaking loudly, clearly and as was his way, direct.

"As we embark on our noble quest to free our glorious land from beneath the Nazi jackboot, more patriots will rise up and join our great cause. This, my friends, will be the final brave march of the partisans!" The two partisan leaders jumped forwards into the cheering crowd, receiving pats on the back, Amerigo handed the men German sub-machine guns popular with the enemy forces, the MP40. Vito approached the armourer.

"I think I need a rifle," said the younger partisan, Amerigo cracked a sly smile and unzipped one of two black heavy duty duffel bags, they were laden full of weapons.

He handed Vito an American M1 semi-automatic carbine rifle, "try this one, it is simple and easy, the right kind of weapon for this job" he recommended, Vito examined it and happily slung it over his shoulder.

Amerigo lifted the two duffel bags and along with the Vito, joined the throng of resistance soldiers. The giant band of rebels walking along the road was drawing a lot of attention as they passed, Men and women would leave their homes, with weapons ranging from carving knives, pitchforks or for a select few even shotguns and joined the forces, growing the army bit by bit. Then men distracted themselves, from the journey they were embarking on and the operation they had to complete at the end, by introducing themselves to the other patriots. Vito was surprised how quickly they had reached the granite crucifix, that sat by the crossroads 'the House of our Saviour'.

"We will rest here, we have some other troops to join us, they will be meeting us here," Walter addressed the Italian civilian army.

The men collapsed around the cross. Vito lay down with his back against the cold giant cross and shut his eyes, to try and catch up on his much-needed rest, unlike the others, he had been informed that he would be assisting Sal and Walter with causing a diversion by attacking and blowing up a Nazi chemical laboratory and then being involved in the breaking out the slave labourers from the jail on the fortified Gothic line. Even if he was lucky enough to survive these high-risk enterprises, then he still had to continue with the rest of this armed rabble for its final conquest of attacking Albert Kesselring's secret fortified headquarters, at the small town of Sant'Oreste and end the Nazi oppression, held on this beautiful country, that he had adopted as his own.

He did feel honoured that they trusted him enough to participate and take on these hugely important assignments, but wished he could have at least one night's rest between missions. As they waited for their reinforcements to arrive, Amerigo went around the newest members and exchanged their rustic weapons with more advanced lethal weapons, with very basic instructions how to use them.

Vito was in a limbo, where he was not totally asleep, but yet not totally awake, he dreamt, but still aware of the men around him, time did not exist.

A call and rushing of men brought Vito out of his dozy state with a start, he looked around. All the volunteers were taking cover, Vito was confused for a time, the sky had turned darker and down one of the roads of the juncture they could see a fleet of vehicle headlights, heading in their direction at speed. Vito fell back and dropped to the ground beside Salvatore, who was on a single knee, with this weapon ready to use in a moment, Vito cocked his rifle and took aim at the approaching vehicles, which they could make out by their shape that they were a selection of both cars and trucks.

"Do not fire," called Walter. "Let them identify themselves. We do not want to shoot any allies," he was looking through a pair of binoculars watching the transports.

He turned to Salvatore and whispered, in a low voice so no one but Sal and Vito could hear, "They are flying Bandiera d'Italiaflags." Sal looked to his comrade with surprise. The Bandiera d'Italia was the red, white and green, Italian national flag, but what did this mean?

As the auto-mobiles got closer, there was a dust cloud hovering over the transports. Vito's finger was poised tightly on the trigger; this could turn into a fire-fight in a matter of minutes. If a property they had passed contained a Nazi informer, then this could be an attack and the operation could end before it had started.

The cars sped towards them at an alarming rate, as they approached, Vito could see what Walter had mentioned, each of the vehicles had Italian flags flying from their windows or makeshift flags fitted to the rear of the pickup trucks. The partisans readied their rifles, if it was an attack the transport would stop short of them and then all hell would erupt. But the cars did not slow they kept driving straight on, coming to a short, abrupt stop, in a parallel line, only six feet away from the army of resistance fighters. There was an absolute silence as the dust began to settle. This was too close, the partisans, who had seen battle before new to draw their side arms and knives, ready for close quarters combat.

A tall man wearing a thick, long, black overcoat and matching fedora hat on his head stepped from the side door of the lead truck. Vito cracked a smile and rose to his feet, he straight away recognised the man, who was wearing his common attire, it was their black-market friend, Alfredo. Then another door opened and another, other men and women began jumping from the back of the trucks. Vito recognised each one of them, they were the Torino resistance, who had frequenting the cafe the evening they had captured the pair of Gestapo agents, it took his comrades a little longer to realise who these people were.

Walter was the first to approach them and shook the hand of the Torino resistance leaders.

"Giorgio, you gave us a fright," he said.

Giuseppe appeared beside Vito and grumbled.

"Bloody city dwellers, this is meant to be a clandestine operation flying their bloody flags like a god damn parade!"

"Well over two hundred armed men marching down the road, cannot really be called covert," replied the youngest rebel.

They watched as Salvatore greeted Giorgio, who in turn introduced the British SOE, Captain Michael Lees, Vito could smell trouble brewing, so walked up and joined his two resistance leaders upfront. The British soldier had just listened to the plan from Walter and was replying.

"I think as I am the only real soldier and have been trained in all the dark arts of modern warfare, I think it is only right that I should take charge of this attack," he said.

"This is not your country!" said Vito, coming round to Salvatore's way of thinking.

“We are all soldiers; we are just not constricted by military red tape. My men will not follow a god damn foreigner,” spat Sal, staring daggers at the Special Operations Executive.

“And nor shall I,” added Walter.

“And if the Colonel won’t then you will not have many men under your command. These men know and trust him so if he won’t follow you, they won’t!” finished Vito.

“I say, settle down old boy,” said the English captain, motioning to his aggressors. “I meant no offence. But I just meant to say that I have the experience. I could help.”

Sal looked the man in the eyes and said in a low, menacing voice.

“Experience? What do you think we are, boy scouts? This is our country and we will defend it our way, with our men, following their rightful leaders.”

“But any advice you may volunteer would be gratefully appreciated,” added Walter, his high tone of voice turning friendly. Sal tore his deathly glare from the British agent and turned his back on the foreign soldier.

He spoke to the Torino captain, “How many people do you have here?”

“The entire rebels of Torino. One hundred and twenty-three. But we should wait, there are more coming.” Giorgio said composing himself after the partisans had confronted his foreign friend, clearly not what he had expected.

This intrigued Vito, he could not see anyone missing, even the three thirteen- or fourteen-year-old girls were here, armed to the teeth. Seeing this pleased Vito slightly, he was no longer the youngest partisan, at least not in this army.

“More? Who are we missing?” questioned the younger partisan soldier.

“We conveyed your message further along the line, to some of the smaller partisan cells; we considered that you had probably forgotten to contact them. They are converging and should only be around six or seven minutes behind us.” Walter checked his watch.

“I hope you are right. We do not have much time to spare.”

***

The Torino’s leader was not wrong, only a few minutes later a group of forty-eight armed men and women, were seen walking down the road in their direction. It was a combination of multiple different miniature cells. One was a strict communist cell, all wearing the red communist stars with the hammer crossed with sickle logo of the communist Russian Red Army. A rebel group who had Libyan members all wearing the traditional Pashteen Hat Caps and a Jewish resistance group, the men all wore their skull caps, with long beards and the younger men wearing ringlets. Not to mention some family cells and other smaller resistance groups, including some black men for Abyssinia (now Ethiopia) who had joined the partisan groups after the Italian army had invaded their African land.

The two groups met up together over looked by the giant stone Christian symbol. It seemed somewhat appropriate that this collaboration was being made under the ever-watchful eyes of the lord. The civilian resistance army was now over three hundred and fifty men strong and they marched on through the dark, crisp night time air.

Chapter 32

Vito, Walter and Salvatore, split off from the military might, leaving Matteo and Giorgio in command of the military might of the people and went their own way. The trio were lying in a grassy ridge overlooking the rather mundane rectangular structure below. They had hoped to use the cover of darkness to aid them, but morning had caught up with them and the beams of the bright morning sun could be seen rising on the horizon.

This was not all bad, it meant that they could see what they were doing, but it also meant that the Axis powers could see them. But with some good fortune it would mean that the base guards would be tired from a full night on watch and be totally unprepared for a stealth attack. But on the other hand if the night duty had already been relieved by the day shift, the sentries would be refreshed and this could make the attack all that much harder, especially when you consider that the three attacking combatants had not had much rest within the last twenty-four hours.

Walter was scanning the complex with his field glasses, pausing every a few seconds when he spotted yet another patrolling sentry, he then handed them to Salvatore who did the same.

"The odds are not in our favour," he whispered in a mumble. This did not fill Vito with a great feeling of confidence and when he was passed the binoculars, he could see precisely what the lone patriot was talking about. Walking around the miserable looking concrete building were at least four guards on each side, wearing the standard charcoal grey uniforms and coal scuttle helmets, with the red, white and black shield, the flag of imperial Germany with the Armenian runic SS on the opposite side.

Vito cursed under his breath, these were not normal German soldiers, they were Schutzstaffel. There was an extra guard watching over each side from the flat roof top and on every corner sat another Nazi goon, manning an MG34 machine gun with a steel shield plate. It reminded Vito of the top-secret base he was assigned to defend in France. If these extra defences were not enough, on the white washed walls, spaced out every five feet was a black cylinder, these were surveillance cameras.

This was a fortress. The partisans would have to cross open land, down the ridge, before getting to the top-secret property. They would have to descend the grassy slope, without being seen from the soldiers above, take out the guards on ground level quietly, without being spotted by the cameras, then enter the building against the unknown defences that were hidden from view on the inside, plant the explosives and escape again all without setting off the alarm or at least not raise the alarm too soon, after all the whole reason for this attack was to draw defensive guards away from the wall fortress. This was going to be their hardest challenge yet.

"Jesus Christ, this is impossible!" Vito said in a low voice. "There must be another way to draw the men away from the Gothic line!"

Walter took the binoculars back from Vito and his eyes were once again drawn back to their objective below them. It took the loan partisan a couple of minutes before he turned to his two comrades who were looking at him with bated breath.

"We need to cause a diversion, to draw them away from the front," he finally mentioned.

"That is a death sentence," commented Vito.

Salvatore added, "I will do it."

"No. This was my plan, it is my duty," he went back to scanning the building and continued, "there is a door in the centre. Once the kraut guards move from their posts, make straight for the door, I will meet you on the inside." The partisan stated "Salvatore, give me your weapon."

"What's wrong with yours?"

"It has a suppressor, I will need to make some noise, I will take out a couple of guards from the roof and then use yours to shoot the guards below to persuade the others away from the side. Vito, leave your rifle here, it will be easier for you, to use the side arms inside."

With that Walter took Sal's machine gun and crawled back down the slope and ran to their left. *He is bloody insane!* Vito thought to himself, *but even through his mad plans he is somehow able to survive*.

"How the hell has he lived so long?" the junior partisan asked his captain, who removed his Colt.45 revolver and chuckled before replying,

“Only god knows.”

The duo removed their pistols and watched the Nazi defenders carefully. Vito looked behind them where the sun had risen; at least the light from the star would blind any troops looking in their direction. Vito picked up the field glasses and his focus went back to the compound. Whist scanning the soldiers on the roof he saw the single guard on the right side of the building crumble to the ground. Seeing their downed brother in arms, the men on the rooftop ran to his aid and looked out towards the southern horizon, for the armed aggressor. Yet the men on the ground were at this point completely unaware of any threat.

Even without any bi-optical instruments, Salvatore could see the commotion happening on the top of the construction. Vito heard his leader mumble something about making ‘the shot.’ Their eyes were now fixed on the guards on the street level, then they would only need to worry about the static cameras, but as these were pointing diagonally outwards, if they kept close to the concrete walls there was a chance of getting into the secret laboratory unseen.

The sound of gunfire erupted from the South of the compound, distracting the German soldiers and with a total disregard to protocol or to their duty; they rushed to the support of their comrades, leaving the east end of the compound completely undefended. The two resistance soldiers could not hesitate, their lone comrade only had a limited amount of time and ammunition, as soon as the defenders realised that they were only fighting one man, it would become obvious to them that this was a diversionary tactic of some sorts.

The duo darted sideways down the slope and directly over to the wall, if they had been caught on camera then it would have only been for a fraction of a second. With their weapons at the ready and their backs flat against the wall they edged towards the reinforced metal door. With little hope Vito tried the door handle, it was locked, he had expected no less and gave a single nod to his leader. They had anticipated this turn of events, Sal withdrew a small flat, black leather pouch, from his back pocket, that contained twenty thin metal shards of various sizes and shapes and with Vito watching his back, Salvatore got to work picking the doors lock. Every second Sal worked on the lock; more anxious Vito became. The resistance leader cursed under his breath, every time he slipped or missed something.

“Come on, come fucking on!” Vito whispered harshly.

“This is surgery, my friend” murmured Salvatore, “one more click” and with that there was indeed a metallic click from within the door. “Ready?” Vito aimed his pistol to the door and even though he was relieved to be getting inside and out of the precarious situation, he decided to make a sarcastic comment to try and lighten the life-threatening current atmosphere that could be cut with knife.

"Never!" Salvatore gave the reinforced metal door a tug and it flung open, Vito with his arm at full length, with his finger poised tightly on the trigger entered first, followed by Sal who shut the door behind them. Unlike the outside, the hallway they found themselves in was pristine, with clean white tiled floors and walls, the whole place had the stench of antiseptic fluids.

With their side arms at the ready, they had not a clue what type of defences this building may contain. They edged down the corridor step by step; listening for any sound, the air inside was still and silent, making this research facility a spookily scary place. Not helping the duos nerves. They passed a couple of empty laboratories, the place seemed desolate. Checking around them Vito followed his friend and captain into one of these vacant laboratories. It was exactly the same as the hallway, except for the entrance which had windows pointing into the corridor.

Along the walls were metal shelves with chemical components and a metal table with various concoctions. In one corner there were silver barrels piled up, with a red diamond shaped label on each, featuring a flame symbol above the words Entflammbare Flüssigkeiten (flammable liquid).

"What the hell were they making?" questioned Vito looking around at all the chemical equations chalked on boards and scientific equipment.

"I guess whatever this is," Sal held up a small transparent zippier bag with a red swastika printed in the bottom left corner, inside was white, with a pinkish hue crystal like powder.

"Well, what is it?" Vito asked innocently.

"Amphetamine Sulphate," came a voice from the doorway, causing the two men to spin on their feet and aim their pistols towards the intruder, who raised his hand with a smile. It was Walter, the two men instantly lowered their weapons.

"Jesus Christ, Walter!" cried Sal, still keeping his voice low, as they had not yet made sure that the area was clear of enemy troops. "We nearly bloody shot you!"

"How the hell did you get in?" asked Vito.

“Trade secret,” jested Walter smiling at his own humour, “no, I gave those sons a bitches the run around and got them so confused I was able to just slip through the door.”

Sal rolled his eyes, ‘of course, he had’ and he went back to examining the bag of strange powder. He began quizzing the lone patriot.

“So what is this Ampher…Amphet—”

“Amphetamine Sulphate?” Walter helped the rebel leader.

“Yes. What is it?”

“Follow me,” said the lone patriot. He led them down the static white hallway, his two associates kept their weapons drawn, with their eyes darting all over, they were not as calm as their friend. He led them to another similar white tiled room, with a metallic chair in the centre, with heavy duty brown leather straps and multiple monitors with tags to be connected to the head of the subject, to measure brain functions.

“For years, the German forces have been trying to create some sort of super soldier. One who has extreme stamina, moves quicker, stay awake longer, even one which will not go down when you shoot it. This place is where they are trying to develop the drug, this is where they test it on their men.”

“Does it work?” asked Vito picking up a similar bag, that Sal had pick up, from a metallic side table, thinking that this could be useful for the upcoming mission.

“Partially, but they do become hooked on the drug, some of them have even been known to overdose on it, they have a seizure, foam at the mouth and ultimately die,” Walter advised them. With that comment Vito chucked the specimen back onto the table.

“Let’s blow this place,” said Sal sternly, taking off his backpack and opening it to reveal the immense sticks of dynamite inside. The men set about going from room to room planting sticks of dynamite, as near to the barrels of the flammable substance as they could and joined the extended fuses to a longer one that Walter had set up in the hallway.

The trio stood by the exit door that they had entered through previously; Walter drew his pistol and pulled out a Zippo lighter. Then looking at his counterparts, he knelt down and lit the end of the fuse wire. They had no time to spare, the three men burst out through the metal door and shooting at any Nazi unfortunate enough to be in the partisan’s way and they ran until they had got out of view over the ridge, with bullets flying over their heads, which only ceased by the apocalyptic explosion once the fuses flame had run its course.

The immeasurable, furnace like heat from the inferno was overwhelming, yet the trio had no time to celebrate their triumphant victory, they were behind schedule and should have been half way to their second objective by now, the men made haste towards the Gothic Line. Whose guards were on full alert and heading in their direction by road, meaning that they would have to travel cross country to avoid running into the reinforcing enemy troops and re-join with their fellow countrymen.

Chapter 33

The three partisans travelled through the vast fields of sweet corn. Walter grabbed a couple of sweet corn cobs, in the husk, to cook at a later date. The trio had to drop flat to the ground every time they heard the rumbling of transportation lorries coming up the road, this happened several times throughout their journey Vito tried to count how many transport lorries had passed them by, if asked he would have said thirteen, but if the truth be told he had lost count after eight. The sun was now high in the sky and the operation was long behind schedule. But all those who had previously served in the military new one thing, military operations were never punctual.

It took the triumvirate just over two and a half hours before they were able to reconvene with the rebellious army or partisans. The civilian mob had taken refuge in a giant basin of a dried up lake bed, obscured by overgrown reeds. The threesome was met by embraces or shaking of hands by their closest friends and pat from their other allies, pleased to see their safe return.

"We were beginning to worry about you guys," said Alfredo shaking Vito's hand warmly.

"It is good to see you, my friend" the partisan replied. Walter had already separated from the throng and was at the side of the basin, observing the strengthened fortress wall of the Gothic line with his field glasses. He soon returned to the band of rebels.

"The plan was a success, I only see a single guard patrolling a twenty meter stretch of the wall, they seem to have taken the outside guards from the door of the prison. This will make our job a lot easier," he informed them.

"Okay prison break team, follow me. Giorgio, you wait until we are up by the wall and then you lead the men westward, you will find an unmanned, partially built section of the wall, where you can cross."

Sal, Vito, Emiliano, Matteo and Giuseppe, who had taken one of Amerigo weapon filled duffel bags, all congregated around Colonel Valerio, awaiting his command. The open ground ahead was level with little to no vegetation to hide them as they approached the enemy position, but if they timed it right, they could cross when the enemy soldier had turned its back. The colonel watched the patrolling sentry carefully, they could tell the careful movement of Walter's head as he traced the movement of the wall guard that the man was now walking away and then their fearless leader said the word they both anticipated and feared.

"Now, follow me, rapido!" the six-man squad darted from cover and in a crouched run began to traverse across the open plain.

Suddenly their leader harshly whispered.

"Down!" the men fell onto the flat earth and with baited breath, merging into the ground. None of the men dared to move, Walter was watching the enemy soldier on the fortifications, once they were once again clear to travel, Walter gave them a signal to proceed towards the German defences, once again keeping as low as possible the team raced for the wall, each one of them eyed up the monstrous construction, for any sign of the returning sentry. They repeated this several times.

Only once they were stood, with their backs against the reinforced wall did they once again feel able to breathe freely. The men huddled together in a small group. They were beside some concrete steps, which led down to a metallic door, above the entrance way it had a white sign with the bold fraktur lettering 'Gefängnis' (prison).

"The prison is down here, they will most likely have no fewer than two guards in there," whispered Walter, Giuseppe leant forwards.

"We can take four easily," he cocked his gun.

"Not a single shot or we will be in trouble, we must use our knives," Walter commanded. "Vito bang on the door, tell him that one of them has been ordered onto the wall." He looked towards Giuseppe and said, "The second he exits you kill him, before he can make a sound".

The large resistance fighter gave a grim smile, as he removed a razor-sharp Bowie knife from his belt. Vito took a deep breath and carefully descended the stairs. There was a round peep-hole in the centre so the prison guards could see who it was before opening the door, the bilingual partisan stood to the side of the spy-hole and gave two hard knocks on the door. There was no response, Vito looked up the stairs to his comrades, Walter mouthed the words, for him to try again, the partisan did as he was ordered. He waited a few seconds longer, when the shutter of the peep-hole opened and someone looked through.

"What is it?" came a German voice.

"One of you have been ordered to help reinforce us on the wall," replied Vito, he hoped this ploy would work as they only had one chance.

"We are prison guards not wall sentries!" came a harsh reply, Vito looked to Walter who gave a rolling motion with his hand, implying that Vito should continue to push.

"Hey, I don't give the orders, of course, I can always tell them you refuse." Vito paused "But you could be court marshalled for insubordination," he urged calmly. There was a moments silence before a reply came.

"Okay, okay, I will be up in a couple of seconds," Vito retreated back up to the wall, the men had concealed themselves behind a conclave in the walls structure.

No one coming up the stairway could see them until it was too late. Keeping to his word, approximately thirty seconds later the door opened and out came a clean-shaven lean soldier wearing a black SS uniform, wearing a matching black forage cap, with the skull and crossbones insignia on it. Obviously, the prison sector was under Schutzstaffel control, hence the man's objection to working on the wall. The Nazi goon grudgingly walked up the stairs. Giuseppe did not hesitate for a second, he jumped on the soldier and with a paw over the surprised prison guards mouth he slipped his blade into the nape of his victim's neck, killing him instantly.

"Vito, dress into his uniform and tell the other one that you are relieving him. We will take care of him and you get the prisoners out," commanded Walter. Now the partisan understood how this man got his reputation, he took risks.

Vito, not too happy that he was the one taking all the risk in this particular challenge and was sure Walter would reap the benefits. But following his order Vito stripped off the dead German and dressed into his uniform, it was much lighter, more comfortable and warmer than the Wehrmacht uniform that he had worn in his past life, stature obviously had its benefits in the Reich. Taking off the holster he looked inside it.

"Son of a bitch!" he murmured as he saw a Luger, his favourite side arm, this was his now. Checking the German warden's pockets he found a switch blade, with a black handle and in silver was the Nazi insignia, so he slipped this in his boot, it could become handy later on. As he perched the forage cap on his head, his troop looked at him with a smile.

"So how do I look?" he asked, Sal replied.

“If we didn’t know you then you could pass a one of those arse-holes.”

Vito was not quite sure whether he should take this as an insult or a complement. But if it serves its purpose, then that was all that mattered. Vito took a deep breath and descended the stone stairs, attached to a hook on the stolen trousers he found a set of five keys, one he recognised as a locker key and one belonged to a padlock, most likely for a footlocker, one fitted a vehicle and he assumed the other was for something personal, he flicked through them and found one that matched the keyhole in the door. He slipped it into the lock and with a decisive turn the door opened, Vito took a second quick glance to his group of comrades before entering the subterranean confined lock-up.

The underground prison was a single large room, with eight metal barred cages. The atmosphere down here was cool and damp, with a distinct smell of human waste, there were no toilets here, each cell had a single bucket, shared between the five to ten occupants. Vito made a point not to look at the detainees, but strode directly over to the guard, wearing the similar attire. He had hardly noticed the disguised partisan enter as his nose was deep in an adult magazine.

“I have been commanded to relive you,” he told the German, who looked thrilled by the news. He put the magazine down on a small wooden table, which had a single propane lantern and a large ring with a set of keys, one for each cell.

“These guys won’t give you any trouble,” said the prison warden “They have had their meal for today and they will go back on work detail in the morning.” With that the German walked from the underground room, to meet his fate with the waiting partisans.

As soon as the door closed Vito grabbed the large ring of keys and went to the first cage, it had seven men inside all wearing British uniforms, they looked battered and worn.

“Do any of you speak Italian?”

“Yes,” said one of the men, who was sat in the corner, he rose to his feet and walked up to the bars to look, what he assumed was his captor in the eyes, “I do.”

“I am with the resistance; we are here to get you out.”

The man looked at Vito suspiciously. The door to the sub-terrestrial detention centre opened, making Vito spin round with his gun drawn, to see Emiliano standing in the doorway, carrying his friend’s clothes.

"Jesus, you could have given us some warning, I almost shot you." Vito was thankful that he was not of a nervous disposition as many of his friends would have been dead by his hand by now, if he had been.

"I am sorry, my friend," pleaded Emiliano, entering the confinement area, seeing the man enter, with his partisan armband, lit up the faces of the detainees. Unburdening his colleague with the clothes, he handed the ring of keys to him. "I got you another Luger magazine from the second guard," he said passing Vito the spare pistol magazine.

"Thank you. Unlock these guys whilst I get changed," ordered Vito, disrobing himself of the Nazi clothing.

Emiliano went from cage to cage unlocking each one in turn, giving Vito the chance to observe the occupants, recognising them mostly by their insignia and badges that they continued to wear with pride, in one there were seven British, next nine, of whom he assumed by the insignia, were Gurkhas, three Americans, who was caged with a pair of Indian Sikhs, five Canadian and one of the cells had nine men who looked like Italian civilians, but Vito knew that they must be partisans.

The final cage Emiliano did not unlock. It was smaller and there was only one occupier, he was sat at the back with his head down, wearing a German uniform. Slipping on the partisan armband Vito joined his friend at the cage door.

"Wer bist du?" Vito asked his identity, the prisoner stayed silent "Wer bist du?" He repeated louder, the man replied in German.

"My name is Hermann, Hermann Schröder."

"Well, private Schröder, what did you do to find yourself in this shit-hole?" questioned the partisan.

"I am a deserter," the man said, wearily rising to his feet.

"Bullshit!" Spat Vito "deserters are shot."

"Normally, yes, but fortunately they are short on labour here, so they thought it would be easier to make me work on the wall, rather than execute me. Let me out and we can go our separate ways," said the German approaching the metal fencing.

Just then Sal and Giuseppe entered carrying the corpses of the two Nazi prison guards and dropped them on the ice-cold floor. The pair of newcomers looked to Vito, for an explanation.

"He said he is a deserter," Vito informed him, "he wants us to release him."

"Leave him," commanded Salvatore harshly, Emiliano interjected.

“If we leave him behind, he will yell the place to high heaven.”

“Open the cage.” Giuseppe growled, Emiliano did as he was bid, the German soldier took a step back, as the door was swung open. Giuseppe stepped into the cage, towering over the soldier and then, drawing his blade he slashed the young Nazi over the throat. Blood sprayed from the wound covering Giuseppe face, Vito and Emiliano stood where they were in horror, they were not squeamish but neither had ever seen so much blood.

The incarcerated German, clung his hands over his wound, with no avail as the blood seeped through his fingers. Sal turned to the escaped prisoners of war, greeting the partisans, who he evidently knew personally.

“We are the Italian partisan army, on our way to attack the headquarters of the German infection, currently controlling out land, Albert Kesselring. You will be joining our ranks. Now remain quiet and follow my associates out where you will be given a resistance armband to identify you as one of our band and a weapon. Vito, Emiliano get them out of here.” The few Italian speakers translated to their liberated fellow countrymen.

The two young partisans then led the freed prisoners of war out of the underground fortifications, the men breathed in the fresh air as if it were in short supply and squinted in the Mediterranean sun. They were each given a tricoloured partisan armband by Walter who introduced himself to his new alias, as Colonel Valerio. Before the small military squad, keeping tight against the wall, in single file, made their way along the Nazi defences.

Chapter 34

The team of partisans and escaped prisoners of war eventually arrived to a section of wall that had nothing but the concrete foundations, the area looked like the site of some type of massacre, there were slaughtered German bodies splattered all over. This is where the civilian army had passed and must have covertly eliminated the sentries guarding this area. This made it easier for the second wave to get through to the south of the Gothic line. The men walked through the work area, carefully weaving through the concrete work and perturbing metal bars, yet still keeping their weapons at the ready. No one knew how long the demolition of the chemical plant would keep the Germans at bay and when a shift change may be due.

They re-joined with the army of freedom fighters, three miles from the wall, at a derelict barn house, the people had settled both inside and out, there were a number of camp fires where the partisans were boiling pots of coffee and cooking some morsels of meat. They welcomed the newcomers warmly giving them each a mug of the warm brew and Matteo went from one of the escapees to the other, fixing any injuries that they had sustained at the hands of their fascist German captors. Whilst the armies' leaders congregated together to discuss their next steps, they were now in enemy controlled land and danger was all around. Vito sat around one of the fires and got out his pipe, as he smoked his tobacco, he spoke with the Italian speaking rescued Englishman.

"Who are you guys?"

"We are a British Green Beret commando unit; we were dropped into Italy to scout out the Gothic line and were ambushed." The British soldier explained, "the last eight months, we have been forced to work on the construction of the wall, we did what we could to sabotage and slow down the job, but you can only do so much."

"Well, getting you guys out should hopefully draw it to a standstill," Vito said encouragingly.

"We can only hope. But I worry that they may force locals to finish what we had started." This did not sound very good to the young partisan and went over to Salvatore to convey what he had just heard.

"I expected as much," said the rebel leader solemnly, "but if we succeed with our mission, then we will not have to worry about it. They will soon retreat and the wall will be abandoned."

It was eventually decided that the partisans would rest here that night to recover from the sleep deprivation, that many including Vito were suffering from, giving them all a chance to recuperate from their injuries and fatigue.

The following morning, the resistance troop left at first light, it had been the first time Vito had slept properly for over seventy-two hours and as he awoke, he felt refreshed. Yet feared what was still to come. The army, along with their new found allies marched proudly down the streets, small teams of partisans joined the hostile patriotic contingent, raising the civilian troops even more, this was no longer a mob, but an entire country up in arms.

As they marched along the road, some of the British escapees began whistling a tune, Vito did not recognise. So he turned to the Italian speaking English soldier and asked him about the tune. He was informed it was a British song called 'Colonel Bogey' and began translating some of the words, making Vito laugh out loud, the English had a strange sense of humour to be able to make jokes about testicles.

They marched along the roads for a few hours with no problems of any sort and it seemed that the occupying forces were completely unaware on what was approaching from the northern unoccupied sector. They were only an hour away from their designated objective, when they saw an axis military transportation vehicle approaching, there was a wave of rifles being cocked, ready for any intransigence this vehicle and its occupancy could cause, but they did not waver but continued to approach, the Nazi transport.

The sea of armed rebels walking down the road directly towards them, it did not seem to bother the German driver as the lorry continued to travel towards them, it did not look like it would stop, Walter put up a hand indicating for the civilian force to stop. The men stood stock still in the centre of the streets, showing their defiance.

Aware that the men before them would not falter, the driver braked hard stopping just twenty feet from the resistant band of 'terrorists'. Walter walked up to the driver's side door.

“Aus!” he ordered the man out; the German driver was not paid enough to risk his life and followed the command. “Vito, tell him to get on the floor face down.” Vito did as he was asked, “ask him who is in the back.”

“He says it is a prisoner transport.”

Silently Walter signalled to half a dozen of the men to follow him, this included Vito, Salvatore and Giuseppe. The partisan leader led them round to the back of truck. The men took aim to the back as Walter tore open the flaps, as expected sitting there were a couple of junior Nazi soldiers, they looked at the men aiming their weapons at the two men. Walter gave a single worded command.

“Aus!”

The two teenage troops raised their hands and exited the lorry. There were five prisoners in the back of the truck, one older man, three younger men in their late teens and a female around the same age as the three younger men.

“Vito, take these two bastards over there.” Salvatore ordered, pointing to the edge of the street, Vito directed the pair of captured Nazis over to the side of the road, above a small ravine. As the hostages exited the lorry, Vito could not control his anger at these scums and without an order he shot each man in their chest. And looked back to Sal, who was surprised by his comrade’s malicious behaviour.

“I didn’t have any rope,” shrugged the young partisan, swinging his rifle onto his shoulder. Salvatore just gave a small laugh and turned to question the people that they had just rescued.

“So who are you?” The older man stepped forward.

“My name is Frosino, these are my three sons and my daughter.” He took note of the men’s armbands and continued, “We had heard about your cause and joined up with a small cell of partisans on our way to meet up with you all. We were attacked, the others were shot and they took us captive, to work as labourers on their wall defences.” The man explained, his nerves were showing as he spoke quickly without a single pause.

“Amerigo!” Walter called out, “give them a weapon!” he ordered.

“Could we use the truck?” suggested Emiliano. Salvatore looked in the back of the truck before answering,

“It will only carry twenty of us, or thirty at a push and they will find it suspicious if they are not expecting a transport truck.”

"He is right," agreed Walter. "But they will not be expecting three hundred partisans walking down the road either, but I think I know which will surprise them more." The men laughed, thinking about how shocked the enemy forces would be seeing this colossal army approach them.

"Unless we are spotted," Vito interrupted, "it is not like we are inconspicuous."

"The kid is right," said the newcomer, Frosino, "we are in hostile territory. Our group was only small but we got ambushed by the Hun."

"Maybe we should split into smaller groups and meet up closer to the objective," suggested Salvatore, looking at the army's leadership. Walter was in quiet consideration for some time, making the other men feel uncomfortable, when he finally spoke it felt as if some shackles had been released.

"Yes, it is not a bad idea. Salvatore, you take ten men and scout out the surrounding area and especially the entrance of Monte Soratte, we need to know what defences they have. We will split the rest of the troop into smaller groups of twenty men. We will take different routes, this way we will rouse less suspicion, if we are seen. I will take the truck with twenty men through the nearby towns to investigate troop movements. We will meet at the church of Eremo Sant'Antonio, it is remote, on a ridge, it should be able to house all of us, it is surrounded by a wall, with a large gate, it can be easily defended. We can post lookouts, who can view the entire valley and alert us if any Nazi patrol comes too close."

It was clear the lone partisan was speaking as the thoughts came to him. With that said, Vito immediately volunteered to go and assist the man that he most respected, the leader of the woodland rebels, Salvatore.

Chapter 35

Receiving a rough pencil sketch from Colonel Valerio, Salvatore chose his ten-man team from his own forest camp partisan band, the civilian soldiers he could trust, this included Vito, Giuseppe, Matteo and Emiliano. They walked past the driver who was still laid face down on the floor, quivering with fear.

"What are we going to do with this son of a bitch?" asked Giuseppe, he had a malicious glint in his eye, without looking at the downed man, Vito drew his pistol and fired a single shot to the Germans head. Giuseppe glared at his comrade with jealously.

"I guess I'll have to dress in his uniform then and be the driver" said Walter, looking at the executed Nazi, giving the impression that he had intended the German to drive. "We will be setting up road blocks on our way back to the church."

As they left, Walter was still arranging separate teams and choosing their squad leaders, Alfredo was one of these leaders and was directing his group over a freshly ploughed field.

"Let's go lads" said Sal boldly, leading them in the opposite direction than Alfredo's crew.

The team of patriots trekked over pastures and fields, darting across roads and through field overflow ditches. Sal kept checking the rough drawing, before changing the direction, whenever they got too close to a road or a building of some type. They made good time considering the number of diversions they had to take. Soon they were walking over a grassy knoll, but it was not natural, there were multiple ventilation shafts, feeding air to an underground complex of some sort.

The team were silent as they edged forward, the slightest sound could travel through the air tunnels and they did not want the occupants to know of their presence or at least not yet. They kept low scanning the horizons all around them, being spotted would instantly cause suspicion and could result with them being sent to concentration camps for the rest of the war, with the possibility of the German command bunker, being on full alert, in time for the Italian rebel attack. As the ten-man team edged forward the grassy hill split into two, to reveal a deep ravine, with sheer cliff faces on each side and lead to a massive blast door, clearly this was the doorway beneath the mountain.

On guard duty outside were more than half a dozen Nazi soldiers, wearing thick grey uniforms of the Wehrmacht and coal scuttle helmets. On a couple of chain leads were a pair of ferocious looking Doberman dogs. The men were lying flat on the ground, peering over the ridge.

"I fucking hate dogs," mumbled Giuseppe, peering over the edge.

"It won't be easy getting through that lot," remarked Matteo.

"No, it is a bloody bottle neck," agreed Salvatore, "it is a kill zone!"

For once Giuseppe did not make some kind of snide comment about cutting the men's throats, but said exactly what Vito was contemplating.

"Could we not just lob down a couple grenades down there?"

"No, that will alert all on the inside and we don't want to give them too much of a warning," commented their leader.

Vito suddenly had a brain wave.

"What about the van?"

"What about it?" questioned Sal.

"Well we could reverse the Nazi truck up to the entrance full of armed partisans. When they approach to investigate what is going on, we jump out and slaughter them," Vito explained.

The whole team looked at each other, it was not a bad idea and could work, but that was up to the partisan leader, Walter. Sal gave the order to fall back, so they could go on to rendezvous with the remainder of the civilian band, who would be assembling at the aforementioned Eremo Sant'Antonio church. One at a time they slunk away from the observation point, to meet at the bottom of the ridge line.

With no sign posts to direct them, they had to rely on the vague directions they had been given by Walter before they had left their resistance comrades. The group of forest dwellers took full advantage to hide, using the natural terrain, travelling along hedgerows, hiding beneath the woodland canopy, taking cover in ditches and refraining where possible to avoid open spaces. They found themselves following a tributary of the giant Po River, which would take them close to their destination, the water was little more than a trickle but it was low enough to keep them mostly undercover.

As they trundled along the flowing water, they could see a road ahead, that crossed the waterway on a small stone-built bridge, the centre of the bridge had been blown away, possibly a sabotage attempt performed by a partisan cell or British SAS squadrons which were rumoured to be orchestrating sabotages to try and hinder the enemy force, awaiting the arrival of the Allies who were approaching form the south.

The demolished part of the bridge had been replaced with wooden planks, reinforced with thick iron guiders beneath, to make most vehicles attempting to cross it possible once again. The troop froze, when they heard the distinct sound of a motorcycle approaching, the chances of it being civilian was slim to none.

Salvatore pointed to the bridge and the troop sprinted to take cover beneath the low overpass. The men stayed quiet as they could hear the bike move closer and then to all their shock and horror the motorcycle stopped directly above them, the men dared to breath. Had they been spotted? Had they done something to arouse suspicion or warrant a closer inspection?

They sighed in relief when the bike revved its engine and continued along the road, the squad was about to move off, when they stopped and remained beneath the stone bridge, there was the low rumbling of vehicles and even more worrying, tanks. The motorcycle before must have been the scout, which travelled before a convoy to make sure the coast was clear and then would give a signal, usually a white flag so it was clearly a visible, to inform the military convoy that it was safe to continue.

As the first transport drove overhead, Giuseppe cocked his weapon and whispered "Let's take these beer swilling bastards!"

Sal instantly put a hand on his comrade's weapon and whispered harshly, "This is *'not'* our mission! We have to get back to the church without the Germans being aware of our presence." Giuseppe tried to violently pull his weapon from his leader's grip, but Salvatore's grasp was iron tight, he looked his man straight in the eye "Giuseppe, do you understand?" he said harshly.

"Si, capisco," Giuseppe said reluctantly as the tracks of a tank rolled above their heads, putting a strain on the metallic supports.

Five more transports drove over the bridge, from what they could make out from their secluded position, deciphering from the sounds of the engines and the wheels or tracks of the vehicle above them, they could figure the vehicles consisted of a jeep, two transportation lorries, another tank and what only could be conceived as a half-track, the sounds echoed around the alcove, almost deafening the men, hiding there. They remained motionless for a couple of minutes after the low rumbling sound had died away and they were sure that they were clear to continue on to their destination.

They arrived at the church of Eremo Sant'Antonio before too long, it was perfectly positioned as Walter had explained, on 'higher land', giving a perfect three-hundred and sixty degrees view all around, with only one gravel road leading up to a twelve-foot cast iron bar fence. Just before you reached the surrounding white washed walls, hidden beneath a giant Italian oak tree, they recognised the Nazi truck that they had hijacked, indicating that Walter had already arrived. They looked up to the turret style wall to see armed partisans watching their approach. Identify their guests the large fence opened. The church was breath-taking with giant white pillars on either end, with an open bell and massive giant windows all around.

Looking around the men had built small fires around the grounds, cooking small scraps of meat, bubbling soup in cast iron cooking cauldrons and pots of coffee, cooking over the open flames. There were rustic ladders leading up to a parapet around the wall where the partisan guards and lookouts were stationed. As they looked around the camp, they noticed a band of rough looking men that they did not recognise, most had stubble covered chins, many wore naval or sailor's hats, each man wore cross body ammunition belts, most of them were smoking hand rolled cigarettes and gave the men an evil glare as they entered.

Doing what they could to look natural the men walked casually to the centre of the churchyard, yet none of them had let their guard down, they did not know who these new people were and until they were confirmed to be allies, they would rather err on the side of caution. They became slightly reassured when Walter and Alfredo approached them, shaking the men warmly by the hand.

"I guess we are the last back," said Matteo looking around at the relaxing partisan movement around them.

"No, we are still awaiting one more squad to return," said Walter "what news of Monte Soratte?" he asked the new arrivals. Instead of reporting in front of his men Salvatore took Walter aside and they spoke in quiet voices together.

"So who are all these new guys? Where did they come from?" Vito asked his black-market friend.

"They work with me," the man replied proudly, "we use the Po River to transport our illicit goods north, so we have small ports along the river for reports on enemy movement on the water and for refuelling. I spoke to one of the cells and they contacted others, along the river. They brought food and ammunition, not to mention joining our ranks." He smiled.

"They want to join our army?" Vito was surprised; these weren't soldiers but back-alley market traders.

"As I told you before my friend, we are not just traders of illegal goods but we are also partisans," the man chuckled. There was an urgent cry from one of the lookouts.

"There are some men approaching!" Vito, Alfredo and Walter ran over to the ladders and climbed up onto the parapet. They looked over the wall and saw a team of twelve men walking quite casually up the single gravel road, as if they were on a holiday hike. Walter called down.

"It is okay, it is Giorgio's team."

Vito peered at the men and could just make out the Torino rebel leader. As they got closer, the men down below opened the gates, to allow them access.

As promised Walter had set up booby traps on the roads, taking advice from the English Special Operations Executive, they fitted explosives, connected to pressure pads, into slits cut into trees. When a vehicle was to set off the charge by driving over one of these pressure pads, the tree would not only crush the vehicle beneath, but also create a roadblock at the same time. This was a common tactic used by the allied forces and one that was taught to resistance groups, for this very reason.

That night many of the partisans made their bed inside the house of God. But Vito had decided to sleep beneath the stars; he had never been too fond of churches, even when he was forced to go on Sundays when he was a child, by his devoutly catholic parents. It always gave him the shivers and knew he would not get much sleep if he attempted to rest inside the holy house. The night air was cool with no breeze, the sky was dark with no moon, lying beside the smoking embers of a dying fire kept him warm. He took a night time walk on the parapets, where partisans were on guard duty.

Ahead in the distance he saw an orange glow which illuminated the horizon, what was happening was obvious, it was that of a city ablaze. The destructive power was terrifying, but the glow on the night horizon was awe inspiring. The Allies were dropping incendiary bombs, to destroy the Axis infrastructure. He could not be sure what city was burning, but he found himself giving a small prayer for the innocent civilians who would perish on this attack.

Once he finally decided to sleep on the ground outside, he looked up into the night sky, he had never seen so many stars before, that glistened like diamonds in the black heavens. In his home city of Dresden they were mostly eclipsed by street lighting and since he had come to Italy, he had become too intoxicated or preoccupied checking around the horizon for Axis troops, but for tonight at least he was safe and could relax and admire the shapes in the sky.

Chapter 36

The following morning was the day they had been preparing for, the day of the attack which could end the torment and occupation of their noble and historic land. The area was alive since sunlight, people preparing themselves for the mission to come, every man and women there new that this was their best chance of freeing their beloved country and each person was willing to sacrifice themselves for the cause. Amerigo handed around extra loaded magazines, ammunition belts and American and Russian hand grenades to as many of the rebel fighters that he could.

Walter, who wore a red military style beret, with the golden star of Russia emblem on his head, climbed the parapet to address the assembled freedom fighters, everybody fell silent to hang on the fearless leaders every word.

"My friends, my countrymen, you have all answered the call of your country to liberate ourselves of the German oppressors who believe that we were born to serve them. We stand together as brothers; I cannot promise that we will all come back alive but whether we survive or fall we are all heroes here and it will be an honour to serve among you!"

There was a sense of pride as people applauded and saluted their general. Two of Alfredo's black-market colleagues got out a pair of banners displaying the Italian flag with the star and the letters CLN in the centre. Informing that they would be leading the parade of men to their victory, Vito considered this to be a bit too much, but was sure it could inspire confidence as the armband does that every member of their army proudly wore. Walter took Vito to one side.

"We are going with the plan that I believe was your brain child" he said, Vito was taken back, he was sure that Salvatore would have tried to take credit for it. "After we have taken out the guards, I want you to lead the rest of the troops forward."

"Me? But what about Sal or Alfredo or Giorgio?" questioned Vito in a panic, he was not a partisan leader, he was a soldier, just another man.

"No, I am in charge and I say you, the others agree. But once we are inside, I want you to take two men and severe all the communication lines and make sure they cannot be reconnected, use these," he commanded handing Vito a pair of handmade wire cutters, made by two flat bits of iron, with a sharpened rivet, possible to cut through mesh fencing easily. These were often used by Prisoners of war, to escape the camps they were held at.

Not only was Vito to lead the charge but he was now also responsible for severing all communications to delay any possible reinforcements. Vito thought for a moment, he knew Sal and Alfredo, the two men he trusted the most would have their own missions, so settled on his good friend Emiliano and fellow squad member Matteo.

Soon after, following the van filled with twenty armed men driven by Walter, the patriotic army left the confines of the holy land and marched proudly off to secure their victory over the German forces. Vito knew, as everybody knew and had come to terms with in their own way, this battle could result in his death but, again like everyone, he was willing to take that risk. On the leading corners of the army of men the two banners flew proudly in the wind, making the men marching behind stand tall and proud. They were to be the liberators of Italy. They were quiet as every patriot among them got into the zone for the struggle ahead.

Walter stopped the van at the entrance of the ravine and turned around, the entrance was around the next corner. This is where they had to wait for the truck team to clear the entrance way. Walter gave a salute to his troops and began to reverse the truck around the bend, every member of the band held their breath. They could hear the dogs barking and the call of the German sentries, the engine ceased and a barricade of weapons fire erupted the sound travelling down the rocky ravine, then silence, not a sound, had the mission ended as quickly as it had started?

The young partisan leader felt unsure of his next move, he could feel all eyes were on him, he was in charge of the army, it was his decision, if they marched round the corner and the Germans had not been vanquished then in the tight quarters the death toll would be extravagant, but if they charged round with their weapons firing and Walter's team had done their job, they could kill their comrades, the odds were hurting his head but he eventually came to a decision.

He pointed to two men, who belonged to the city partisans and without a word signalled that they should peek round and report back of what they see. The men watched the two nimble partisans run to the bend, Vito unslung his rifle and there was a clicking as people switched off the safety catches on their weapons. The two men appeared in the centre of the ravine, gave a whistle and waved the men over.

"Let's go!" Vito said loudly so all the rebels could hear.

And with the banners held high the army of civilian freedom fighter moved forwards. As they turned the corner, they saw the giant circular door carved into the side of the mountain, Walter and all his team were standing over eight slain German soldiers and two dead Dobermans.

The giant blast proof door was still open, which meant that, though there was gunfire the alarm had not yet been raised. The two banner bearers stuck their flags into the ground by the entrance and took up their arms, then with Walter, Vito and Salvatore in the lead, rifles up ready to use at a moment's notice the army entered the restricted, secret underground headquarters of the Nazi power in Italy.

The tunnels were dimly lit, the walls were whitewashed and every so often, in fraktur writing was a motto of Nazi Germany such as '*Ein Volk, ein Reich, ein Führer!*' translated as 'One people, one country, one leader!' or '*Heute Deutschland, morgen die Welt!*', 'Today Germany, tomorrow the world!' and one which made Vito sneer, said 'Lang lebe unser ruhmvoller Führer!', 'Long live our glorious leader!' These slogans sickened Vito down to his stomachs, making him feel even worse was that he had once believed and rallied behind these words.

There were also small paintings on the walls of idealistic images of the soldier's homeland Germany, painting of castles and green pastures, to remind the German people of the fatherland and what they were supposedly fighting for. The army continued on deeper and deeper beneath the earth, all of a sudden, the three leaders stopped they could hear footsteps approaching along the concrete floor. The three commanders dropped to their knees, aiming their weapons down the corridor, with the men behind them doing the same.

They waited as the footsteps came nearer and nearer then around from a corner walked three young German soldiers talking and laughing among themselves, seeing the malicious looking rebellion before them they froze with their mouths open, but soon fell when a barrage of gunfire tore into them. And as if the secret bunker had just awoken an alarm sounded and red lights began flashing all around, there was no hiding it anymore; the final battle for the Italian people had begun.

Chapter 37

Every corridor they passed a group would splinter off from the army to investigate, destroy infrastructure or kill the enemy troops. Random gunfire could be heard as the partisans came across combatants. The army swept through the headquarters with relevant ease and only stopping when they came upon a group of soldiers, bewildered by the number of rebels they were faced against. The civilian army suffered very few casualties in the first few minutes, apart from a couple of minor flesh wounds, received by ricocheting bullets.

The first major gun battle was when they turned a corner and found themselves in a giant area filled with concrete pillars, piles of crates and barrels. The moment the partisans entered the large room, gunfire erupted, with bullets whizzing past their heads, the partisans darted for cover, many of the rebels refused to break cover but would fire blindly from where they had taken shelter. Walter and Vito were hidden behind a wooden crate, over the din of the gun battle, he yelled to his associate.

"Over there" he shouted, pointing to an open, arched doorway with a word written in block Fraktur on the white wall above it 'Kommunikation', Vito gave a nod, he knew that was his team's objective.

The younger partisan took a brief peek over the box to see hundreds of enemy antagonists, spraying bullets over their heads, impaling themselves into the wall behind the resistance soldiers. Looking around they could see that the attacking forces had taken a few fatalities and a couple of minor casualties, yet most were wisely keeping their heads down.

Vito got out a Russian F1 hand grenade and pulled the pin, keeping the paddle held down, to hold off the seven second fuse to ignite, he looked along the line of men, to his comrades, the ones who were carrying the explosives did the same. Vito was still in command of the attack and once Vito saw most of his soldiers were ready, he lobbed his grenade over his barricade, the other men copied their attack leader.

Most of the resistance soldiers ducked their head down and covered their ears to protected them from the cataclysmic, apocalyptic fulmination, that dominant shock wave and shook the foundations of the subterranean control centre, making the reinforced walls crack. Vito risked another stealthy peer over the top. He could hear German troops crying for their mothers, they were sprawled all over the room, some were missing limbs, whilst others, if not dead, were limping away using the cover of the dust cloud that had erupted during the explosion.

Vito looked for his two team members who would join him to severe the bases communications and cut it off from the outside world. Matteo was behind a pillar near the doorway they needed to exit through, fastening a belt around Frosino's upper leg as a makeshift tourniquet, the lower part of his leg had been ripped open by weapons fire. Emiliano on the other hand was taking cover behind a pile of weapons cases, Vito caught his eye and with a wave of his hand directing that they should advance forwards to Matteo's position. He shook Walter by the hand.

"Good luck, Colonel Valerio," he said, the lone partisan gave a nod.

"And to you, my friend," he replied, then he turned to speak to the remainder of the army, "Move forward men, capture or kill!" he cried, whilst Vito and Emiliano convened with Matteo and the rest of the rebel army pushed forwards, exposing themselves from their hidden positions and charging towards the enemy position with their weapons firing rapidly.

"How is he?" he asked Matteo as the resistance veteran stuck a morphine syrette into Frosino's arm.

"He will survive."

"Good, we must go, we will come back for him," Vito instructed without compassion, they had to focus on the mission and could not be distracted. His two associates both had different guns to their team leaders, Vito's Enfield, Matteo carried a Browning M1919 when Emiliano carried a Bren light machine gun, both were destructive weapons they were mostly used on a bi-pod but could be used just as easily by hand.

Vito led his two comrades through the archway and down the narrow spiral brick stairs, with their firearms up and at the ready. It was dimly lit, but they moved slow, ready for any Jerrie soldier who could emerge in the flight of steps below them. They took each step at a time, as they continued down, they could begin to hear the static clicking of electronics. The men entered a low roofed tunnel like basement, along the wall were massive devices with small round plug ports and wires connected to others.

In the centre was a smoking barrel and two men chucking in a load of paperwork from a couple of removed drawers, the partisans did not hesitate for a second and slaughtered the two junior soldiers.

"Emiliano, stick a load of that paper work into your bag, we will send them to the Americans, it could help with their invasion," ordered Vito. At a small wooden desk was a Nazi lieutenant, with ash blonde hair and a bullet wound to his head, spraying the wall with blood, in his hand he had a military issue Luger revolver, on the table sat an empty bottle of schnapps and an equally empty glass.

"Fucking coward, he must have heard us coming, had a drink and shot himself!" said Matteo. Vito got out the wire cutters he had been given and began to cut the wires, he looked to his two associates and reconsidered.

"On second thoughts make this thing into Swiss cheese," he commanded his associates, the two men took a step back and began riddling the mechanisms with bullet holes.

Once the small flickering lights had ceased their chaotic flashing, did the men continue deeper into the underground base? They went through one room and then another until they came to what looked like a hospital wing. There were beds along either side, with motionless Nazi soldiers in each, they all had some sort of wound. At the end, in long white coats stood a male doctor and female nurse with their hands raised. Vito looked at the lifeless patients, there was something severely wrong here, he turned to the doctor and decided to see if these hospital workers spoke Italian.

"What the hell is all this?"

The doctor replied, "Please, they kidnapped me from the local hospital, to help them with the wounded. But they are all dead," Vito looked at the corpses, "we were ordered that if the base was infiltrated, we should poison the injured to spare them interrogation, they thought it was medicine. They did not suffer," the man explained.

"Damn their suffering! You a medical professional, you have taken an oath to save people, not murder them," Vito growled.

"Please, we had no choice," the nurse spoke up. This angered the partisan. He was disgusted, they may be German troops, but no man deserved to die this way, no matter their nationality.

"We all have a choice," said Vito and fired a single shot into the abdomen of each of them. They fell to the white tiled floor as blood seeped from their open wound. The trio continued deeper into the Nazi headquarters, ignoring the dropped men.

***

The three partisans entered an empty room after empty room, with more Nazi slogans and German landscape works of art on the flaking white painted walls. After countless barren rooms then entered what looked like a small cafeteria, with lines of wooden tables, where some of the occupants had etched quotes such as 'Die Deutschen immer vor dem Ausländer und den Juden!' translated as 'The German always before the foreigner and the Jews!' and swastikas, etched possibly with the use of a Hitler youth knives, tables and metallic chairs.

There were Nazi, swastika banners hanging on the walls and propaganda posters, such as one Vito had seen many times before and help inspire him to sign up for the army. It was a picture of Hitler, holding the Nazi flag, wearing a medieval style suit of armour. This was meant to give the impression that if you were a Nazi soldier you would go into history as a hero, like the knights of old.

On the opposite side of the room there was a waist high wall, something did not smell right. Vito remained in the doorway, carefully observing the room, there were a couple of dead Nazi soldiers on the floor, but no sign of any partisans. Then Vito raised his rifle, he saw a shadow move from behind the low wall, he took three steps back and backed behind the cover of the wall.

"On the other side of the room, behind the wall," he whispered to his comrades. His counterpart's weapons would be more effective against concealed combatants. The two men stepped into the doorway and opened fire. Over the din of a rapid gunfire, Vito heard a yell from the other side of the room.

"Mettiti al riparo! Il capo è giù!" They were speaking Italian, these weren't German troops, they were Italians! Vito swiped his hand across his throat, signalling his men to hold fire. Vito had to be careful, it was not unheard of for the Nazi regime to have members of other nations in their ranks or could this be some of the final remnants of the evil Blackshirts?

"Surrender in the name of the Italian resistance, the CLN!" he shouted across, there was a temporary hesitation before they responded.

"Who is it?"

"Vito"

"You fucking idiots! Friendly fire!" came a reply, "It's Flavio, you just shot or team leader Alfredo!" the trio lowered their weapons, they had been shooting on their comrades and wounded the black-market partisan and one of Vito's most trusted friends, Alfredo. Vito's team revealed themselves with their hands raised, to show they were not the enemy and walked slowly towards the walled defensive position, where three partisans rose to their feet.

The two of the men Vito recognised, Flavio and Pietro, the third was a brutish of a man, with a messy brown beard, a lazy eye and a malicious look, he flipped a match in his mouth, by his attire, Vito classed him as one of Alfredo's black-market associates. They approached their fellow rebel soldiers, as they walked around the small wall and in a puddle of his own blood they saw Alfredo lying on the floor brandishing multiple bullet wounds to the torso.

Vito dropped to his knees beside his friends, he was still alive, the young partisan took his injured partner by the hand, as Matteo attended the man's open wound, Emiliano stood stock still in shock as he looked down at their fellow fighter.

Alfredo coughed up some blood indicating that some internal organs had been compromised.

"Cigarette" he chocked, Vito rifled through his counterparts, overcoats, pockets and found his stainless-steel cigarette holder, snapped it open, removed one of the ultra-slim cigarettes and put it between his friend lips. He then turned to the other black-market dealer and took the match from the man's mouth, struck it on the floor, finally lighting his partner's tobacco product. Alfredo grabbed Vito's collar and pulled him closer, so that he could whisper in his younger friend's ear.

"I am sorry, kid. Go to the room above the cafe, beneath the red floorboard, I have something hidden there, take it. Find your mother," he urged, he then began choking on his blood.

"It is a gut shot," whispered Matteo, "he won't make it, all I can do is give him some morphine, to make him comfortable."

"Do it," ordered Vito. Matteo took out a morphine syrette and stuck it into their dying friend's leg. It took immediate effect as Alfredo's breathing levelled up.

"More," insisted Alfredo.

"I can't, it will kill you," said Matteo apologetically.

“Nothing can stop that now. Give me more!” he persisted Matteo looked at Vito, who gave a reluctant nod. Matteo took out a second syrette and stabbed it into his leg. Alfredo’s closed his eyes and began to blubber slightly, his breathing slowed further. Vito nodded to Matteo to inject his friend and brave comrade again, Matteo did as he was bid.

Alfredo ceased breathing and Vito felt his comrade’s hand go limb in his. By now the young partisan had tears streaming down his face. He let his emotions loose and gave a scream of anger. He picked up his past friend’s cigarette holder, it would not be much use to him but it was something to remember him by and slipped into his trouser pocket.

“See you on the other side, brother,” whispered Vito, closing his friend’s eyes.

“We should go to the control centre,” said Flavio, covering Alfredo’s face with his own camouflage coat, “Salvatore is waiting for us there!”

They moved on with the intention to collect the dead body of Alfredo when they left the subterranean base for the last time, along with the other fallen comrades. They eventually arrived at the biggest room, the Nazi command centre of Italy. There were two men on guard outside the room, they welcomed the men and the five other men enter before their distraught leader Vito, who wiped off his tears from his face before entering.

Chapter 38

Vito entered the reinforced room, against the long wall were a group of twenty or thirty German soldiers who were down on their knees, under a single armed guard. There were approximately eighteen partisans standing around the room looking at the captured soldiers with disgust. Vito looked to his left and saw standing in one corner, leaning against a wall and still wearing his red beret, was 'the Colonel', Walter Audisio, who looked in Vito's direction and gave him a welcoming nod, which the youngest partisan gave in reply. He looked around the large room, he saw that many of his resistance brothers in arms had been wounded, some more serious than others.

"Vito, I am glad you are safe. Come over here, my friend," called Salvatore from the opposite end of the chamber. Vito walked slowly to his commander.

"Alfredo's dead," he informed him solemnly, he could see the rebel leader bite his tongue as he absorbed the sobering news. He eventually stated.

"He was a good man, a true patriot. He will be sorely missed," Vito had to agree, he had only met the black-market partisan twice before, but he would have been happy to call him a friend. Salvatore interrupted his thoughts.

"Come, my friend, I have someone I want you to meet," he said putting an arm around Vito's shoulder and directed him to an opposite corner, where a small group of his counterparts were huddled. Salvatore pushed aside his comrades to reveal, an elaborate vintage desk with a framed black and white picture of Adolf Hitler and the man who was now standing in front of them, in a blue, field Marshall full dress uniform, wearing around his neck a black iron cross with the swastika in the centre, the date of the beginning of the war 1939, the cross was topped with crossed swords beneath the oak leaves, declaring it as the highest honour of the Nazi empire, this Maltese style iron cross was known as the Knight's' Cross of the Iron Cross with Oak Leaves and swords and the owner carried a golden monocle in his right eye.

Sal continued, "Even though we could not find the kraut who murdered those many civilians, SS Obersturmbahnführer Kappler. We did though find this man. Vito, may I introduce you to the man who orchestrated the 'Rote Tag' and also the man who controls the invading forces in our glorious country, Generalfeldmarschall Albert Kesselring."

Vito could feel his head fill with red mist as he looked at the Axis officer. Vito looked at the man known as 'Smiling Uncle Albert', yet his famous wide smile had disappeared, his face was stern and completely changed the officers appearance.

"All traitors to our Führer and the Reich will pay. Heil Hitler!" the highest-ranking German in Italy bellowed at the top of his voice.

"He is all yours, my friend" whispered Sal, appalled by the officer's outburst, he slipped a bayonet into his associate's hand. Vito took a step closer to the German officer, with his death could come the end the war. The officer straightened up his uniform and said in good Italian.

"Come on then, you dirty son of a bitch wop!" Vito stepped forwards, grabbed the officer by the scruff of the neck and pulled him closer, then he whispered into the man's ear in German,

"I am as German as you are!"

This surprised the German commander so much that the single corrective lens fell from his eye and with that the partisan plunged the blade deep into the Nazis gut. The partisans gave a small applaud as the most hated man in Italy fell to the ground choking on his own blood. But this was not enough for Vito, this monster had been responsible for the death of his love. The red mist had totally encompassed him and all he could see was the deceased corpse of his love as he sat astride the officer.

The partisan continuously plunged the knife into the man's chest in frenzy, spraying blood over himself. Even after the man had passed Vito continued, the once grand Field Marshal's chest had become a bloody mess. Sal allowed this bloodbath to continue for another minute, before commanding a couple of guys to pull him off the corpse, which took them their total strength. They held Vito back until he had calmed.

The captured Nazis were sat quietly against a wall trembling with fear. Vito, with the German officer's blood splattered over his face and soaked into his clothing, he looked a terrifying sight, he looked at the pathetic display, as he wiped the blade clean with a filthy cloth rag, all eyes were watching him, not the partisans nor the Nazis had ever seen such a bloodthirsty display.

He dropped the rag to the floor and walked the line of the German prisoners, eyeing up each one as he passed. He locked eyes with a Gefreiter, equivalent rank to a lance corporal, who he recognised from a past that no longer existed. It was once his childhood friend, Stefan, he must have been reassigned to Italy when he had eventually been promoted. Vito instantly broke off the gaze and continued down the line of captives, hoping he had not been recognised. "Siggie?" question Stefan making Vito shiver "Siggie? Ist das du?" Vito turned, still holding the bayonet in one hand, strode directly over to his old and in a past life best Nazi friend. He leant forwards to look the Nazi direct in the face and said in Italian.

"The name is Vito! Now shut your hole you fucking kraut!" as he spoke he pointed his blade at the Germans throat, as a warning for the man to back down. Out of the corner of his eye he could see Salvatore looking at the two of them suspiciously. Doing his best to ignore his commander's gaze he continued down the line observing the sad display. Before he knew it, Sal had walked around the back of his men and materialised, as if out of the dense air, by Vito's shoulder.

"Do you know that Boche Gefreiter?" He asked quietly.

"No, of course not. He must be confusing me with someone else."

Sal did not react, but speaking louder said, "We need to keep one alive, so he can deliver our message through their ranks and warn them what happens when they hurt our people. Fear is our best weapon, it will destroy their moral." Vito knew only too well what was to come next, "you choose the one to live." Sal's voice returned to a whisper.

The younger partisan was fully aware that this was a test. This German, Stefan, had recognised Vito and risked his life, even at this stage of the war, if his true identity was revealed, his life would be forfeit, no matter of what his past exploits had accomplished, not to mention the aspersions it would cast on the Maquis.

Once again, he had to prove himself to the people he had now come to consider as his friends and family. He walked back along the line of condemned troops, each man knew the fate that awaited him, Vito's gaze passed over Stefan, if he chose his former friend, it would confirm Sal's suspicion and he would be under close observation, never to be trusted again. Eventually, his eyes lingered on a young private, he could not be a day over seventeen years of age, he had tears in his young eyes and was trembling with pure dread.

"This one," Vito pointed out the lad with his knife, "he's barely old enough to shave."

Salvatore nodded his approval of the decision.

"Tell that scum that you have just saved his life, for today at least" as he signalled to a couple of his men to remove the trooper from his brothers in arms.

"Congratulations, kid," Vito said in German, "you get to live another day."

The two partisans dragged the conscripted youth over to a wooden chair and bound him to it with rope. The young soldier started blubbering and pleading, clearly not registering what Vito had said.

"Please no. Please don't kill me! Mother."

"Giuseppe, shut that god damn bastard up!" commanded Salvatore. Giuseppe who was watching the pathetic display with some humour, removed his filthy, metallic grey, neckerchief and stuffed it harshly into the boy's mouth, muffling his cries. Then something that none of them had expected happened, the young soldier gave a whimper and a dark patch appeared in the trousers around the young man's groin, a deep yellow liquid emerged, flooding the chair and trickling to the floor.

"Shit! The buggers only pissed himself!" Laughed Giuseppe, making the assembly of partisans break into laughter. Vito leant against one of the cold reinforced concrete walls and packed his pipe with tobacco, whilst the remaining Axis combatants were made to rise to their feet and face the wall. Five rebels aimed German MP40 sub-machine guns at the apprehend men awaiting their leader's command. Salvatore looked around at his army of civilian fighters, men who refused to live under a fascist dictatorship, neither that of Mussolini or Hitler, men who took up arms for their country and freedom. He spoke to them loudly.

"These scums think they can control us! But we here have proven them wrong! This is the price that you must pay if you slaughter our people, our men women and children!" He turned to the marksmen and said a single word "Fire!"

The room flashed in light as the gunmen opened fire, the solid reinforced concrete walls ricocheted the sound, the remaining partisans watched as the backs of the invaders were riddled with bullets, dropping them dead. Vito had thought he would have some feeling of remorse, witnessing his childhood friend being executed but he felt nothing. His friend was a Nazi and he had no longer any emotions towards the followers of that cult. Vito quite calmly lit a match against the wall and went to light his pipe, when he saw something that made his blood turn to ice. The bound Nazi soldier, whose life he had just spared, from the same fate, was wearing a silver chain, but it looked out of place around this young soldier's neck, it looked too feminine for a soldier of the Wehrmacht.

The partisan stepped forwards and pulled it out from under his tunic. It was a pendant, an oval turquoise surrounded in silver. Vito recognised it in an instant, he had seen and admired it before, it was a gift from a mother to her young daughter, it was Elvera's pendant. In his mind's eye he could see this young soldier shooting the young Italian maiden and then if that wasn't enough, bending over the fallen female, unfazed by her malicious slaughter and tore the jewel from her tender neck.

A red mist encircled the partisan once again and without realising what he was doing he had dropped his blade and taken out his Luger, pointed it at the young youth's head and squeezed the trigger, the powerful pistol removed half to the young soldier's face.

Sal turned in a startle, "What the hell happened?" He asked in dismay.

Vito did not reply, instead knelt down and removed the necklace from the Germans neck. Seeing the silver pendant, Salvatore nodded and said, "So that was the Nazi who slaughtered the young Elvera."

Vito, found it hard, he had just avenged his love, this had been the single thing that had made him so ruthless over the last eight months. He thought that taking vengeance for his love's death, would make him feel fulfilled but instead he now felt a strange sense of emptiness. All of a sudden, he filled up with emotions and before he knew about it the youngest partisan, crumbled into a corner of the room in uncontrollable tears. No one reacted, everyone knew what the man was feeling, every man in the resistance had lost someone, whether a friend, family or loved one. And now with victory the anger they had once held inside them had vanished and their whole life had changed, in the blink of an eye.

Chapter 39

Vito, along with Salvatore and the Torino city partisans returned Alfredo's body back to his home city, in northern Italy. Where the religious partisan, Pietro, took it upon himself to inter the black-market trader, partisan and true hero of Italy. He was buried wearing his resistance CLN armband as a jingoist. Before their close friend was buried, the former rebels covered their comrade's coffin in the national Italian flag. He was given a patriot's funeral, yet even though the war was almost over, the Italian resistance still had to remain on high alert, in case any Nazi sympathisers decided to avenge the assassination of their only link to the German, National Socialist leadership in Berlin.

The wake was held at the cafe that Vito had first met the Torino resistance, the atmosphere was sombre, yet a lot of alcohol was passed through the lips of the mourners. But one thing lingered on Vito's mind, the message he had been given by Alfredo, his eyes continued to linger on the stairway leading to the room upstairs. The partisans and black-market traders who had come to pay their last respects and eventually, the men retired one at a time, taking an early night, they had all been given rooms at the homes of city dwellers. So that after the daring mission they had just been on, then they could sleep at least one night in blissful comfort.

Vito woke before day break and crept from the house he had been staying at, silently. The elderly partisan couple who owned it had been welcoming and served them a mind bogglingly tasteful meal, it was a fish platter, beyond compare, it was a rare luxury, it consisted a variety of fish all egg washed, coated in seasoned flour and then deep fired. They even served battered squid, which Vito was sure he would not find appetising, yet was pleasantly surprised.

The former partisan wondered down the quiet streets, heading back to the city's rebel coffee shop, he peered through the business windows, it was deserted, this is what he had hoped, yet he needed to get upstairs and the only route up was from the inside. He tried the door, it was locked, Vito checked the streets, it was all quiet, nothing was stirring, so Vito turned his back to the door and with a stern backwards kick, he cracked open the door. He paused, in case the sound had roused anyone, the area stayed desolate.

He side stepped into the uninhabited bistro, every step echoed around the area, he drew his pistol, he could not be sure that this place was completely unoccupied, some of the grievers may have decided to stay here. Vito carefully made his way up the wooden staircase, each step creaking as he put his weight upon it and into the room he would have been staying at on his previous visit.

He looked at the floorboards and a single floor pane different from the others, it was a deep cherry red colour, this must be the one Alfredo had mentioned with his dying breath. With a final look around he drew the flick knife he had taken from the body of the prison guard, from his boot. He fell to one knee and began to pry it up, it took a few tries and he was beginning to wonder if he was right, had Alfredo been delirious through shock? A few more minutes of chipping away and with a distinctive crack the board came loose. What Vito saw beneath took him by surprise.

In a small wad of Italian notes was approximately one-hundred Lire, a pair of blank identity cards, with the stamps and ink to make it look official, as well as three ration books and ten packs of the ultra-thin cigarettes that he had often seen the black-market trader smoke. Alfredo had given his friend a treasure trove, a way for him to live a new life in relative freedom beyond the war.

Finding a candle in a clay candle holder on a writer's desk, Vito went to work forging a new passport for himself, using a newly assumed name, lying had become so second nature and changed the place he lived to Torino, in case he was challenged in the northern hemisphere, he still had the one given to him by the Maquis for when he got further South, the third card he kept to alter when he had decided of a place to reside for the remainder of his life.

He slipped the money and other items into a small tanned haversack and walked carefully down the stairs with his gun still drawn. He walked directly into the back room and straight over to the refrigerator, upon opening it he saw three filled baguettes, wrapped in grease paper, he grabbed these and put them into his sack. On the side he took a small jar of olives and a half bottle of red wine, with a cork in the top.

He had enough to keep him for a few days travel, he replaced his pistol and went to the counter, he put one of the newly acquired twenty lire notes down and grabbing a scrap of paper and a pencil he wrote 'Sorry about the door..." he paused, he was going to sign it, but he had never signed anything under his assumed name, the French forger had forged the signature in his identification, before he received it, but he had never had to use it, so he decided to sign it with the single letter, not only his assumed initial but also the symbol for victory *'V'*. He then strolled casually from the establishment.

The young man walked leisurely through the bleak, deserted city, heading south after a good hour the streets began to wake with people, newspaper vendors and stall workers were preparing to open their businesses. As he reached the southern end of the city, he found some bikes chained up to some railing. Vito approached one and with the wire cutter he had been given for the attack at Monte Soratte, using them he snipped through the chain, he instantly stood up straight and looked around in case the owner was nearby, seeing nothing suspicious he took the cycle and began biking along the road heading south.

He felt slightly sad to be leaving his friends and brothers, who he had bled and fought with, side by side for the last five years. As he cycled along, he felt a small tear run down his face as he thought of his comrades, they had been his family since he had come into this country and considered him as one of their own, having ultimate trust and faith in him.

He travelled by bicycle for several hours following the Po River, until he got to the small town of Campagnino, he was travelling too slow by bike and he needed to increase the speed of his travel, so as not to bump into any if his comrades travelling south, he did not want to have to explain his departure, making his decision to leave all that much harder. He disembarked his bike and began to scout the streets, he knew exactly what he was looking for.

He saw an old town pump in a square and with a few pumps he drew some of the water, he splashed some into his face and cupped a couple of mouthfuls for him to drink, this helped him to decide his next step. If he was caught committing this crime, he would be arrested and spend the next few months in an Italian prison. He walked along the quaint streets until his eyes caught what he was looking for, it was an old grey Topolino or "Little Mouse" which was the nickname for the Fiat 500. The vehicle was unlocked and Vito remembered the conversation he had had with Alfredo about hot wiring cars and revealing the wires, cutting a couple of them and crossing them, revving the engine to life. And he sped off, continuing his race to get to the southern tip of the country. He had to make small diversions when craters from bombs or downed vegetation crossed the road, making it impassable.

He had just skirted the outside of Rome, travelling via side roads as much as possible when was met by a wooden table blocking the road. The former partisan was worried, this was not normal, there were no properties around here for the item of furniture to come from. As he was contemplating his next step, there was a metallic tapping on his side window. Vito was shocked, there was a gruff looking man, pointing a revolver, similar to Vito's Luger, in his direction. Vito took a deep breath and wound down thc driver side window.

"Sì?" he asked coolly.

"This is our road, you must pay to pass," replied the man savagely. Vito looked around, he was surrounded by these ruthless men. These were bandits, "fifty lire, now!" the man continued.

"We have vanquished Mussolini and those Nazi bastards. Come on guys, we are free." He could see a flare in the man's eye.

"We were all members of the Blackshirts. With the downfall of our great dictator, we lost our income. So we now must go back to what we know best. Now pay, now!"

This made sense, many of the Blackshirts were criminals released to work for the fascist dictator. With the many weapons and ammo dumps left by the Nazi troops, there was no shortage of weapon supplies, these men knew how to live outside the law and the layout of the land. With lawlessness across Italy, these men were free to take what they could, the only way they knew how, illegally.

Before the man had mentioned, his praise of, Mussolini, Vito had considered saying that he was a partisan, with the hope of being let passed without having to pay a fine, but forcing these men to lose their job, he thought better of it. The former partisan reached round to his back pocket and felt the grip of his own gun, he hesitated, if he had not noticed the large band of bandits around his stolen auto mobile, he may have taken the risk of shooting his assailant but in this certain situation it would prove to be futile, instead he reached into his back pocket and began to count out the notes, the criminal reached through the open window and grabbed the whole wad of bank notes and then chucked five lire back to Vito, with two words, "for fuel".

The bandits removed the blockade and the former partisan continued his travels south, a bit poorer.

Chapter 40

After the ultimate attack against the Nazi forces many of the partisans went their separate ways, with the knowledge that the war would soon be over and they could return back to their friends and families, crossing the Gothic line, when there were no more Germans to guard it.

With the assistance of the Italian rebels and intelligence that they had recovered, the Allied soldiers had pushed across the Po Valley in northern Italy and German forces in Italy finally surrendered on May 2nd, 1945 and two days later Berlin fell to the Russian red army, with the supposed suicide of the Reich's führer, Adolf Hitler. On the celebration of Italy's liberation, Walter Audisio delivered the body of their former, much hated, dictator Benito Amilcare Andrea Mussolini's body to the Italian population in the country's capital city, Rome, who subsequently lynched the corpse for all to see.

With the freedom of Italy now restored, the partisans disbanded and had to do their best to integrate back into society. Some, including Salvatore, had decided to remain in the woodland and become loggers. A few had moved to one of the cities to make a living as market traders, others went to the coast to become fishermen and a couple even went to the country's capital, Rome, to follow a dream of having a career on the stage.

Vito on the other hand continued to travel down south, by hitch hiking, by bus or rail and when he needed to, he would even resort to stealing another car. The men and brothers in arms he had left behind, a bit put out by his sudden disappearance. Had all assumed he had travelled to Naples to find his mother. But Vito went further south to restart his new life, as a real Italian citizen, with a brown leather pouch full of stolen golden lire.

Epilogue

Seventy Years Later

Outside a picturesque olive grove on the rolling hills of the small Italian island of Sicily. Sitting, as he did every day, in an old twine rocking chair sat a lean man of considerable years, absorbing the scorching afternoon Mediterranean sun. He wore a wide-brimmed straw hat, on his silver haired head, he had a matching white brush moustache sitting on his upper lip, he carried an oval turquoise pendant, surrounded by silver on a silver chain around his neck, his clothes were old and moth eaten.

No one knew anything about this strange bachelor or how he had been able to afford the purchase of the substantial olive farm and the locals rather avoided him and very rarely spoke with him, if they did, they would have noticed a slight German accent, which had slowly become more distinct over the years of solitude, in between the fluent Italian. There were rumours of this elderly man being a Nazi general who escaped to Italy after the war, but no evidence or facts, could be uncovered.

On a small round wooden table beside him sat a well-used, beautiful clay and amber 'oily' pipe, a stainless-steel cigarette case, a small empty brown leather pouch and in a modest silver frame a black and white photo of a women with natural Italian features, the picture looked old and worn, bleached by the sun, but still clearly visible. In one hand, his thin nimble fingers held a glass of ice tea and in the other hand he played with a single golden Italian Lire that glinted in the sunlight as he flipped it in the palm of his hand.

The Facts

When most of the characters in this book are fictional, there are some who were real, but their demeanour or demise may have been altered for the book. So here are the facts.

Adolf Hitler:

Adolf Hitler was a German politician, demagogue and Pan-German revolutionary. He was leader of the Nazi Party and rose to power in Germany as Chancellor in 1933 and Führer in 1934.

Clemens Rüter:

Clemens Rüter, was a German soldier, stood guard on the crest of the hill overlooking the clearing where the four men were tied to stakes in front of the firing squad and he took three snapshots. Rüter went back to Germany after the war and the camera, with the film still in it, was left untouched for forty years. Shortly before he died, Rüter told someone about the camera and the three images.

Benito Amilcare Andrea Mussolini:

Benito Mussolini was an Italian politician and journalist who was the leader of the National Fascist Party. He ruled Italy as prime minister from 1922 to 1943; he constitutionally led the country until 1925, when he dropped the pretence of democracy and established a dictatorship.

Heinrich Himmler:

Heinrich Luitpold Himmler was Reichsführer of the Schutzstaffel and a leading member of the Nazi Party of Germany. Himmler was one of the most powerful men in Nazi Germany and one of the people most directly responsible for the Holocaust.

Jean Pierre Moulin:

Jean Pierre Moulin was a French civil servant who served as the first President of the National Council of the Resistance during World War two from 23 May 1943 until his death less than two months later.

Yvette Lundy:

Yvette Lundy was a member of the Maquis during the World War 2 and began supplying forged official documents to escapees from a camp at Bazancourt and to Jewish families. She assisted the Communist Marcel Nautré and others, avoiding detection by the authorities, as well as providing shelter at her brother Georges' farm for Free French fighters parachuted into the region.

Lundy was arrested on 19 June 1944 interrogated by the Gestapo, she was subsequently imprisoned. During the interrogation, to protect her brothers and sister (René, Lucien, Georges and Berthe) who were also working for the resistance. She was then deported, first to Saarbrücken (prisoner number 47360).

Simone Segouin:

Simone Segouin also known by her alias Nicole Minet, is a former French resistance fighter who served in the 'Francs-Tireurs et Partisans' group. Among her first acts of resistance was stealing a bicycle from a German military administrator, which she then used to help carry resistance messages. She went on to take part in large-scale or otherwise perilous missions, such as capturing German troops, derailing trains and blowing up bridges. She was present at the liberation of Paris. She was promoted to lieutenant and awarded the Croix de guerre. After the war, Segouin became a paediatric nurse.

Walter Audisio (Aka Colonel Valerio):

Walter Audisio was an Italian partisan and communist politician. He was imprisoned before the second world war for his anti-fascist activities. As a senior partisan he was involved in the death of Benito Mussolini, possibly being the individual who killed the dictator and his mistress. After the war he served as an Italian deputy and later as a senator.

Albert Kesselring:

Albert Kesselring was a German Generalfeldmarschall of the air-force, the Luftwaffe during the second World War who was subsequently convicted of war crimes in July 1960. In his military career that spanned both World Wars, Kesselring became one of Nazi Germany's most skilful commanders and one of the most highly decorated, being one of only twenty-seven soldiers awarded the Knight's Cross of the Iron Cross with Oak Leaves, Swords and Diamonds.

Herbert Kappler:

Herbert Kappler was a key German SS functionary and war criminal during the Nazi era. He served as head of German police and security services (*Sicherheitspolizei*and SD) in Rome during the Second World War and was responsible for the Ardeatine massacre. Following the end of the war, Kappler stood trial in Italy and was sentenced to life imprisonment. He escaped from prison shortly before his death in West Germany in 1978.

Claretta Petacci:

Claretta Petacci also known as Clara Petacci was the mistress of the Italian dictator Benito Mussolini and was executed with him by partisans.

Captain Michael Lees:

Captain Michael Lees led the spring 1945 SOE/SAS mission to destroy the key German Army HQ in northern Italy, with the aim of shortening the war and saving countless Allied lives. Leading from the front he was shot five times but miraculously survived.

All other characters in this book are totally fictitious and any similarity in appearance or demeanour to anyone dead or alive, is totally coincidental.